Copyright © 2023 by Lashell Rain

All rights reserved.

No portion of this book may be reproduced in any form without written permission from the publisher or author, except as permitted by U.S. copyright law.

This novel is a work of fiction.
All characters and events portrayed are products of the author's imagination and are used fictitiously.
Cover done by Miblart

Revised Edition.

THE OSPARIA SERIES
BOOK ONE

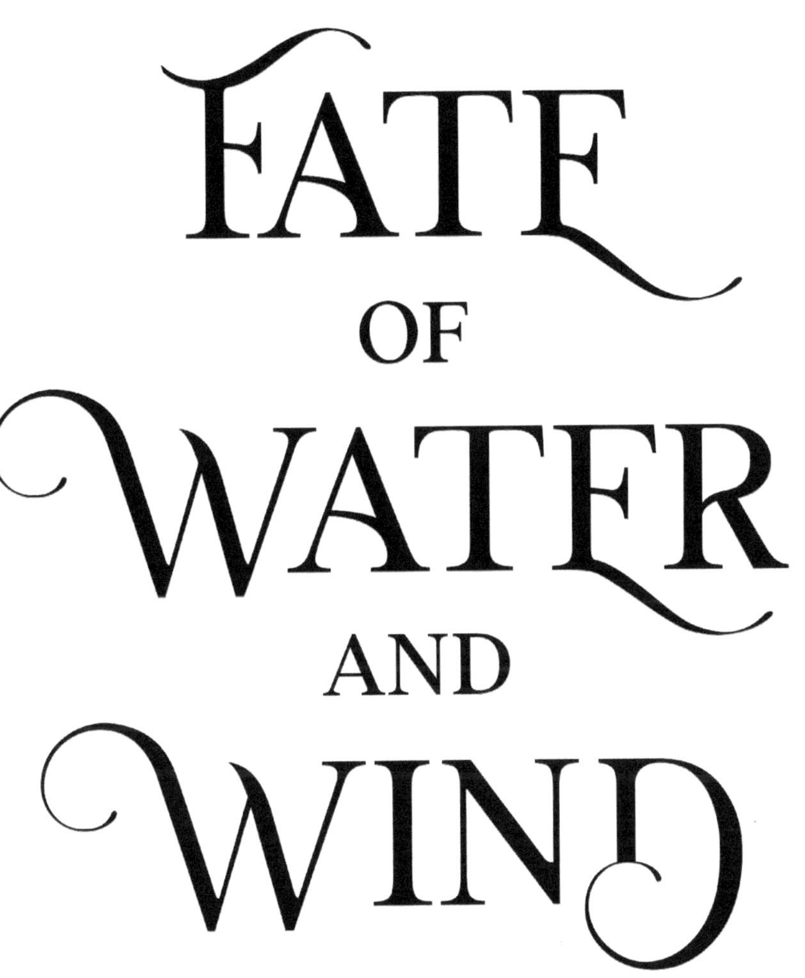

FATE OF WATER AND WIND

LASHELL RAIN

CONTENTS

Content Warning   IX

Dedication   XI

Emelyn & Ace   XIII

Map Of Osparia (left)   XIV

Map Of Osparia (right)   XV

1. Chapter One   1

2. Chapter Two   9

3. Chapter Three   23

4. Chapter Four   29

5. Chapter Five   35

6. Chapter Six   47

7. Chapter Seven   54

8. Chapter Eight   70

9. Chapter Nine   80

10. Chapter Ten   87

11. Chapter Eleven   94

12. Chapter Twelve   104

13. Chapter Thirteen   111

14. Chapter Fourteen   120

15. Chapter Fifteen   133

16. Chapter Sixteen   142

17. Chapter Seventeen   156

18. Chapter Eighteen   163

19. Chapter Nineteen   171

20. Chapter Twenty   178

21. Chapter Twenty-One   184

22. Chapter Twenty-Two   191

23. Chapter Twenty-Three   203

24. Chapter Twenty-Four   210

25. Chapter Twenty-Five   217

26. Chapter Twenty-Six   225

27. Chapter Twenty-Seven   231

28. Chapter Twenty-Eight   248

29. Chapter Twenty-Nine   253

30. Chapter Thirty   270

31. Chapter Thirty-One   287

32. Chapter Thirty-Two   294

33. Chapter Thirty-Three   299

34. Chapter Thirty-Four   306

35. Chapter Thirty-Five   309

36. Chapter Thirty-Six   316

37. Chapter Thirty-Seven   328

38. Chapter Thirty-Eight   338

39. Chapter Thirty-Nine   350

40. Chapter Forty   360

41. Forty-One   364

42. Chapter Forty-Two   367

43. Chapter Forty-Three   370

44. Chapter Forty-Four   384

45. Chapter Forty-Five   390

46. Thank You   400

Acknowledgments   401

CONTENT WARNING

Dear Reader,

This book contains mature content.

Material includes:

Explicit sexual scenes, graphic violence, talk of genocide, violence through fire, imprisonment/captivity, torture, loss, grief, war, attempted SA (not by the MMC)

To those who have unseen wounds—

I see you.

OSPARIA
HEAVENSREACH
THE DOCK MARKET
LINTAWA BAY
SIRENS PASS
SWAMPS OF ILLUSION
WOODHAVEN
WESTWELL HARBOR
CAPITAL CITY

ESORA
NEW POINT PEAK
ERS OF
YNUA
EMBER
THE WESTERN WYVERNS
IMPERIAL DISTRICT
IRON ISLE HARBOR

CHAPTER ONE
EMELYN

The steep rugged mountainside had turned into a web of snow and ice. We had been climbing Heavensreach all morning, determined to reach the highest peak where the pojo tea leaves bloomed. This had become our yearly tradition, honoring our loved ones that had fallen to Ember's cruel soldiers.

Ace trudged through the knee-deep snow in front of me, leading the way to our spot on the mountain. Nobody came up here anymore, this was a tradition we had started together, something that was strictly ours.

As we made it over the snow-capped peak, I looked over the open horizon. It reminded me every time we made the climb how this place got its name. The clouds floated lower than the mountain top and as the sun set in the distance, it was as though you could step out and walk on them. Lovely pinks and purples cascaded through them like a door to another world. It was just as breathtaking this year as it had been the last. I turned away from the open expanse and that's when I saw it.

The destruction.

The ruins that were once a bustling, beautiful city full of laughter and life as Sky-Elves flew above the mountains were now nothing but charred wood and stone left behind from the crumbling buildings and homes.

I looked to see Ace on his knees a few paces from me, kneeling on the cold ground of everything he once knew, reminiscing about his way of life from before. His thick hooded cloak wrapped around him for warmth and concealed his feathered ebony wings that he kept tucked into his back and his extended pointed ears; a common trait amongst his kind. Ember had come, seeking the destruction of every Sky-Elf, and they had almost succeeded.

Life in Esora was never the same. Every inch of ground held a memory of a loved one, a people nearly extinguished for standing with the Sky-Elves against Ember. I'd lost both of my parents on that battlefield, and Ace had lost his alongside me. It burned the memories of their deaths in my mind, the way the fire Fae soldiers scorched the earth, mountain, and our people. Ace and I had made a promise to each other after we lost everything; we'd stay together always.

Living every day in Esora, repeating our tragedies became too much, and as long as Ace remained hidden, we were free to explore the world. Ember had already taken too much from us, and we refused to let them have any more control. They'd sentenced us to be orphaned, but we wouldn't let them sentence us into a life of misery. We always kept an eye out for more of his kind, but never had success.

We had all suffered losses from the war, but I couldn't imagine what it would be like living in a world where your entire kind had been extinguished from the wrath of Embers Fire Fae. My thoughts often drifted to that day, when we'd first heard word of Ember's upcoming attack. It was said in the letter before the war started that Ember believed the next chosen was amongst the Sky-Elves.

I'd asked Ace a million times over the years if he was sure he wasn't the Peacebringer. Sometimes he'd sign to me his frustration with the question and assure me he wasn't, other times he'd tell me to fuck off. The thought made me chuckle under my breath and pulled me back to reality.

I walked to his side. "Ace," I whispered, but he could still hear me.

He lifted his hand without looking in my direction and signed, "give me a minute, Eme."

I nodded and stepped away. This was something he did every time we visited Heavensreach, paying respect by kneeling to those that had been forgotten.

I moved back to the mountain's ledge taking a seat to admire the beautiful view, my feet dangled over the edge of the blissful scene in front of me, the blanket of pillowy landscape beckoned me into it's embrace, but what lay just beneath was a long free fall to death.

before we set up camp for the night and picked our tea to drink around the fire. We would head back down the mountain at dawn to visit our village, and Willow, for a while before we went on the move again. We hadn't seen her since last winter. Normally we tried to visit every spring and winter when pojo bloomed, but last year we were too far in our travels to get back in time. We always sent her letters during our time away, though.

Ace clapped a heavy hand on my shoulder, letting me know he was ready as he helped me to my feet. Loose strands of his dark-brown hair had fallen from his half up bun and framed his lightly stubbled face. Feathers laced into the hair he had pulled back. His cheeks and longer, sharper ears were chapped from the icy winds. I was sure his face matched my own from the journey up here.

He draped an arm around my shoulders as we walked the short distance to the tea trees that had grown back after the war. We picked the leaves in silence. The only sound was the rustling trees blowing in the chilly winds of winter. Our visits were bittersweet. I'd learned over the years that grief never got lighter. We had just gotten used to carrying the weight.

After we picked the pojo, Ace quickly flew us down to the cliff side we had grown so fond of when we were kids that jutted out along the front of Heavensreach. It barely rose above the bristled tops of the nightoaks. He started the fire, placing the small kettle over it, and I bended the water from my skin into it with a flick of my wrist. I pulled the moisture out of the leaves, drying them out, before Ace threw them in as I watched the treetops sway among the foggy skies as the last of the sun's rays disappeared. Spicy cloves and cinnamon cleared my sinuses as the tea steam wafted from the pot.

Ace handed me a cup a moment later and I bended the drink into his and mine. I took a long sip. Its heady flavors brought the heat back to my limbs, and a warmth filled my chest from the memories.

"I can't believe it's been a hundred years…" I spoke and Ace sighed under his breath.

"Me neither." He signed, holding up his glass to clink it against mine as we stared off and enjoyed the views.

"Mai lao kahi." Forever as one, I whispered it to myself, bringing my hand to the moonstone hanging from my neck and gripped it softly, running my finger over its smooth surface. Ace grunted his agreement. The words were a sentiment to both of our kinds, one that united our people against Ember all those years ago and one that we continued to use between one another. As long as we had each other, we knew everything would be okay.

After finishing my third cup of pojo, Ace was chuckling under his breath at me. "What? It's been a year since we didn't come back in the spring and missed the blooms. I'm enjoying it now." I smiled, and he stood, dusting himself off before packing up what little belongings we brought with us.

"You ready?" He signed and offered me his calloused hand. I looked over the cliff side at the darkened night sky one last time before nodding to him and taking it. "Don't puke on me." He signed, and I rolled my eyes before he took a step off the cliff side and we free fell. My stomach flopped, and my tea sloshed around in there in a way that made me queasy. Fear slithered through me from the weightlessness but I didn't scream. I had grown used to the feeling of it over the years of traveling with Ace through the skies in the dark.

Mere inches from the ground, Ace's wind blasted from his free hand and feet, slowing us almost completely as our knees bent to absorb the small impact as we landed on the soft, snowy forest floor.

Ace never used his bending or wings during the day. We did our best to keep him hidden at all times, but if he needed either of them, he'd use them in the dead of night, taking advantage of the darkness. It was difficult for him at the beginning of all of this, but he's grown more used to it now.

The walk down the worn path to the village was swift. We had made the journey so many times it was a mindless walk. My feet were numb in my wet boots, but the dim light floating outside Willow's small hut of a home was like a beacon calling to us in the distance. She had told us she'd leave the lantern outside. Within a few more strides, I heard the wind chimes and trinkets hanging from the surrounding trees clanking in the breeze before I saw her plump, short silhouette step out into the frigid air bundled in layers, with a small blanket draped over her shoulders. As if she had stayed up late waiting for us, listening for our steps. She grabbed the lantern and held it out in our direction.

"Ace, Eme, is that you, child?" She called, and I answered.

"It's us." A bright smile stretched over her shadowed features as she held out her arms, preparing for our embrace. Ace and I wrapped our arms around her. Her scent of white tea and herbs surrounded us. Home. We had made it home.

CHAPTER TWO
EMELYN

I jolted awake to the sound of two pans clanging together, ricocheting off the walls in the tiny house.

"Rise and shine," Willow called out from the living room. Which was also the kitchen and dining area. Our house was old and small but it was plenty for us. Willows nurturing over the years had always made this place feel like more than it's worn furniture and scuffed wooden walls. Ace and I slept in a nook tucked off of the main room of the house, big enough for two beds a few feet apart and not much else.

I could hear her shuffling around in the open space. "Breakfast is ready," Willow called again and Ace groaned, wrapping his wings around himself like a bat, as I shoved my pillow over my face. The sun wasn't even up for the day yet. The only light was the large lantern that sat on the worn dinning table and the small wood burning furnace tucked in the corner keeping the place warm. Ace and I had been spoiled during our travels away, not having to ever wake up before the sun. Our mornings had been lazy and unhurried, often spent exploring our surroundings, or staying on top of our training. Our days were filled with adventure, as we roamed through forests, scaled towering mountains, encountering strange creatures and ruins hidden amidst the wilderness. We would share stories by the campfire under the starlit sky. One of my favorites was Ace getting his ass kicked by a naked dwarf in a pub. But regardless, as we journeyed, our bond only grew stronger.

Willow yanked the blankets off of Ace and I. "Come now, child, there's work to be done."

"Come on, we had a long night... Can we do the chores later?" I asked, rolling my eyes, I knew the answer would be no, but it was worth a shot. She scowled at me as if it was an absurd thought. The look made the wrinkles that crowded her eyes and mouth look deeper, adding to her already old age. Ace and I were over a hundred and, for the most part, still looked the same as we did when we were teens other than a few battle scars. Among the creatures of our world, the Fae held the distinction of having the longest lifespans, their years stretching far beyond those of mortals.

Following closely behind the Fae were the Sky Elves and Earth Dryads. Though their lifespans were not quite as extensive as those of the Fae, elves and dryads could live for centuries. Beyond that, the lifespans of creatures grew increasingly shorter. Humans, dwarves, orcs and other mortal races lived but a fraction of those years, their lives fleeting in comparison.

I had always wondered how old Willow actually was, but she never would say, only that she had been around long enough to know a thing or two. Her lively attitude never dulled and whether she was five hundred or five thousand, I wouldn't expect anything less.

I was worried she'd douse me with her water bending, so I rubbed the sleep from my eyes and sat up on the bed. "Okay, okay, I'm up," I whined and grabbed one of my boots and threw it over at Ace, who had started snoring again. He jumped from the heavy leather thudding against his chest. He stirred awake and gave me a mean mug, but dropped it when he saw Willow scowling at him next. "What should we do first?" I asked, and she spoke and signed back to both of us.

"First, let's eat, then you both can head to the village to pick up some herbs for me from Lyn, and grab me a new pot from the blacksmith. After, you can head over and check the fish nets so we'll have something good to cook for dinner tonight." Her scowl switched to a smile as she sauntered back into the kitchen area of the house, her long dress swishing at her ankles. Her loose gray braid hung down her back, swaying with each step. I looked over at Ace rubbing a hand down his face, surprise pasted there that I was sure matched my own.

"You're letting us get you a new pot?" I asked, dumbfounded. In all the years we lived here I could count on one hand the number of times Willow replaced something. She would fix and repair until it became unusable. For over fifty years we nagged her to get a new pot since the one she used left a savory taste on anything she cooked. Instead of replacing it, she'd scold us for having childish taste buds.

"All good things come to an end, child, and that pot has met it." She said over her shoulder, as if she hadn't fought us tooth and nail over it for half a century. I looked forward to food that wasn't altered by an ancient pot tonight. Yet, despite the distinctly flavored meals, dinner with Willow had always been one of my favorite things. Every night she would make dinner while telling us a story, a lesson, on fantastical beasts that roamed our lands while other stories were teachings on things. I could already smell the aroma of milk, ginger, and lemongrass as Willow worked her magic. Whether it was succulent grilled fish marinated in a tangy sauce, fragrant rice dotted with fresh herbs, or a colorful array of vegetables stir-fried to perfection, every bite was always delicious.

They were some of my most cherished memories of our time with her, and although it had been years, the woman never stopped blessing us with her stories.

I think she could live 100 long lifetimes, and never run out of knowledge to share with us.

"What made you want to replace it?" I asked, still shocked that she wanted a new one.

"The bottom cracked last night after I made dinner. That's why I could only greet you with a hug and not a warm bowl of stew to go with it," she said, grabbing her fur coat and draping it around herself to fight off the winds before she stepped out into the cold. Her words filled me with warmth. In the past, she had always greeted us with some food or some herbal concoction that tasted horrible but was good for our soul she'd say. I figured she didn't last night because it was so late. I guessed wrong.

Ace put on his leathers and shoved his boots on and I did the same. Excitement about a pot seemed silly, but I couldn't wait for Ace and I to pick her the perfect one. Though, I'm sure regardless of the quality we got, Willow would use it for the next century.

Ace and I walked out into the open room, Willow's plants that jutted out from the living wall to the right were plush and bright even in the winter. The big leaves, vines, and herbs were the only thing that separated her room from the rest of the house. She'd always kept a small conservatory in her home in case anyone ever needed tending to. She was an elder Kumai teacher, after all. Her knowledge went far beyond being a healer, and it had always been one of her passions.

I walked toward the exit. What was this crazy woman up too now? Ducking out of the front door with Ace on my heels. He was extra careful passing the living wall putting a wide girth between himself and the plants. He probably didn't notice but the laugh bubbled in my chest from a memory and I had to hold it back.

The first summer we spent with Willow she told him to be weary of the wall, but he hadn't mastered tucking his wings in yet, so when he accidentally brushed them against it, he had itchy rashes over his entire body and patches of feathers falling out for weeks.

I found Willow standing over the fire pit wielding water and oats over the flame to cook us breakfast without her pot. The murky oat water twisted around the flames until it was thick goo and then she wielded it into the two bowls she held in her other hand.

"Have to make due with what you have, child," she said and Ace and I chuckled at her creativity. We wasted no time as we gulped down our bowls before leaving them in the wash bin on the table in the kitchen.

Willow ushered us back out of the door with her hands full, I offered to help but she pushed me and Ace along. "Be careful out there, child," she called to us over her shoulder as she walked over to her wagon kicking up snow. Her hands full of skins and furs to take and sell in the dock markets at Lintawa Bay. She would make more money for them there rather than selling them in the village.

"You too," I said, following behind Ace, who grunted with a wave of his hand. He wasn't a morning person, and I think being away from our daily routines with Willow made it even more obvious. I laughed under my breath as we trudged through the snow. The icy winds sliced through my bones leaving a tingling sensation on my skin until my body grew used to the frigid temperature again. the pristine white landscape stretching out before us in all directions. I patted Gigi, Willow's horse, on the nose. feeling the warmth of her breath against my palm as she snorted softly. She patiently waited for Willow on the trail, already hooked up and ready for the trip to the markets. her sleek coat gleaming in the soft light of dawn.

The sun, being barely a sliver over the horizon, illuminated the frosted trees with a warm, honeyed light. It let me know Willow didn't waste any time this morning regardless of how late of a night we had. That woman never stopped working.

Ace's walk was brisk in front of me, his boots crunching through the snow. "Hey," I called, but got no answer. "Ace," I tried again, nothing. I rolled my eyes, bended the snow at my feet, forming it into a ball. I threw it, sending it flying into the center of his back with a satisfying thud. He paused, rolling his shoulders to shake off the snow before he turned to face me, a mischievous grin spreading across his face. The corners of his eyes crinkled with laughter as he met my gaze, the warmth of his amusement melting away the chill of the morning air.

"You're going to pay for that, Eme," he signed.

"We'll see," I said, before darting into the woods at my fae speeds in the village's direction. He chased me and I saw snowballs fly past my face as I weaved through the trees.

After a few minutes, he came out of nowhere on my right and tackled me, moving as fast as the wind, before he pinned me to the ground.

"You cheated, you're faster with your bending." I huffed out my words, trying to catch my breath.

"You started it." he signed with a scowl.

"Yeah, I figured it would put you in a better mood, you grump."

"I'm not a grump."

"Are too." I signed before flicking my wrist turning the snow to water and dousing his face with it. I chortled under his hold, but I couldn't contain my full belly laugh. My laugh made him laugh as he rolled off of me. He sighed, scrubbing his hand down his damp face.

"You do that every time." He signed before he raised his legs slightly and used his body's momentum to lurch to his feet in one swift motion. Then he offered me a hand, and I took it.

"I doubt I'll stop anytime soon," I said, dusting the snow off from my clothes. We moved through the trees until they opened up to my village. Loud chatter filled the air. Horse's hooves clopped, and wagons creaked with the comings and goings. Women played with their children in the morning's snow before they headed off to their Kumais to learn as the sun began to rise.

Homes and small shops sat in uneven rows, Some were constructed of rough-hewn timber, their sturdy frames reminiscent of log cabins, while others boasted elegant stone. The paths lined with wooden or metal signs jutting from the roofs of the shops with their business names written on them in an array of different fonts.

When I was younger, we would have to travel to the dock markets often, but our village was large enough now, you only needed to go occasionally if you were looking to trade for more coin, but we could find most things here.

Our home had grown over the years, and my father would have loved to see it. The thought made my hand move to grip the moonstone necklace that he gifted me all those years ago that hung around my neck. It had always been a silent comfort.

I walked down the path carved through the snow as people passed us, giving us warm smiles and waves now that they realized we had made it home. Our people were friendly, but after the war, we hadn't particularly grown close to anyone other than Willow. I think a lot of them carried a small seed of resentment after Ace and I left a few years after the war.

Our fathers had been leaders. We would have been the next in line, but once we knew the village was in good hands, we left. Ember hunted the Sky Elves, and still were as far as we knew. So we explored Osparia, running from the memories home held.

I glanced up to the sign that read Lyn's Herbs & Spices and Ace held the door open for me as I walked inside.

"I'll be right with you!" Lyn called from the back room before hustling up to the counter. "Ah, Ace, Eme, so good to see you! What can I get you? Willows usual?" She asked cheerily, her long brown locks intertwined in an intricate braid that draped over her shoulder, with small white flowers weaved into it. Her attire mirrored her sunny disposition, a flowing dress of vibrant purple that danced around her ankles with each step. Glass vials and large jars filled with dried plants and herbs sat on the shelves next to dead, preserved creatures for witches' brews and stews. Sometimes I wondered if Lyn practiced witch magic, I had never seen her bend, and her shop opened up here about half a century ago. Fairly new compared to those that were here during the war all those years ago.

My gut twisted thinking about what sorts of things Willow had fed us over the years from these jars, but knowing she preferred fresh meat from a hunt eased my roiling gut. Lyn grabbed a basket from under the counter, already prepared for Willow's next order.

"That'll be three coppers." She spoke with a smile to me, but I watched as she eyed Ace walking around, looking at the large vials of preserved creatures as I tossed the coins on the wooden bar that separated the front and the back of the store. Lyn didn't sign, or at least she hadn't over the years of us coming and picking up Willow's orders. Not many people knew the language anymore. But she always gazed at Ace with curiosity of what he could be.

"Thanks so much for your time," I said softly while grabbing the basket of herbs.

"No bother at all. We love Willow. I appreciate her business. Tell her I said hello."

"Will do." I turned and tapped Ace on the shoulder, nodding toward the door, bringing his attention back to the present instead of the weird looking preserved bird in a jar. Or was it a dragon? I couldn't be certain.

"Thanks again," I called over my shoulder before the door shuddered closed behind me.

"Where did Raul's place go?" I signed to Ace, and he shrugged, glancing around at all the signs. Last year he was only a few shops down from Lyn, but now his shop wasn't there anymore.

We meandered through the markets, stopping a few times at new places of business to grab a snack, and to see how much the village had grown since we visited last year. Eventually we found Raul. He had moved to a larger building with the growth in his business. No snow sat atop his roof. No vines wrapped around his building like they did with most of the others. Black smoke barreled out of the metal looking chimney jutting out of the top of his work place. We walked into the hot, dry space. The heat from the coals made sweat bead down my back. The clanks of hammered hot metal ricocheted around the room.

Glancing at all the weapons he had on display, hanging from large metal hooks, along with the large pots and pans he had beautifully crafted. The wooden benches they sat on so worn from the weight of them they had indentions from the pots scoring circles into the dark wood. I meticulously picked up and looked at them all. I settled on the largest one that looked the closest to what Willow already had. The thick metal pot weighed a ton.

I grabbed the basket of herbs from Ace and let him carry the hefty pot. He rolled his eyes at me, carrying it effortlessly as Raul came from the back hallway. Blackened gloves lined his hands and his clothes were covered in soot and wet with the sweat of his labor.

"And what do I owe the pleasure of seeing you both here?" He asked and signed. Raul had fought in the war with us all those years ago. He knew our fathers, so he knew the language of the Sky Elves.

"Willow is in need of something new." I said, and he gave us a weary look. He swiped a towel over his forehead while walking over to the counter. His short, blonde hair fell over his brow.

"I never thought I'd see the day," he said, giving us a smile. Ace sat the cauldron looking pot on the counter, but Raul raised a hand. "It's on me," he said and Ace shook his head.

"You know we can't accept that, it probably took you forever to–"

Raul cut off Aces signs with his own.

"It's fine. Maybe giving it to Willow for free will have her visiting me for business more than once a century," he said with a chuckle.

"You're sure?" I asked.

"Positive. I have to get back to work, but tell Willow to visit sometime," he said, leaving us with a smile before he left for the back of the shop.

Ace grabbed the pot from the counter and sauntered toward the door while I tossed in a handful of coppers into the small tin can that sat on Raul's counter. He deserved a payment and he couldn't turn down a tip.

CHAPTER THREE
EMELYN

Ace and I made it back to Willows with herbs and a new pot in hand by the middle of the day. We left them both sitting on the table in the house. She wouldn't be back from the dock markets for a little while longer, and I wished I didn't have to go to the fish nets with Ace because I wanted to see her light up when she saw her new pot.

In all the years I had known her, I couldn't remember a time she had got something new rather than making do with what she already had. But I also knew she'd string us up by our toes if we didn't bring her something home to cook in it.

The crashing waves against the craggy shore below beckoned my attention. We were so close I tasted the salt in the air. Ace walked ahead of me, grabbing the first metal post jutting out of the snow dusted ground, and yanked it free from the cold soil with one quick pull, revealing his strength.

The posts kept the nets pinned to the shoreline. I looked over the edge and watched the dark waters of Draynua slam against the front of the narrow, rocky cliff face we stood on. This place had always been fruitful with fish, but the small drop was still terrifying. It wasn't necessarily the rocks or the water that I feared, but the beasts that were in it.

"Are you going to help me, or are you just going to stand there?" Ace signed with his free hand while the other held the weight of the first net, his arm muscles strained and shook against the sway of the ocean.

"Okay, okay, grump," I said, and he scowled at me. I walked a few feet from him to where the next post lay and tugged it free, letting it drop to the ground as I gripped the fish net with both arms. Ace stretched his arm down the net with every pull, dragging it back on to the shore. Fish flopped wildly as he yanked them out of the water.

I used my fae strength to tug my own net to shore, but it didn't budge. Not even an inch. I tried again. My arms shook from the amount of muscle I was using, but it wouldn't move. We had done this every morning while living with Willow over the years and I wasn't weak by a long shot, but the net barely moved any further, no matter how hard I fought against it. The line remained taut.

Ace dragged in the last of his net. Large fish lurched and twitched as he moved them away from the edge. I tried again and again. My knuckles ran white against the grip, but I yanked harder each time until it suddenly fell slack.

"Are you getting weak on me?" Ace joked as he sauntered back to me, but the vibration that shook my chest from the animalistic purr that came from the cliff's mouth made him stop in his tracks. Water sloshed up over the edge as a clawed, webbed paw braced the land. I stumbled back as Ace yanked two daggers free from the straps across his chest. The creature used the last of its strength to haul itself onto the soil.

"Move, Eme," Ace signed, but the beast didn't attack. It raised its eyes to look at me on shaky legs. A water linx stood in front of me before it rolled to its side from exhaustion, heaving for breath with our nets tangled around its body. It had feline-like features. It was huge, larger than three men. Its jagged fins ran from the top of its head to the tip of its tail. The colors faded from a deep scaly blue to a bright red. The color was definitely a warning to those who came near it.

Its cat-like face had long whiskers on either side of its mouth full of razor-sharp teeth. Its breaths came out long and hard, guilt tugged at my heart, I knew the poor creature would die if we left him this way and my soft heart couldn't handle that. I took a step toward it and Ace slammed his arm in front of me.

"Are you out of your mind? It'll kill you." Ace signed urgently, his gaze darting back and forth between me and the trapped lynx.

"Ace, it's hurt, it's trapped in our nets, it's our responsibility to set it free."

"Great, so you have lost your mind." He scoffed, his face edged with frustration as he glanced warily at the struggling animal again.

"Just shut up and help me." My tone firm as I stepped closer to the ensnared creature, hiding the slight tremble of my hands.

"You're on your own for this one." He signed and tossed me one of his daggers. I rolled my eyes but stepped toward the beast slowly, no sudden moves. Ace stood to the side in a fighting stance, ready to strike if necessary. When I crouched down next to the animal, his head shot in my direction with a snarl, showing me its teeth and bright orange eyes.

"I'm here to help," I spoke soothingly, wanting the linx to understand I wasn't a threat. The animal watched me intently but didn't move. I cut each notch in the net carefully. As I sliced the net away, I noticed the linx was a boy. The net was tangled around his body from his largest dorsal fin down to the flat, pointed end of his tail. I pulled the last of the net off and stood, and the creature pounced on top of me, pinning me to the icy ground. My efforts to communicate that I wasn't a threat had obviously failed. Cold water dripped from his colossal frame and seeped into my clothes as he hovered above me. It sent a chill down my spine. The beast still hadn't attacked but I still turned my head away from his sharp teeth and hot breath. Ace readied to strike.

"No! Wait…" I yelled. My chest rose and fell as my heartbeat pounded in my ears. The linx purred, the sound soft and mellow before he released me. He sauntered back to the edge and peered over his shoulder at me before leaping back into the depths of Draynua.

A heavy sigh shuddered out of my body as my adrenaline subsided. Ace walked to me and kneeled next to me.

"Are you hurt?" he asked, and I shook my head, still reeling from what had happened.

"You're crazy, you know that." he signed, helping me to my feet.

"Life's no fun if you're not." I said and he forced out a laugh at my response.

"Interesting..." The unknown voice rasped and sounded ancient from behind us. My heart stopped, and I was unsure if I was breathing. Ace and I turned in the voice's direction and my eyes went wide at what was leaning against the tree. Ace was as still as a stone next to me. The water linx was nothing compared to the creature before us.

The kappa.

CHAPTER FOUR
EMELYN

His black leather-like skin shone still wet from the waters he emerged from. His taloned fingers and toes were long and boney, just like the rest of him. Loose strands of stringy, damp, black hair barely hung from the sides of his scalp surrounding the small bowl-like dome that sunk into the center of his skull. He looked up, his dark eyes meeting mine, and I thought back to every story mother Willow had ever told around the fire.

The kappa was a creature of all knowledge, he sought kindness but loved fear. There was only ever one alive at a time. If they died, their soul would be reincarnated again with all the knowledge from before. Some believed they were chosen by the gods to harbor the knowledge of Osparia, similar to how the different gods chose parts of our world to bless with the abilities of bending. Others believed they were just another cruel creature of our world.

Be unafraid, he feeds on others' fear.

Kneel and always show him kindness. He's addicted to kindness.

If he offers a truth, you must fill his cap.

Her words echoed in my mind the moment the kappa stood straight. I let out a breath.

"How are you today, sir?" I spoke as respectfully as I could, kneeling before him. He pitched up a brow before bowing back, placing his lanky arm over his midsection.

"Feeling rather benevolent today, Emelyn," he said, rising with a cocked grin on his tight-leathered face. As terrifying as he looked, his voice didn't match the witt rolling off of him.

"How do you know my name?" I asked.

"The kappa knows all things, and through the kappa, all things are known. I'm surprised being raised by Willow didn't teach you that."

"You know Will—" I didn't finish my question. His statement had already answered it. I hadn't realized when Willow told me the kappa was the creature of all-knowing that she had meant it so literally. I wondered what it was like to carry all the answers of the world on your shoulders.

"Well, if you know my name, Kappa, I feel it is only fair I should know yours," I asked happily, painting a polite smile on my face. The kappas' smile stretched from ear to ear. It was wicked and horrifying, but I didn't let it show.

"My my my, I've lived through every dark age and war, and I have never had someone ask me my true name." He gave me a bemused look. "First you save the linx from death, and now you ask the kappa of his true identity? How rejuvenating." He stretched out the last word. His voice was a deep rasp that made gooseflesh coat my neck. Was that what drew him here? Showing kindness to a fellow beast? I assumed so.

"All man and beast, regardless of how scary they may seem, have feelings," I said and his smile wavered, his face growing more serious.

"I want to offer you a truth for your soft heart, Emelyn."

"What do you mean?" I questioned, glancing over at Ace as he watched our conversation in stunned silence.

"If you are willing to fill my cap, I will not only give you a truth... but I shall tell you my true name." He took a step toward me, but I didn't move. I couldn't. I was doing my best to keep my nerves in check.

The kappa kneeled to the ground and tilted his head down, letting the dark murky water from the hole in his scalp slosh to the snowy forest floor, leaving it empty. I could tell it hadn't been emptied in years. Moss and slime had grown within it. "But remember, a truth from The kappa can be life changing." He glanced up at me with a wry grin as I stood there for a beat and hesitated for only a moment before I waved my arm and bended the water from my skin into his cap, filling it to the brim with fresh water.

He stood so close his lanky body towered over me, and his eyes glowed as they pierced through me and rooted me to where I stood. His voice deepened into something that sounded unworldly, guttural, and terrifying.

"You are the wielder of all the elements, the next bringer of peace, the one chosen to restore this world." As he spoke a jolt of power so painful formed in my gut, coursed through my veins, and awakened something within me I never knew was there.

The world shook beneath my feet as the kappa dissipated from my line of sight. All I could see was a blinding light that jutted into the skies above me and pulsed into the ground at my feet. Veins of light infected the earth, spreading at my feet.

A set of rough hands pulled me into a hard chest. Ace had pulled me into him. His hands cupped my face as my vision returned to normal and the bright light faded. His eyes looked me over.

"Eme, Eme, are you okay? Can you see me?" he signed frantically. His azure eyes filled with concern. I understood, but the shock of the revelation of what had just been told to me was too much. I shook my head, trying to make the shock subside. "What did you do to her?" Ace signed aggressively toward the kappa, hissing under his breath. The kappa's eyes narrowed in on him at his lack of kindness–respect.

He cocked his head so inhuman like that it reminded me of the monstrous stories told around the fire about the things the kappa was capable of. The things he had done. I pulled myself out of my dazed stupor before Ace got himself killed.

"Sir..." I chimed in, "my esteemed ancient one... If you would be ever so kind as to explain what just happened?" I filled my voice with smooth indulgence.

"Hmmm." He growled, low and lethal, as if my words soothed something within him. "Aren't you just a jewel, Emelyn." His voice stretched the last syllable of my name. "There's no need to explain what you already know."

Ace eyed me, letting the truth settle between us. I turned to the kappa who had backed away to the wood line. He looked at us one last time with that sly grin back on his face before he dissipated into a black puddle in the snow. He never told me his name...

He'd left me in a wake of truth, I struggled to believe, but the kappa didn't lie. He couldn't. The moment he spoke it, I was whole, the light filled my chest and reveled with my incarnation leaving me to deal with the reality that my life was forever changed.

I was the chosen one, the Peacebringer. I always had been.

CHAPTER FIVE
EMELYN

Snow crunched underfoot as Ace and I hastened through the dense woods, dappled evening light playing across our faces. The urgency in our steps felt as if it almost disturbed the usual calm of the forest, rousing the birds and any other creatures out here.

Ace's arm muscles tensed against the weight of the fish in his grasp, their silver scales glinting like coins tossed into a wishing well. The string was heavy, but he bore it as if it were as light as the air he commanded, his jaw set in determination. We had been successful in our catch today, the nets yielding generously, but the bounty felt like a burden given the gravity of what we'd learned from the Kappa.

"What the hell are we supposed to tell Willow, Emelyn?" Ace stopped abruptly to sign to me, finally breaking the silence between us, the tension was tight in his shoulders.

I cast a sideways glance at Ace, his cerulean eyes reflecting a storm of emotions I struggled to quell with. I knew whatever lay ahead of us was going to be a whole knew type of hell. But I didn't want to think of that right now.

A bead of sweat trickled down the side of my face, I drew in a breath.

"Nothing... we don't have to tell her or anyone else anything, at least not yet."

"Nothing? Dont you want to think about it? You're the fucking Peacebringer, the very thing Ember has a bounty out for and you want to just pretend you're not?"

My heart clenched at his words, and I halted, turning to face him fully, the stream beside us babbling obnoxiously. The setting sun cast dim light through the leaves. I saw his chest rise and fall with each breath, saw the way his eyes searched mine for something—anything—that resembled a plan.

"Watch your fucking mouth," I shot back, my voice a mix of command and vulnerability that only Ace could draw out of me. My eyes blazed with the intensity of the waters I commanded, yet they held a plea for understanding. "And yes, at least while we're here. Once we leave we can deal with it then."

Ace's expression shifted, the hard lines softening. He understood the weight of what I had to carry better than anyone. Hell, he had done it for years.

"Even if we wanted to hide it," Ace continued, as wind whipped the rustling leaves, I wondered if it was his, "she'd see straight through us. She knows us better than that. We've never been able to keep anything from that woman."

"If she notices, we'll tell her, if not, we keep it to ourselves, we'll figure it out once our visit is over. Neither of us know where to go from here and I don't want to get Willow involved."

As we neared the edge of the woods, the outline of Willow's home emerged. A part of me longed to confide everything to Willow. Yet, another part clung to the illusion of normalcy, to the notion of an evening untouched by fear or duty from this never ending war.

"Alright," Ace replied finally, the tension in his jaw giving away his reluctance to let the matter go. But he respected my wishes, falling into a silence that enveloped us as effectively as the growing shadows. Ace took the lead as he walked to the house, He sent his wind to touch all of the chimes in the trees, making them louder than normal, enough for Willow to know we had made it back home.

The wooden chair groaned under my weight as I shifted, trying to find some semblance of comfort at the small dining table. The air felt heavy, between Ace and I. Ace sat across from me, his eyes fixed on the grain of the table, seeming so engrossed in teh pattern of the wood to distract himself.

Willow moved about the kitchen with practiced ease, the clink of pottery and the scrape of utensils the only sounds daring to disturb the quiet. Her back was turned, but I knew she was aware, her senses had always been as sharp as a knife.

When she finally turned around, her gaze swept over us, gentle yet piercing.

"Something's wrong with you two, did something happen today?" Her voice cut through the stillness. Ace and I exchanged a brief, fraught glance. eat crept up my neck, betraying my calm facade. I drew in a slow breath, hoping my voice wouldn't waver at the same moment Ace began to sign something.

"Nothing out of the ordinary," I said.

"Just a long day is all." Ace signed.

She didn't seem convinced, her eyes narrowing just a fraction as she studied us, "are you sure child?" She pressed.

"Yes," Ace and I chimed simultaneously, my voice and the quick movement of his hand overlapping in a clumsy display. We were like two kids with their hands caught in the cookie jar, wide-eyed and guilty without uttering a confession at all.

Willow chuckled dryly, a knowing lilt in her tone. "Yeah, that's not suspicious at all, child." She said it with an affectionate shake of her head.

She moved around the small space with practiced ease, serving us our dinner as if it were any other night. Except tonight was different. A generous spread of fish, its skin glistening under the dim candlelight, lay next to the smoked pika, which let out little tendrils of steam as if it had just came out of the ground. The sides were lined up meticulously: root vegetables roasted to caramelized perfection, wild greens dressed lightly with vinaigrette, and a basket of warm bread filled the air with its comforting scent. This was a small feast in comparison to the dinners we usually had.

"Your acting as if you caught a cat in the nets, what happened out there today? You were fine this morning," she pressed again, her eyes locking onto mine as she took her seat across from us. It was as though she plucked the imagery straight from my mind—how did she manage that? It wasn't a small cat but it was a feline creature all the same.

"Like Ace said, it was just a long day," I murmured, reaching for a piece of bread in an attempt to occupy my hands. I tore off a chunk, the crust giving way with a satisfying crackle. Ace had already submerged himself in his plate of food. I guess his logic was he wouldn't have to respond if he was holding bread and silverware as he stuffed his face.

The chair scraped against the wooden floor as Willow stood, the soft rustle of her skirts hushing the room. "Well, I'm sure you'll be whipped back into shape in no time," she said, her voice carrying that age-old wisdom that seemed to see straight through to one's very soul. "Maybe your favorite dessert will cheer you up. I almost forgot." She sauntered into the small kitchen area.

I exchanged a glance with Ace, a silent conversation passing between us. We loved Willow, but desert? The way she moved on from the topic instead of digging deeper to figure out what was bothering us? Who was this woman.

"Okay, what's going on with you? Is it a special occasion?" I asked as she walked back over to the table with a plate of cloud berry bread. It was something she only ever made for special occasions.

Willow set the plate on the table. "Oh no child, I just missed you both is all," she said, and there was a sincerity in her tone that made my heart swell. "And I figured your first full day back would be long. Oh, I also got a bottle of Ace's favorite Gin from the markets." She moved to open one of the small cupboards under the counter and there was the bottle unopened as she grabbed it and it clanked against the table as she set it down.

"Thanks Willow, I could use a drink after today." He signed I scowled at him from across the table. Underneath the table my foot found his leg and I kicked him. The swift kick was meant as a warning. His body jolted slightly, a reaction masked by a chuckle that bubbled up out of him.

"You know, you didn't have to do all this just for us coming back," he continued, his eyes glancing over the feast one more time, the desert the Gin. "We'll be sure to come back sooner next time." Ace finished and I realized he was probably right, had she made such a meal because we had stayed gone so long? Guilt filed me, not just from that but from the things we were keeping from her. We finished the rest of our food in a silence that wasn't quite uncomfortable anymore. Afterwards Ace and I gathered the plates and began cleaning. Willow always enjoyed the cooking, it was the clean-up she never cared for so we always took care of it for her while we were here.

With the last of the plates wiped clean, I set them aside and leaned back against the counter next to Ace. Willow moved with a grace that belied her years, stepping between us to place a bottle of gin on the worn wooden surface. Her hands were steady, but there was an odd tension in her shoulders that caught my eye.

"Now, go enjoy yourselves," she began, her voice carrying the familiar warmth. "Oh and I'll take care of the chores tomorrow simply because of the amount of fish you brought home. You did good today, you deserve it." Her smile was as comforting, but it didn't quite reach her eyes.

I glanced at Ace, trying to gauge his reaction. His posture was relaxed, but I saw the quick flicker of confusion in his gaze before he masked it with a nonchalant shrug. Something about everything Willow had just said felt off.

"Are you sure?" I found myself asking, even as I mentally craved the respite she offered. "We don't mind helping out."

Willow waved off my offer with a dismissive flick of her wrist. "Nonsense. You two have been through enough today. Besides, it gives me something to do." She turned away, busying herself with a stray pot that didn't really need any more scrubbing.

Ace nudged me then, a silent signal that we should accept the gift without further question.

"Something seems wrong," I signed to him behind Willows back.

"I know but I think we should just accept the day off, especially after what happened today." He signed back his eyes wide.

"You both better not be talking about me," Willow said and the glanced over her shoulder giving us another smile.

"Thank you, Willow," I managed, my voice softer than I intended.

"Of course, child," she responded, still with her back to us. "Now shoo, both of you. Enjoy the night air."

With a last glance at the woman who had become our anchor, Ace and I stepped out into the cool embrace of the evening with a bottle of Gin in hand.

We had wandered into a clearing that seemed as though it was waiting just for us, with a large nightoak offering its trunk as a seat. I settled back against the tree, the bark pressing into my skin through the fabric of my shirt, grounding me in the moment.

Ace circled around, gathering kindling before dropping to the forest floor. His wings folded neatly behind him as he used the twigs and dried leaves, coaxing a fire to life quickly with one of his daggers he kept draped over his chest and a stone.

The bottle of Gin Willow had given us sat between us in the snow, already more than half-empty, condensation beading on the glass. It was good stuff—smooth with a hint of juniper and something else. I grabbed it and took another pull, feeling the warmth spread down my throat and settle in my belly.

"Remember that time at New Point Peak where we had to run for our lives because the soldiers rushed us, and you got an arrow in the ass." I couldn't help but chuckle at the memory, even though it had been a close call.

Ace snorted, a sound that rumbled deep in his chest, and shook his head. He reached for the bottle, his hand brushing mine. "Yeah, I remember," He signed. "Good times," He tilted the bottle toward me in dry humor before taking a long pull from the bottle.

I laughed again, tipping my head back against the tree. The firelight played across Ace's features, softening the sharp angles of his face as he attempted a scowl at me.

"I wouldn't have gotten hit if you would have kept the glamour up but nooo you thought we were in the clear." he signed.

I rolled my eyes, shifting to get more comfortable while pulling a few strands of loose hair behind my ear. "Hey, don't blame me, you're the one who wanted to go there to try the Gin, not me," I retorted. A playful note threaded through my words as I snatched the bottle from him and then gave it a little shake, "This is definitely better than theirs." I said before taking another drink.

The night had draped itself over the forest like a thick cloak, and the stars peeked through the canopy. It reminded me of someone...When Ace and I were wounded and dying during the war a man cloaked in black had saved us from the woods, I often wondered about where he was now.

Ace chuckled, the sound rich and warm in the cool night air bringing me back to the present. "I needed to know," he admitted, a sheepish grin flashing across his face for a fleeting second.

We sat there, enveloped in the somber quiet, each lost in our private contemplations. The fire popped, sending a shower of sparks skyward, a fleeting attempt to reach the stars that watched us.

I broke the silence with words heavy enough to sink into the cold earth beneath us. "All this time, we thought it was a Sky Elf, hell I even joked that you were the Peacebringer over the years. But it's been me all along." The truth hung in the air, as tangible as the smoke from our fire.

"Damn the mother, what the hell do I do Ace?" My voice cracked a little and I choked down the emotions with another swig of the Gin.

Ace got to his feet and moved the short distance to sit closer to me. Draping one of his wings around me like a little cocoon before he signed.

"We'll get through this just like we've always got through everything else. Together." He tucked me into him. He then reached for the Gin bottle, and took down the last of it.

I watched the flames dance as twigs snapped in the woods. Ace perked up from the sound.

"You hear that?" Ace signed.

"Yeah, but I'm took drunk to go for a hunt right now," I murmured my eyes feeling heavy and Ace chuckled and agreed. I didn't remember making it back home. I just remember feeling weightless.

CHAPTER SIX
KADE

As I stepped through the threshold the clatter of cutlery on metal trays echoed through the murmur of voices that filled the warship's cafeteria. Soldiers, weary from the day's drills, were hunched over their trays, shoveling down the evening's rations with a mechanical persistence that spoke of their longing to be anywhere but here.

As I made my way between the long rows of metal tables, I caught the tail end of a conversation that prickled my skin. Seth, a soldier known for his loose tongue and arrogance was holding court at one of the tables, his voice carrying over the rest.

"Look, I'm just saying, if Princess Valla was on this mission, at least we'd have something sexy to look at," he crowed, eliciting chuckles from his comrades.

My hand tightened around the tray I had yet to fill, the metal edge biting into my palm. Not because of his crass objectification of my sister—I didn't give a fuck about her—but because of the insinuation that followed.

"Hell, I'd bet she would have already captured the Peacebringer and we'd be back home by now," Seth continued, oblivious to my approach, "and not stuck out here on this warship eating fucking slop for supper."

I stopped behind him, the weight of my silence heavy in the air. A few heads turned, eyes widening as they noticed my presence. The laughter around Seth's table died.

"Is that so, Seth?" My voice was calm, but it carried an edge.

His buddies shifted uncomfortably, eyes darting away, but Seth, ever the bold one, swiveled around and faced me head-on. His chest puffed out like a rooster's, ready to stand his ground.

"Prince Kade," he said, a hint of defiance in his tone.

"Would you like to continue to insult me behind my back or would you prefer we take it to the fighting ring and you can show me just how big a man you are?" I arched a brow, my posture lax.

Seth faltered, his posture deflating as if the very air had been let out of him. "No, sir," he muttered, sinking back down into his seat.

The rest of the cafeteria had fallen deathly quiet, every pair of eyes fixed on us. With a curt nod, I dismissed them, their gazes dropping as I took my tray, filled it, and then retreated back to my quarters.

The hunt for the Peacebringer weighed heavy on my mind, though when did it not? The chosen one was the only one who could stop Ember from completing their goal of dominating this world. For a hundred years, Ember had believed the chosen one was gone, my father hadn't known if they were killed or not in the war between Heavensreach and Ember. No one could give us any clear answers, and all the sky elves seemed to have disappeared to. Considering what Embers Empire had done to Heavensreach it was no surprise that any who lived went into hiding. Since then my father had put a hefty bounty on the Peacebringers head, rumors spread like wildfire after that, of sightings, some were dead ends some weren't but the trail would always go cold after a while. It seemed like it was an impossible task to find them.

Pushing open the door to my room, I found Rhet lounging in front of the flames, his shirt carelessly unbuttoned, an image of leisure. He looked up as I entered, his eyes narrowing inquisitively.

"Something happen with the soldiers?" he asked.

I leaned against the door frame, the tray's metal cool in my hands, and let out a breath that felt like it had been held for an eternity. The room was warm, the fire crackling.

"Nothing I couldn't handle," I began, words slow as I moved and took a seat across from Rhet at my desk.

"Though I don't think it's going to take much more before they turn on me. They are father's soldiers after all." My fork jabbed into the meal, the slop-like substance barely registering on my taste buds. "None of them carry any respect for me, they are only here on father's orders, not mine... Anyway, you look like you had a good time," I noted, forcing down another bite as I eyed the flush over his features.

"We had an excellent time," Rhet confirmed with a grin, sitting up straighter in the chair. He rested his elbows on his knees. With a practiced flick of his wrist, he gathered his hair, tying it in a half-up messy bun that somehow added to his roguish charm. "I plan to see him again soon, it's just hard with, well you know." His hand swept through the air, encompassing the vastness of our floating steel prison and the mission we have ahead of us.

His eyes turned toward the porthole, the sun sinking into the endless blue. It was almost night now. "So where are we headed now?" Rhet asked. "I'm not sure the men will last much longer on the water. The last two places we went, even though we stayed for a few days before getting back on the water, they still weren't satisfied."

I set my fork down, pushing the tray away, "they won't be satisfied until they are back home. But unfortunately for them it's going to be awhile. Any new information come in?" I asked glancing over to my marked up map.

Three sharp knocks on the door pulled my attention.

"Enter," I called. The soldier who stepped through the threshold bore a look of urgency in his eyes.

"Sir, we have an urgent message for you, it was just delivered. It's the Peacebringer, sir," he announced. My heart skipped a beat. My face revealed nothing of my inner turmoil as I steeled myself, fixing my gaze on Rhet. He had been tasked with overseeing communications, his oversight could cost us dearly.

The soldier continued, "It's a fae woman, sir, she's not a sky elf. She's in Esora, she goes by the name Emelyn. I have already told the men to change course, sir."

My jaw clenched involuntarily. "Thank you, dismissed," I said, granting the soldier leave with a curt nod. As the door closed behind him, sealing us back into our private council,

I turned fully toward Rhet. His usual air of nonchalance was absent now, replaced by a tension that mirrored my own.

"About that..." Rhet's voice trailed off as he rubbed the back of his neck. "I hadn't checked for any birds since I'd been back." The confession hung between us, thickening the air.

I didn't bother with a response. Instead, I reached for the crystal decanter on the sideboard and poured amber liquid into a glass with a heavy hand. The drink splashed against the sides, a silent reflection of my frustration. I threw it back, feeling the burn slide down my throat, offering a brief respite from the gnawing tension.

"Rhet, we can't afford these oversights," I murmured, more to myself than to him. The stakes were too high, the weight of everything was suffocating me.

"Kade, I—" He started, then stopped, clearly struggling to find words that would bridge the gap his negligence had created.

"Save it," I cut him off, turning back to the map. My fingers traced the terrain leading to Esora, mind racing with strategies and contingencies. But it was to late for that. She was there and we would be there to. I blew out a breath.

I rolled up the map with care, tucking it under my arm. As I stepped toward the door of my bathing chamber, my gaze fell on the polished blades displayed above the mantle. With a finality that settled in my chest like stone, I whispered into the quiet, a vow meant for only me.

"I'm coming for you bunny."

CHAPTER SEVEN
EMELYN

Sunlight filtered through the small kitchen window, casting a warm glow over the wooden table where Ace and I sat with Willow, our plates clinking softly as we ate. The soft breeze caused the leaves on the living wall behind me to sway. The vines and leaves had grown long and I wondered how long it had been since Willow tended to her plants.

The comforting scent of freshly baked bread mingled with the sharp tang of cloves and cinnamon in the air as we all enjoyed a warm cup of pojo. I watched Willow from the corner of my eye, noting how she pushed her food around her plate more than eating it.

Ace glanced up from his meal, his brow creasing with the same concern that knotted my stomach. We both knew

Willow, strong-willed and tireless, always bustling about with chores or haggling at the market. But these past few days had been different. She'd been still, almost reflective, insisting we leave the work to rest on its haunches while we spent time together.

The silence stretched between us, filled with unspoken questions. Was this change in her simply a rare moment of rest or a sign of something deeper? Last night, as we shared stories and laughter over our strong liquor, even then, there was an unusual softness to her. It wasn't like Willow to let go so freely. Was her age catching up to her? I didn't want to think about that.

"Would you two like to go for a walk?" Willow's voice cut through my thoughts, brisk and bright. "We've been couped up the last few days."

I met her gaze, searching for some clue in her eyes, but found none. She seemed as solid as the earth beneath our feet, yet I couldn't shake the feeling that something delicate was shifting within her. Ace gave me a subtle nod, a silent agreement that fresh air might do us all some good.

"Sure," I responded. We cleared the last bites from our plates. I lingered a moment longer, watching Willow. She moved with her usual purpose but lacked the brisk efficiency that defined her every motion. It had been days since she'd set foot outside for her customary errands:

the market stalls would be wondering where the woman with the sharp tongue and sharper bargaining skills had vanished to. Actually the woman had always been sharp all the way around but not the last few days.

"Willow, are you sure you're feeling alright?" The question slipped out, coated in concern.

"Of course, child, I've never felt better." Her tone was light, almost playful, yet it did little to ease the tightness in my chest. She reached for her cloak, draping it over her shoulders with a flourish that sparked a brief glint of the old Willow in her eyes. "Be sure to wear your cloaks, it's chilly today. Now let's get a move on," she commanded, her words chasing us towards the door.

I watched her stride past the breakfast table, leaving behind the dishes in a disarray. So unlike her, this casual neglect of order in favor of going for something as casual as a walk. But she bickered at us all the same.

"Come along, you two," she urged, already halfway out the door, her voice feigning its usual unflinching tone.

Ace and I exchanged a glance, each of us carrying a silent promise to tread lightly around our concerns. We grabbed our cloaks, the fabric heavy and reassuring around our frames, and followed Willow out into the crisp air.

Something was off when we walked into our village. It was too quiet. Eyes from every fae followed me, and their whispers taunted me.

She's the Peacebringer, the chosen, the reborn...

Their words circled me with every step further we took into our small hole in the world of Osparia. How did they know? We hadn't even told Willow. Willow still stood straight, not even looking to me after hearing the truth of their words.

The sound of a man cut through the soft murmurs. I recognized him. His name was Kai. He was a water fae like me. Like everyone here.

He had been there during the war all those years ago. His skin was bronzed and weather-beaten, bearing the marks of countless battles. His black, shoulder length hair was messy. His boots were sturdy and worn from long treks. He ground his stance in the snow. Despite his rough exterior, he wore a new cloak with fur fighting off the chill of winter. But he was holding chains in one of his gloved hands.

"You lies to us," he said, his tone sure.

"What?" My brow furrowed. I looked around me seeing a growing circle of angry and confused faces.

"Kai, don't–"

He cut Willow off, disregarding her completely, and it made anger rise within me.

"You deserve everything that's coming to you." As he spoke, more male and female fae stood and raised their heads in agreement at his words.

"Kai, don't do this. She is one of us, she always has been, Orion wouldn't want this." Willow spoke up for me, but he rushed at her, stopping when he stood toe to toe.

"Orion is dead. And it would disappoint him that his *daughter*," he spat out the last word, as if I wasn't worthy of the title, "didn't do something sooner."

I stepped forward, throwing my arm between the both of them. I was protective of Willow, his wrath wasn't for her. His words had made my eyes sting. My father was everything to me. He was our leader before the war and wouldn't have wanted this divide within our world–our people.

"How did you find out what I was—am."

"See!" He pointed to me, "she admits it to us all, she is the Peacebringer." He quieted his voice and leaned in a little to close to comfort. "I overheard you in the woods the other day, talking about what you are." He spat at my feet. "And now, Ember is coming for you and we will be free of them by giving them what they desire most." He said as he glared daggers at me, he pulled the snow from the ground, shifting it to water, and twisted the snake-like stream in my direction. I dodged his strike and turned his own water against him, making the water's edge as sharp as a blade, slicing it across his cheek. He turned to me, his wrath fully focused on me instead of Willow now.

He bended again, eight streams of water jutted from the ground like an octopus. Ace stepped up to my side, and I placed my hand against his chest.

"No." I signed, and he stepped down, but remained close in case I needed him. Kai grew closer as he stepped forward, readying to fight me. He finally broke the silence.

"You expect me to believe, all of us to believe, that you didn't know?" He gestured to the growing crowd of fae and other creatures surrounding us now. "You expect us to welcome you with open arms after this? As you stood idly by as the supposed Peacebringer, in a war that's been ongoing for over a century!?" He released a manic laugh under his breath as if he thought this was all some crazed joke. Blooms of smoke barreled from his mouth in the frigid air. "And you have done nothing to stop it!" He yelled, bringing his glossy eyes to mine.

"I fought by all of your sides during the war." I peered around the crowd. "At any battle we came across over the years."

"Except you were the key to stopping it, Emelyn!" His claim made me go quiet. "We lost everything! Our wives, women lost husbands... we lost our children, our homes." He choked over the words. "You could have stopped it... I'm sure you remember my wife, my daughter. She looked up to you, you know, our leader's brave daughter Emelyn, our future leader... and now where are they, Emelyn?" He waited for my response, but the knot in my throat wouldn't let me speak. "Where. Are. They. Now. Emelyn!?" His shouts made an uneasy silence fall over the village.

"They're dead," I whispered. That was all I could manage, but any fae could hear what I said.

"And where did you go afterward? Where did you go after the war?"

"I left." My voice was as quieter than a whisper as I fought back the tears brimming my eyes. If only I had known the powers I possessed. If only I had known how to use them.

He shook his head before lunging for me. Lost in his anger, I turned my head away, preparing to just take his strike.

I deserved it. If I had the power to end this war all these years, and didn't, or couldn't, I couldn't blame him for his wrath. I'd be angry too. Regardless that I didn't know what I was. I should've known sooner than this, figured it out before it had gone this far. I felt as though I had failed everyone I ever loved.

Ace hauled Kai up and over his shoulder before he got to me, refusing to let me take his wrath willingly. Kai spat at my feet.

"I hope they destroy you! This sought after thing we lost everything over! I sent for them and they're coming! They're coming!"

He screamed with angry tears streaming down his face as Ace carried him off until he finally pushed out of his hold and stormed away, kicking up snow. The whispers from before turned into shouts.

"Fuck you!"

"Embers going to come for you!"

"Worthless!"

"How could you!"

Villagers cried, and I took a few steps back, still reeling from everything that had been said and done. All the people I had known my entire life turned against me in the blink of an eye. The only ones on my side willing to stand up for me were Ace and Willow. But the few would never overrule the many glaring at me, their eyes filled with hatred, mirroring everything Kai had said about me. They all believed that I knew and allowed the war to continue, allowing the deaths of all those dearest to them—to me.

"What would Orion think!? Or Ivy!?" A woman yelled from the mob of a crowd. All the eyes, the words, the talk of my parents, buried into my soul. My blood ran cold. The panic rose in my chest as my feet rooted where I stood, my breathing rapid, unable to free myself from their words, more painful than any sticks or stones.

I was suddenly backstage, seeing from a distant spot in my conscious mind, watching the chaos unfold. Their mouths kept shouting, spewing spit from their anger until all the noise faded and I wasn't in control anymore.

I watched from outside myself. My eyes locked on the crowd and the light in my eyes awoke again. Bright and burning. Their faces went slack before terror coated their features. Silence fell as brows furrowed, and lips parted until every fae blew backward away from me, flying through the trees and snow. The only ones remaining untouched were Ace and Willow.

The power came from me. Wind bended in a blast from my chest, uncontrolled and erratic. I didn't know how it happened. The light faded from my eyes and Ace had an arm gripped around me for support. When I came back to my senses, a few moments later, everyone looked at me with fear.

"Time to go." Ace signed and tried to haul me away.

"Wait!" Willow called out to us. "Please, let me know where you end up, and that you're safe... I'm so sorry child, you didn't deserve this. Neither of you." She shook her head before pulling me and Ace into a hug. "Now go, hurry."

We hurried away before anyone had time to recover and retaliate. I peered back over my shoulder at Willow, who stood alone in the cold. The only person left from our past that still loved us, and I didn't know if I could ever return to see her again.

"What happened back there?" I asked as my mind replayed everything over and over again through the few hours we had been walking through the woods. Something more within me stirred in my gut and took over when I panicked at the village. Was I the Peacebringer? Or only a vessel for its power? Was that the same thing?

"Exactly what you think." He responded with his hands as he walked next to me.

"Did I bend the air?" The question came out in awe. I knew the chosen one could bend all the elements, but knowing and experiencing it for myself were two different things. I wasn't in control back there. It was.

Whatever that meant.

I was the chosen one. The thought ran through my mind again. This needed to sink in. I would have to learn and master these abilities and bring peace to our world again. The weight of the responsibility made me gravely ill.

"Are you alright?" Ace asked, and I was sure he had noticed my face going more ashen with every step further we took.

Of course I wasn't alright, I was spiraling.

I cleared my throat. "Yeah... can you–can you teach me something?"

He paused his steps and turned to me after I fumbled over my words. As far as I knew there had only ever been one Peacebringer before me, at the beginning of time, when the gods blessed us with the abilities we have now, they sent the chosen to bring peace, help our world find ballance with our new abilities. Only ever to return and be reborn when we had lost our way. Ember had thought they had destroyed the Peacebringer all those years ago in hopes to take Osparia for themselves. Although they had still been unsuccessful with taking Woodhaven. Legends say, if the Peacebringer is alive, they'll have the abilities to defeat whatever evil defiles the world to restore it again.

But I had seen Embers' brutality before. Ace and I lost our parents to them. We lost everything to them.

I wanted to hide in a hole, but what kind of life would that be? Ember would continue to rage over the world with their cruel tyranny. There was no going back to the way it was before.

I was only an orphan from a small corner within the world of Osparia. I didn't have the ability to take down an entire empire. But I knew the Peacebringer was powerful, they wielded all the elements and when awakened became a deadly, unstoppable force. I was sure there was knowledge about the peacebringer that even the legends and campfire stories didn't tell us about. The outburst at the village proved to me that I carried it within me. Knowing that a war was coming, fueled me to want to prepare. Besides, it seemed like a good way to keep my mind busy.

"I can try." He arched a brow and glanced at the ground before looking back up at me. He stepped forward and took one of his small black feathers that I kept weaved into my silver hair and placed it in his palm. He bended the wind and created a small turbulence around it. It shifted and spun above his hand, but the feather never left the center of his palm. The movement stopped, and he sat the feather in my hand.

"Your turn," he said, and I rolled my eyes.

"That was completely unhelpful, Ace." I huffed, and he laughed. "I've seen you bend the air a million times. That doesn't mean I understand how to do it," I said, and he hummed in contemplation.

"Bending the air is like breathing for me. I don't know how to teach it." He ran a hand down his face.

"What does it feel like?" I asked, and he gave me a puzzled look.

"What do you mean?"

"When I bend the water, it's as if I can feel it running through my veins, like a flowing river. I can feel its current through me. What does it feel like when you bend the wind?"

Ace thought about my question before he answered.

"Weightless." He looked at my scrunched brow and then looked back to the feather. "When I bend the feather, I feel as if every tendril of wind weaves between all of its barbs and encircles it, keeping it in one place but still allowing it to move."

I shook my head. "I'm never going to get this." A cynical laugh escaped me and Ace grabbed me around the waist and launched us to the tops of the trees. I yelped from the speed and chill of the air, clutching the feather in my palm. "What are you doing?" I yelled, and he landed on a large branch big enough for both of us to stand on.

"Making you the feather." He signed and then weaved the feather back into the same spot he took it from in my hair.

"What?" I asked. I was so confused until he glanced at me and then down to the ground below. "No! Have you lost your mind? Now look who's the crazy one."

He shrugged as if maybe he had misplaced his brain.

"I won't let anything happen to you. When Sky Elves are learning the basics of bending, our parents would make us freefall from Heavesreach."

"Yeah, you were all a bunch of nutcases." I laughed, and Ace smiled at the memory.

"No better than getting thrown into a river and hoping you figure out the flow of the water." He signed and I couldn't disagree. "Exactly."

"Yes, but at least you had your wings."

"Eme, listen to me." Ace's features grew more serious. "I already said I won't let anything happen to you."

I knew he meant it, but falling to your death had a way of filling you with doubt.

"Now I want you to feel the airflow between every limb as you fall. That's the best way I can describe what it's like to air bend."

I nodded and then looked down.

Instant regret. My stomach recoiled.

"Ace, I don't think I can–" My body went weightless as fear slithered through my gut, the freezing winds blasting into my face as I fell head first down to the snowy depths of the forest floor below. He had pushed me, and I felt a scream work its way up my throat, but I swallowed it down as I tried to focus. I closed my eyes and leveled out my body while I splayed out my hands and arms, feeling every place the wind touched me. It flowed through my clothes and around my silhouette. I worked to wield the feeling, the air, before it had the chance to get past me.

I wanted to feel weightless. I wanted to float. I needed to stop the winds from flowing past me and to command them to stay under me so it would keep me from becoming a broken lump at the bottom of this tree.

What you want and what you get are two very different things. I continued to fall, and I finally screamed, squeezing my eyes closed, thinking this was the end for me, my best friend pushing me out of the tallest tree he could find. I continued to feel the icy wind whipping past my face. The chill of it almost burned me as it barrelled against my skin. A light tap against my shoulder made me unscrunch my face and look to my right. Ace was crouched next to me in the snow with a smug smile on his face as he leaned his arms against his knees.

I was confused for a minute until I glanced down and saw that I had never hit the ground, but hovered just above it. At first, I thought it was Ace's bending, until I looked at him again and he put both his hands up.

"That's all you, Em." He signed, and I blew out a breath. I couldn't decide if I wanted to laugh or cry. I think I was doing both as we smiled at each other in awe of it all.

"Now how do I stop it?" I asked and with a wave of his hand, I plopped into the soft snow underneath me with an oof. "Could've warned me," I said as I stood, bending the snow off of me and sending it to Ace. He closed his eyes with a sigh when it splattered against his chest.

"We need to work on your block. That way no one can take control of the wind your bending like I just did." He wiped the wet chunks of snow off the front of his leathers and pulled in his cloak, draping it back over his wings. "I guess that doesn't really matter. After all, I am the last Sky Elf." His words hit me in the heart. Though we had never come across any Sky Elves in our travels, I hoped there were more out there.

It had become a habit to cover his wings since he was always in hiding, but did he need to conceal them now? He wasn't the peacebringer...

It was me, and I had to learn to embrace it.

CHAPTER EIGHT
EMELYN

We walked through the dense woods until they opened up to a muddy crossroads at sunset. Patrons were coming and going from our favorite tavern. The large wooden sign posted above the front door read Bells Bar & Brothel. Music and moans came flowing out of the windows on the second floor, while other women enticed travelers from the trail to come up to the whorehouse above the bar.

"I should have known you were heading to Bells." I said, walking behind Ace. He turned but continued to walk backwards up the trail while signing to me.

"I figured we could use a drink, and a good time after everything that happened." He winked and I chuckled with a wag of my head. "Besides, Hinky would never turn us away." He signed. The last time we had been to Bells was last year when we came in for one of our yearly visits. Usually we tried to visit Willow every six months or so, the same time pojo bloomed, but we were far in our travels and missed one. We had a routine when we came to visit. Bells had always been a part of it. I wondered if Hink and his wife, Helena, had missed us.

Stout beer, roasted meats, and perfume assaulted my nostrils as Ace pushed the large wooden front door open with a loud creak. The door was large enough for any race to fit through. This place had always been a safe haven for those that needed somewhere to go, we had learned that early in our travels when we stumbled across it. But now, things were different. I was the chosen one, and I wasn't sure if they would welcome me after I told them. I was still waiting for Ace to scold me for it, but he hadn't, not yet.

I threw up my fae glamour for Ace. I had always glamoured his ears when we went into public places for fear of people realizing he was a Sky Elf. His wings had always stayed hidden and tucked under his heavy woven cloak, but his longer extended ears would give him away if I didn't hide them, making them look like fae ears instead. But now I wasn't sure if it mattered anymore. If Kai had told Ember who I was and sent for them I doubted they'd be after Sky Elves anymore. Better to be safe than sorry.

I threw up another glamour over myself, not wanting to draw anyone's attention. Making my silver hair blonde, and dulling my fae features.

The bard sang tunes from the small step up stage in the far corner. Fae, orcs, dryads, brownies, shifters, along with plenty of other species, all different shapes and sizes, sat around large tables playing and betting on their games of Tile and cards. They drank and ate good food, lost in their own conversations. It was a busy night, and I was glad for the amount of bodies in the room to keep everyone's attention off of me.

Women sauntered around the room in tight busty dresses that hardly concealed anything as they served drinks and food to the easily excited males. Typical. Afterwards, if you wanted more than that, you could go upstairs where the working women had rooms. Downstairs was for business and relaxation, while upstairs was for all the sultry fun your heart desired.

We walked over to the long sleek wood bar that took up the back half of the room. Next to it was a narrow staircase that led upstairs. I pulled out my barstool made of some type of rock, as if they had sculpted it from stones, and it scuffed against the floors. Ace did the same.

There was a mix of dark stained woods and stone throughout all the furniture, creating a dark but cozy atmosphere. Helena was an Earth Dryad. She could bend earth, into anything she needed it to be, so I was sure it saved them coin when a bar fight broke out and they needed to replace anything.

"What can I get'cha?" The Orc barback called out to us as he dried the cups with a well-used rag before he tossed it over his shoulder. His pale green skin looked darker in the dim light of the tavern. He was burly and soft, but still riddled with muscle. The cups looked miniscule in his large hands. A beard in one large braid hung down the center of his chest and his long black hair pulled back into a ponytail at the nape of his neck. He looked up with his warm brown eyes from what he was doing and his bushy brows softened when he realized it was us. His gentle greeting eased some of my worries.

"Hey Hinky." I said with a wave of my hand.

"Haha! Eme, there's my girl!" He leaned over the bar and slapped a heavy hand on Ace's shoulder, almost knocking him from his seat. "Ace, my boy!"

I smiled as he leaned over to give me a quick hug, but his words tugged on my heart from a memory of long ago. I pushed it aside.

"How have you been? It's been so long." His deep voice boomed past his two sharp fangs that jutted from his bottom lip. "I was worried when you didn't visit in the spring." He slid each of us a cup full of some strong amber liquid and Ace and I took it down with one swig. I grimaced at the taste, but my shoulders relaxed as I perched up against the bar. I had needed that drink more than I thought.

"We've been—"

"Hinkleton Tulgan Bell!" A familiar woman's voice yelled from the backroom behind the bar. We could hear her clear as day over all the sounds in the bustling room. She meant business. Hinks' shoulders lurched as he flinched from the reprimand.

"Yes, dear," Hink answered his wife.

"You left the damn meat out again!" She called as she rounded the corner to face him, shoving the large tote of spoiled goods into his stomach. Her dress hugged her full, but short, figure. She barely reached Hinks' chest as she stood in front of him. Her heart shaped ears poked through strands of hair that had fallen from her labor showing her Earth Dryad lineage. Hink took it from her, disappearing through the back, disposing of it, before coming back through the backroom door.

"Stop hounding me, woman. I took care of it."

"Gods, if it wasn't for this stupid bond tethering us, I would've left ages ago!" She started to walk back through the backroom but Hink smacked her on her voluminous ass before grabbing her wrist and pulling her back into his broad chest.

"You'd still love me." He teased, and she huffed a breath, fighting the smile of defeat that tugged at her lips. She raised to her tippy toes, giving him a quick kiss.

"Did you see our guests?" Hink asked, and she looked past him to Ace and I.

"Oh, hey lovelies! How have you been?" She made quick work pouring us both a refill. The fact that she knew our cups were empty showed her expertise of running this place. "Gods, you can't even keep their glasses full, Hinky." She spat, glaring at him before returning to us with a warm smile. Ace and I took down the drinks as quickly as the first.

"We've been good, Helena. How are you?" I lied, wiping my mouth.

"Splendid dearie! So glad you stopped by for a visit." She gave my hand on the bar a light squeeze and reached across to tug on one of Aces cheeks before breezing by Hink and going back to her duties.

"I see things are the same as always." I laughed, enjoying the sense of familiarity. Their interaction was a balm to my spirit.

"Worse... were expecting. Again." He rolled his eyes, but despite his tone insinuating it was a nightmare, he couldn't hide the light in his eye. He loved Helena and I could see his excitement at having a new addition.

"How many kids is that now?" I teased.

"It'll be the 5th, and the last, if the damned woman wasn't so beautiful, maybe I could stay off of her." He chuckled as a small stone flew through the kitchen window that sat gaped open behind him. He rubbed at his neck where it hit before he turned to look at his wife, who winked with a sultry grin on her face. "You see what I mean... damned goddess with ears that can hear from a mile away."

Ace and I laughed as he poured us another.

"Ace." Her voice was like a seductive hiss. Ace looked over his shoulder to where Cherry stood at the bottom of the stairs. Her dark red dress matched her hair. Her legs seemed to go on forever, and so did the slit that went all the way up to her generous hips. She was busty and thick in all the right places with a tight waist. Beautifully fae. Her hips swayed with every step toward us. She wedged herself between Ace and me. Her leg swung over over Ace's lap, wrapping around his waist on the stool.

"Hi Eme." She spoke from her painted lips, but her eyes never left Ace as she faced him and began placing soft kisses on his neck. I could smell their arousal.

"I've missed you so much, Ace. Let's go upstairs and I can show you how much... Just like old times." Her mouth crushed against his and she whimpered from the touch. Ace was Cherry's regular customer. They had been fucking for as long as I could remember, ever since we found Bells.

Ace pulled back and looked at me as if asking permission like a child, and I nodded toward the stairs.

"You're a grown man. Go, have fun." I signed with a wink.

Ace wasted no time, picking Cherry up and placing her feet back on solid ground. He grabbed a bottle of amber liquid from Hink.

"You sure you don't want to join in on the fun, Eme?" Cherry questioned, her eyes filled with hunger toward me.

"You ask every time, Cher, and the answer is always the same." I crooned.

"It's a damn shame. I guess I'll just have to keep fantasizing about it then." She gave me a warm smile before she took the lead and Ace followed her like a lost puppy back up the stairs, taking a long swig from the bottle. I rolled my eyes.

"You sure you don't want to have your own fun?" Hink asked me as he served up another round of drinks.

"I'm sure. I'll be sleeping alone tonight."

"You can drop that glamour Em, everyone knows who you and Ace are. We don't judge here, you know that." His words made me relax further in my seat. I glanced around at the patrons that were too invested in their revelry to notice me anyway.

"Thanks Hinky."

As my glamour fell away, my fae features became brighter. I was sure my jade green eyes lit up, along with my complexion and silver hair. I dropped Aces too. Cherry had already seen every inch of him anyway. The thought made me huff a laugh.

The normal loudness in Bells faded slowly as the wooden door creaked open behind me. My stomach instantly knew something was wrong. Someone had walked in. I glanced up from my drink to Hink, who was nodding toward the back door past the stairs. A warning to slip away through the crowd. I glanced over my shoulder at the men that had walked in. Three of Ember's Fire Fae soldiers stood there, peering around the mass of people in the bar, angry scowls on their faces. They looked chapped and tired from the cold weather.

Fuck, Ace.

I peered back over to Hink, who shook his head again, knowing who my mind had wondered too. He looked toward the back door, telling me to leave.

"I'll take care of it... Go." He mouthed the words, and I didn't hesitate.

I did my best not to draw attention to myself as I weaved through people dancing and gambling. The bard started singing a new song. It was fast-paced and got people moving and I knew Hink had done it on purpose to give me a better chance to slip out the back.

"Gentlemen, what can I get'cha?" I heard Hinky's deep voice steal their attention before I slipped through the back door. Fire Fae weren't all bad. Only the soldiers under the emperor's commands were the ones we had to look out for.

I took a deep breath to steady myself and looked into the night sky. The clouds looked different. They moved quickly, barreling into the sky. My head cocked to the side, taking in the unusual movement. My blood ran cold as I realized I wasn't looking at clouds. I was looking at smoke. A lot of it, that came barreling over the skyline. It didn't take much longer after I recognized the smell of charred wood and coals wafting on the wind.

The village.

Willow.

I took off into a sprint without a second thought, forcing each step against the uneven snow hoping I wasn't too late.

CHAPTER NINE
ACE

I hadn't fucked, touched, or tasted a woman in months. Being constantly on the move with Eme meant we didn't get the luxuries of pleasures very often, and I intended to savor every moment

Spread your fucking legs.

I motioned to her, but she teased me as she lay on the bed. Bunching the fabric of her dress around her hips revealing to me her thick thighs—and nothing underneath it. I gripped the soft flesh and pried her legs apart, spreading her wide for me. I wasted no time as I dropped to my knees and dragged her to the edge of the bed. My head dipped between her thighs. I licked through her wet folds before I flicked and sucked at that taut, small bundle of nerves.

"Ace!" She moaned my name, arching further into my mouth as I devoured her. I hummed and licked as I pushed two fingers in, pounding them into her relentlessly. A growl vibrated through my chest and thrummed across that tender spot I knew would have her screaming for me.

There it was.

Cherry cried out as she ground her hips against my face. I withdrew my fingers and grabbed her plump, bare ass with my hands and squeezed, pulling her further into my mouth. Her movements became erratic. Uneven, as she squirmed under my hold.

She was close.

I let her drag against every flick of my tongue until her thighs strained, her legs trembled, and she came. My tongue savored every drop of her release as her inner muscles clenched around my needy mouth.

My cock throbbed, begging to be released from my now tight pants. We hadn't even gotten undressed before we started playing. When she'd sat in my lap at the bar, she was already dripping for me when I'd slid my fingers over her slick pussy under her dress.

I stood, walking over to the small office table on the other side of the room where the liquor had been abandoned. I snatched it up, taking a long drink before I felt Cherry's delicate hand running over my cock, undoing my pants, and pulling them down so they pooled around my ankles.

My breath hitched in my throat after taking down the fiery liquid as she fisted me. Once, twice. And then her touch was gone as she backed away and slipped her red delicate dress off her shoulders, letting it fall to the floor, revealing her large, firm breasts. She stood completely bare to me.

"My turn." She whispered as she dropped to her knees and urged me to her with a single curling finger. I obliged.

Cherry was attractive, but she was prettiest with her mouth wrapped around my cock. She licked at my tip, making a groan escape me before she opened for me and swallowed me down. Her head bobbed up and down on my thick length as she gripped my balls, kneading and rolling them in her palm.

Skies above.

I growled, low and guttural.

I fisted her hair and swiped my thumb over her tear-stained cheeks as I thrusted my hips in sync with her movements. Saliva spilled from the corners of her mouth as she choked me down, but continued to take everything I gave her. I grunted with every bump of my hard length against the back of her throat, again and again.

My hips pumped faster as I spilled down her throat with a jerk, and she swallowed every pulse of my release. She flicked her tongue over my dripping tip and lapped up every drop of me, same as I'd done to her.

Gods, she hadn't lost her touch.

She pulled back and took a few steps away from me as she wiped her mouth. I stepped out of my pants and took another swig from the bottle before handing it to her and taking off my shirt, maneuvering it around my wings easily. Her eyes lit up with pure feral hunger, and the look alone had my cock ready for her again.

I nodded to the bed and signed, "Show." Over the years, Cherry's picked up on a few signs. She knew exactly what I was asking for. She sauntered back to the bed and spread wide for me as she lay back and ran her hands down her body. The image made my mouth water. She whimpered when her fingers swept over that sensitive flesh between those delicious thighs.

Fuck.

I groaned as I sat the bottle down and stroked my cock as I watched her slowly come undone again. Her moans became breathy as she played with herself in front of me. I pumped myself harder at the sight of her.

"Fuck me, Ace." She moaned and her fingers paused. "I'm so ready for you." She was shaking with need. "Please." She begged, her voice dripping with desire.

I was at the bed in two long strides, crawling on top of her and sinking into her dripping, wet pussy. I threaded my fingers through her hair and held her in place. As soon as her needy walls clenched down on me, I knew I wouldn't last long. It had been too long.

I took one of my hands and ran it down her voluptuous curves until I could circle that taunt bulb under my thumb as I fucked her. I sucked on her peaked nipples as her screams of pleasure echoed off the walls in our room. Her long nails scratched down my muscled back around my wings as she writhed against me. I thrusted harder, faster, until we were both falling over the edge again. Our sounds of pleasure came out as animalistic cries.

My balls tightened, and I grunted my release as hot jets of cum overfilled her and she went slack underneath me. I rolled over to my side, both of us gleaming with sweat. A large pitcher of water sat next to the bed with a two glasses, but I went straight for the pitcher, drinking it from the container before offering Cherry a glass.

"Have I ever told you, you're my favorite customer?" She said as her breathing started returning to normal.

"Every time." I signed, and she grinned, taking the glass from my hand downing the water. The heat and haze from the alcohol had snuck up on me quickly as I got up and stumbled for my pants. My face had gone numb, but I grabbed the bottle off the desk as I yanked up my pants and took another swig. This place had always been where we could take a breather, relax and enjoy the amenities, and that was exactly what I had planned to do.

I walked back over to the large bed and laid propped up against the wooden headboard, my wings tucked effortlessly behind me. It squealed under my weight and I wondered if Cherry and I had broken it. She rubbed her hand over my abs before she straddled me again. She took the bottle from my hand and took the last swig of it before she sat it on the nightstand and leaned in. I opened for her as our tongues danced around one another. She hummed and my cock twitched from the sound. But a knock stopped us from going any further. I cocked my head toward the door, thinking it was Eme before a familiar voice sounded from the other side of it.

"Ace, it's Hinky. We got a situation."

I huffed, but Cherry crawled off of me and sat on the bed. My pants hung low on my hips as I went and opened the door. When I saw the look on Hinks face, I knew something was wrong.

"Where's Eme?" I signed.

"She's gone. Some Fire Fae came into the bar and she slipped out the back, but when I went to tell her the coast was clear, she wasn't there anymore." He spoke and my chest instantly tightened.

Lead sunk into the pits of my gut. I gathered the rest of my clothes frantically from the floor and got dressed quickly before I turned to Cherry, tossing her a small pouch of coin.

"Till next time, Cherry." I signed before brushing past Hink in the doorway. Fear struck me when I heard it. Our warning. Anytime we needed each other, we would call with a whistle.

And now Emelyn's whistle howled on the wind to me.

My blood went cold as I darted down the stairs and through the thick crowd, heading straight for the large front door. I knocked a woman over in my scurry to leave.

"Sorry," I signed as I gripped her arm to help her back to her feet.

Her puzzled hazel eyes, flecked with gold, struck me at first glance before I released her and darted out of the door. Normally I'd take more care, that wasn't the way I intended knocking women off their feet, but my mind was racing. I had to get to Eme.

I hoped I wasn't too late.

CHAPTER TEN
EMELYN

I ran, and ran, as fast as my fae feet could carry me, until my lungs burned, my side ached, and my legs begged for reprieve. Smoke billowed through the forest, causing my eyes to sting, but I didn't stop. Sounds of fighting and women crying carried through the haze. My heart pounded at the familiar sound, pummeling my chest with every hard beat. Snow fell lightly from the storm clouds rolling in, but it never got the chance to stick before the fire turned it to water, making the ground a muddy mess.

The soldiers had ransacked the village, flames engulfing all the small homes, huts and businesses. It all flashed back from the war a hundred years ago, and my stomach sank. How long would this go on? I was so tired of all the bloodshed.

Seeing the devastation unfold before me, memories of the past flooded my mind, each one a sharp, piercing pain that twisted my insides. The raw emotions of fear, anger, and sorrow threatened to overwhelm me, as if I was reliving those dark times all over again.

Water twisted up my arms, pulled from the sloppy ground, as I launched myself forward, trying to lessen the fire's destruction when I heard a familiar voice yell.

"That's her! That's who you want! Let us go! I called you here to take her, you said you wouldn't hurt us!" Kai shouted over the roar of the flames, and the sizzle of snow under the soldiers boots. Every fire fae soldier's eyes turned to me. The one holding Kai by his shirt tossed him to the soggy ground.

Shit.

I stood in a fighting stance, preparing for the worst as they circled me. Water whipped around me like the legs of an octopus readying to strike. I wasn't sure I could take all of them by myself, but I would try.

The first step one of them took, I whipped water at their ankles, knocking them back into the ground with a grunt. Then the rest changed their approach. Flames licked up their arms and legs as the circle grew tighter around me, the heat starting to suffocate my body. The blaze made me lightheaded as sweat beaded on my brow, making my clothes stick to me. The flames took the air from my lungs. It was impossible to breathe. I choked, trying to swallow the air my body desperately needed. I swiped my water at them, but my vision grew hazy from the heat. My water was evaporating faster than I could bend it as they circled me.

Suddenly, something changed. The feeling in the air shifted, like the barrelling black smoke coating the sky. This sensation coated me, calming the blaze, cooling the burning heat surrounding me but filling me with a new sense of dread.

Unease swirled in my gut, making every taut muscle in my body tighter. I wanted reprieve from the heat like a fish needing water. But the fear brewing inside made me want to crawl out of my skin.

I craned my head, looking through the fiery blaze when I saw him.

Kade, the prince of Ember. Heir to Embers throne.

Astride his warhorse, he trotted through the destruction as if this was a normal night for him. He probably enjoyed it. I assumed he was just as vile as his sister, Valla, the same woman who destroyed Esora, destroyed our life—our peace. His honey eyed gaze met mine as he strode by, looking me over once before his eyes returned to me.

His dark, tousled hair fell over his brow as he tilted his head and revealed his full lips curling upwards on one side in a menacing way that twisted my insides. And then he strode away.

His presence was dominating, and demanded attention, especially from me, regardless of the hate I carried for him.

While he pranced by on his warhorse, he held a look on his face I couldn't quite place. It creased across his brow as he looked out toward the fiery slaughter. If I didn't know better, I might mistake it for anger. He turned from it to leave, and it was as if the heat engulfed me again, returning in his absence. My small moment of reprieve was gone. My hatred must have stole my senses.

"Stop!" Willow cried out, and some of the Fire Fae turned for her. I looked to where she stood. She'd clearly been part of the scuffle, but she was alive. I sent gratitude to the gods for protecting her. The soldiers walked in her direction and it lurched me into action. I grasped for any moisture left behind. The sizzle of water and flame lashed into their ankles as I threw my bending at them. My long tendrils of water grabbed at their legs and knocked them away, dragging them to the ground. One man got to his feet and a tendril of my water shot through his chest, covering the ground in crimson.

I got them. All but one.

Somehow, I had missed him amongst the crowd of fae and fire.

He clutched Willow from behind as his flames diminished and he pulled a long dagger from his belt. His fire heated the blade so hot that it glowed a bright red. He held it up to Willow's neck.

"Wait." I slowly let my water fall away to puddles at my feet and raised both my hands above my head. "It's me you want, right? If you promise to leave, I'll leave with you willingly... Please... Don't hurt her." I pleaded, dropping to my knees, ready for surrender. The other fae recovered from the ground and grabbed my wrists, chaining them in irons behind my back.

All my power left me, the iron stealing it away. If I hadn't already been on my knees, I would have collapsed to the ground from the loss of it.

"It's okay, child," Willow spoke softly, "I'll see you again." Her stoic features didn't match the threat facing her life. I saw no fear, only calm acceptance. There were tears in her eyes, but I knew they weren't for herself–they were for me having to watch.

The man holding Willow paused for a chilling moment, locking eyes with me as a sinister smile spread across his face. My heart clenched in terror, a cold dread settling deep in my bones, as he raised his blade it seemed to glint ominously in the firelight, reflecting the flames that danced around us, casting eerie shadows that danced across his face.

With a swift and cruel motion, he moved the blade, slicing through Willow's delicate neck. The air was filled with a sickening sound—a wet, guttural noise that echoed through the chaos—as the blade cut through flesh and bone.

Blood gushed from Willow's neck, dark and thick, staining her clothes and the muddy ground beneath her. The metallic scent filled the air, mingling with the acrid smell of smoke and burning wood, creating a nauseating mixture that assaulted my senses. The sight of her life pooling on the ground, mingling with the mud and turning it into a dark, sticky mess, was a horrifying sight that would be forever be seared into my memory.

Willow's body slumped forward, collapsing onto the soil with a sickening thud, her eyes staring lifelessly ahead. Her once vibrant and lively spirit silenced in an instant, leaving behind only a haunting stillness.

"No!" The word tore from my throat, a guttural cry of anguish and despair that escaped before I could stop it. A sob wracked through me, my body trembling uncontrollably as the weight of what had just happened crashed down on me.

"No no no no." I screamed, weeping, my knees scraping through the mud as I fought the soldiers holding my chains, using my body weight against them. Trying to get to her—needing to ger to her.

hot tears streamed down my dirtied cheeks. The men from behind hauled me to my feet and restrained me, holding me tighter than before with the irons around my wrists. I lurched against them again and again.

The man that killed her cackled to himself. I'd remember the sound of it. The look on his face when he took her from me. The emptiness in his blue eyes. How his dark, wet hair fell over his brow when he jerked the blade. I would end him one day.

He turned away and left her lifeless body behind a few feet in front of me. As fast as the flames started, they were gone, as the fire fae soldiers began dragging me to their warship. I was numb–destroyed once again by the murdering flames of Ember.

With the last of my energy, I whistled, sending it with the wind, in hopes Ace would hear my cry for help. Willow had been one of the few people we had left and now all we had was each other.

CHAPTER ELEVEN
EMELYN

The Fire Fae soldiers crowded me closely as they escorted me back to their large, black metal warship in the distance. But my eyes didn't focus on that. They locked on the back of the soldier's head that had sliced Willow's throat and left her at my feet.

His very existence made every nerve ending in me want to lunge for him and tear him limb for limb for what he'd done. My imagination got the best of me as I thought about every way I could cause him pain before taking his life. Tears still dampened my cheeks, every step away from Willow felt wrong. It should of been me. I should be the one lifeless, while she should still be here. I was supposedly this all powerful thing, the peacebringer, but I couldn't even protect those dearest to me.

My mind was interrupted when the three soldiers behind me shoved me, hard, to my knees and then grabbed me by the scalp and yanked me back to my feet, jerking me forward again. They laughed, and mocked, tossing me around for their enjoyment. The pain from the disconnect of my abilities made me stumble, my legs becoming wobbly.

Fucking iron.

"Move!" One behind me shouted as we made it to the moonlit shoreline where the ship was perched and waiting. The long metal ramp dug into the ground as we climbed it. Every step for me was a chore, with the iron clamped around my wrists. The pang of metal under my boots with every step I took was the only thing keeping me grounded and calm as I tried to focus on my surroundings and ignore the pain tingling through my limbs. I made note of every turn and hallway as they moved me through the narrowed halls of the ship, but the haze of iron clouded my mind.

A small metal door appeared at the end of the one we were traveling down. It had a large locking mechanism attached to it and I assumed this was where they kept their prisoners. As the man who killed Willow opened the door and walked inside, he stepped down a flight of stairs leading to the belly of the ship. I followed, feeling a thick fog of pressure consume me as I walked through the threshold, making me fall to my knees. He moved to the side, letting me tumble down the metal stairs.

I gasped for breath from the magic that enchanted this space, and the impact of the fall. I tasted blood, and my head pounded. This magic, on top of the iron already around my wrists, dying almost sounded pleasant right about now.

The murderer cackled under his breath before hurrying down the stairs and grabbing my arm, he dragged me by rows of cells before he threw me in one.

"Don't fight it. You won't be getting out of here." He spat next to me before he sauntered over and undid my cuffs. It relieved the pain but my body was so weak. This space had some sort of enchantment, keeping those within these walls unable to use their bending. Weakening them. I looked along the ceilings and could see the bloody markings that kept this place bound by whatever magic they had used. The only person that would be able to bend in here was whoevers blood they had used for the markings.

Smart.

I didn't know enough about enchantments to know how to break them. I'd have to change that after I got out of here.

"Don't get any ideas, pet." He said as he walked back out, slamming the cage behind him. All his buddies snickered under their breath. There were seven of them, including the man I hadn't taken my eyes off of since the village. "Enjoy your new home." He sneered and the rest of them taunted me with nasty remarks as they walked away, heading back up the stairs, and slamming the metal door. The loud clanking sound of the lock sealed me in. I was trapped, caged like an animal, unknowing what fate lay ahead.

I looked around the large space, searching for anything I could use as a weapon. The metal floor was cold, and wet. I could hear the squeaks and pitter patter of rats' feet around the room. I glanced at the other cells but saw no one. A few skeletons littered the empty cells, which didn't seem promising for me.

The cell next to me had one in it, and I slid my arm through the bars and tried to rip a bone away from it. I had no weapons, they had stript me of everything. A bone was better than nothing. I snapped it off the skeleton, and it splintered, giving it a sharp end. Perfect.

I could kill him if he got close enough. I stood, the metal wall lined with the small of my spine as I leaned back against it for support. The rock and uneasy sway of the ship departing against the waves outside made me slide back down the wall to the dirty floor.

The water was so close beyond the wall I could feel its pull to me, even though the magic kept us apart. I was sick. Nauseous. My body was so tired and weak. I was so cold. I laid on my side, the wall at my back, and tucked the sharp bone under me. The icy chill of the metal ship seeped into my bones without the warmth of a blanket or the comfort of a pillow.

My mind wandered to the day we returned to the village. Willow welcomed us back home from our travels with open arms, warm eyes and a smile stretched across her face. I focused on that as hot tears streamed down my face and the darkness of sleep consumed me.

The loud screech of the metal door opening tugged on my eyes as the light shone in and a hooded figure stood at the top of the stairs. I sat up, hiding the sharp bone from view as I waited for what was coming. For all I knew, this person could do unspeakable things to me, kill me if they wanted.

I got to my feet as they approached the cage, keeping my guard up and preparing for a fight. The man walked over and pulled down his hood, looking at me with amber eyes through the bars.

"Calm down. I'm here as your escort. I'm not going to hurt you." His dark, shoulder length hair was wavy and half pulled up, while loose strands framed his face.

"What does Ember want from me?" I wanted to figure out how long they planned on keeping me alive, if the emperor wanted me dead so bad, why hadn't his soldiers killed me in Esora.

"Knowing my father, my guess is your head on a platter so he can scare the rest of Osparia by taking away their last shred of hope. But you probably don't want to hear that, so I'll give you the optimistic answer, he just wants to talk."

"Real reassuring." I huffed as my eyes glared daggers at him. I'd put his fathers head on a platter first.

"Come on, we're going to the deck. My brother is waiting." He gave me a cocky grin, and I noted the similarities between Kade and him. They were definitely brothers by the resemblance. Both princes of Ember.

"Your brother? What's your name?" I asked.

"Prince Evereht Corvus, the youngest of my siblings, call me Rhet, I'm used to living in their shadows by now." He gave me a small bow. "At your service, Emelyn," he said sarcastically with a wink, and I rolled my eyes.

"You're quite the character, it seems." I gripped the bone behind my back, still leaning against the wall. He nodded toward the door.

"Come on, there is something you need to see." He unlocked the cage and turned, walking back toward the stairs, giving me his back as if he wasn't worried I'd kill him. "Leave the bone. You've been in this room for too long. You wouldn't stand a chance against me." He shouted confidently over his shoulder before making it to the door.

Startled he knew about the bone, but even more so surprised why he didn't take it from me. I let it fall to the floor though, because he was right. Lifting my arm at the moment was a chore. Everything felt weighted down and I couldn't remember the last time I ate. How long had I slept? My eyes burned with tears, how long had Willow been gone?

I shut them down. I'd grieve alone in my cell, away from prying eyes.

I followed behind him silently as we walked up the stairs, through the door, and down the long halls they had dragged me down before. Fire torches lined them, casting a warm glow of light.

Walking out on the deck of the ship, the temperature shifted and suddenly I was freezing. Snow was falling heavily now, and they had stripped me of my cloak and weapons when the soldiers took me. The lap of the waves crashed against the ship, tempting me to flee or run but I was so weak. Something made me pause. Something more than the treacherous weather.

Prince Kade stood with his back to me, looking out over the ocean. I peered over at Evereht. All he did was nudge me forward. No other soldiers were out here and I wondered how long I had been out in that cell. The darkness of night casted over the cloudy sky, making it seem dreary and colder than it already was. A fog had settled over the water.

When I was captured and taken to the ship, it was in the middle of the night. Now we were surrounded by water, and it was once again nightfall. I had to have slept the day away.

I stepped up to where Kade was leaning his forearms against the long, sleek, metal rail looking over the waters of Draynua. He wore all black. His honey eyes gave me a sympathetic side eye before he looked back out to the open water. The expression seemed genuine. I didn't like it. I noticed then that the ship wasn't moving. It had stopped, they'd dropped the anchor.

"Why aren't we moving?" I asked, never looking at him, keeping my eyes fixed on the open expanse of water and fog.

"Because there is something you need to see." His voice was soft.

"What is it?"

He nodded out to the sea. Thick fog lingered over the surface, but in the distance a faint glow appeared through the storm, the size of a firefly. It swayed and bobbed gently with the water. I understood what I was looking at. I tried to swallow past the lump in my throat but couldn't as I choked on a sob. I didn't want to cry here.

The same memory from long ago when I watched my father's light fade out to sea was shoved to the forefront of my mind, except this time it wasn't my father who I was saying goodbye to.

Willow...

They had sent her out, said their last goodbyes, cast her small boat, and sent the flaming arrow to its mark. I gripped the railing, trying to stand on my shaky legs. Tears fell freely. I didn't care anymore. This was his fault. His men did this.

I turned without another thought and lunged for him. He didn't block my first few attempts to attack, finally he grabbed my wrists and yanked me against his muscled chest, unable to get free of his hold, I had lost the fight, in more ways than one. Grief tore through me, escaping in uncontrollable sobs. If he hadn't been holding me against him I would have crumbled to the floor. I had nothing left.

"I'm sorry." He apologized. The sincerity in his voice only sparked more anger..

"You did this!" I screamed.

"I–" He tried to speak as I stepped back, tearing my wrists from his hold.

"Stop." I spat at his feet before turning back to the faint glow, now fading, and whispered my last goodbye with what little dignity I had left after weeping into my enemy's chest.

"For eternity, let the light of the Mother find you and bring you peace on your next journey. Your fight in this life is finished … Until we meet again." I choked over my words, my final goodbye, as I gripped my moonstone necklace. It was the only thing I had left from my father. He wore the matching one as he left this world and told me he'd always be with me. That sentiment was the only thing bringing me comfort at the loss of both of them now. Clutching the pendant so tightly it made my hand ache, I tried to center myself again. I took a few deep breaths, regaining my composure as the faint orange speck in the distance faded to nothing.

I turned away and saw Rhet standing by the entrance of the hall we had come out of earlier and without looking back, I stalked up to him.

"Take me back to my cell." It wasn't a request, it was a demand, and luckily, he didn't give me any snark as he glanced at his brother before leading me back down to my cage. I didn't dare look back at the prince on the deck of the ship, but I could feel his eyes burning holes into my spine.

CHAPTER TWELVE
ACE

The frigid temperatures of the night sliced into me as I flew through the thick snow and icy winds. A storm had blown in while we had been at Bells. I soared above the tall trees, but with the heavy clouds and fog, I could barely see more than a few feet in front of me, even with my eagle eyes.

I knew the land well enough that it didn't matter that I couldn't see. I landed, seeing the blackened wood of the homes that fae were trying to fix up by hacking down trees, cutting new timber to start rebuilding just enough to get through the weather and the rest of the night.

An ominous silence had fallen over the land. One that I had recognized from another time. While some of the fae worked trying to make their homes suitable for the storm, others walked past me, never looking me in the eye. Something more was wrong and my stomach twisted in knots.

I walked down some of the narrow paths until I found what I had hoped wasn't true. Kai sat next to a bedroll, and as he was laying the blanket over the body, I got a glimpse of the face. Her face.

Willow.

My legs strode to him. Grabbing him by the shirt, I flung him up against a nearby tree, his feet dangling. My wings outstretched in anger, coming out from under my cloak. I kept him pinned with one arm. I signed with the other.

"Where. Is. Emelyn?" My heartbeat pounded in my ears. I didn't want to believe Willow was gone. I couldn't. Not yet. Not until I knew where Emelyn was. Had I lost her too? My mind whirled as I spiraled in my grief.

"They took her." He gasped out the words as I released him and he fell into the snow.

I sank to my knees next to the bedroll. Knowing exactly who lay underneath it.

"I know what I did brought them here... But I truly am sorry about Willow. I didn't know that's what they would do. She didn't deserve this." He tried to clasp a hand to my shoulder, but I pulled away from him with a snarl.

"Leave. Before I kill you where you stand." I signed.

His eyes went wide. He gathered up enough to know to walk away.

My hands shook as I placed them under the thin fabric and flipped it down, revealing Willow's face. Her dark brown features were all the same, her smile lines and crows feet relaxed. She looked as if she was sleeping peacefully.

I brushed her salt and pepper hair away from her face and placed my forehead against hers. Willow was the closest thing Eme and I had for a parent after we lost everything in the war. And now Willow was just one more thing Ember had taken from us.

Warm tears burned against my chapped cheeks. I pulled her into my hold and squeezed her tightly. She had always greeted us with a hug anytime we would come back home for visits—but I was to late. A sob wracked through me and I tried to swallow down the lump in my throat, but it only grew larger the harder I tried. There was no use in trying to hold back.

I broke. For the first time since my parents died, I fell apart on the cold ground, the snow soaking into my trousers. My shoulders quaked, my wings sagged, and my cries muffled into her limp body as I held her tighter.

I was numb. Either from the cold or from the loss. I couldn't tell.

I spent the rest of the night and most of the next day tirelessly and meticulously molding out a small wooden boat for Willow to be sent off in. I hadn't cared about the wintery storm. Emelyn wouldn't have wanted me to come for her until after Willow was taken care of. She'd kill me if I left her like this.

By the end of the day, I hadn't slept or eaten. My only concern was giving Willow the last goodbye she deserved.

None of the villagers talked to me. Either because they didn't sign or because they didn't want me here. Some elders looked at me with pained expressions, they knew Willow and loved her but they also knew what she had meant to Eme and me. I still couldn't believe she was gone.

I was beginning to think maybe our lives were about learning to accept goodbyes.

People had come and went, the only constant Eme and I had was each other, and now with Willow being gone, I didn't know how many more losses I could handle—we could handle. Eme would be fine until I could get to her—she had to be.

Two elderly fae women approached me while I worked on the small wooden boat that I would send Willow off in tonight. She laid a few feet away, covered under a tree.

"We could clean her up for you." One of them, Pricilla, offered. They had been friends of Willows. They were some of the elder Kumais, teachers of the village. Willow had always loved teaching the younger water benders of their healing abilities, how to use medicinal herbs, and so much more. She was the most knowledgeable woman I'd ever met, and I was lucky to have had her as my guardian for as long as I did.

I nodded to them. "Thank you." I signed, and they gave me a sad smile.

"No need to thank us, dear," Pricilla replied kindly, sorrow weighing her features. Using their bending, they rolled the snow in tandem under Willow and gently moved her to their small hut.

I used my bending, to smooth the wood with long strokes of my wind and the dagger I kept in my boot to finish carving out the wooden boat. I hadn't made one in a long while. Eme and I had lost people over the years, our parents being the most heartbreaking, but since then, never someone as close to us as Willow.

I took my time with every stroke of the wood, ensuring it was perfect, but a small part of me knew it was because I wasn't ready to say goodbye.

After long hours of carving and bending, my callused hands chapped and were covered in splinters. When night fell, I finally finished it. I walked over to Pricilla's small home, where they had prepared Willow. I was grateful that they had because I wasn't sure I would have been able to.

They had cleaned her, brushed and braided her hair, and put her in fresh clothes. Ones that weren't stained with blood and mud. I blew out a breath and cleared my throat.

"Are you ready, dear?" Priscillas's voice broke the silence.

I sighed, "Yes." and she gave me a nod. I moved to pick up Willow. Cradling her lifeless body against me, I tucked my wings into my back as I walked out of the small hut and down to the shore. The walk was one of the longest walks I had ever taken in my life, but also one of the shortest, because this was it.

I could hear her soft lullabies, sung late at night when we were scared or restless, or the stories she would tell us around the fires. I remembered the gentle touch of her hands, soft and comforting as she tended to mine and Emelyn's countless wounds over the years. Moments of laughter—moments of pain.

I steadied myself as tears blurred my vision.

The boat I had made already swayed gently at the water's edge. I carefully laid Willow down before I stepped away and pushed the boat off the shoreline. The snow fell lightly, and Pricilla walked up to me with a bow and arrow. The other elder fae woman walked over to me with a torch. I put the arrow over the fire and it sparked to life. Ready to be shot out to its mark, I took aim. Pricilla and the other elder recited the words from my mind. The last goodbye. My last goodbye.

"For eternity, let the light of the Mother find you and bring you peace on your next journey. Your fight in this life is finished… Until we meet again." They spoke together, and every word sent the stake further into my bleeding heart. The arrow left my fingers, flying and hitting it's mark. I watched as the flames slowly devoured the small boat. I sat there until it was nothing but a faint glow, and then nothing at all.

I didn't know how long I had sat on that shoreline, but I knew Emelyn was alive, and now it was time to get her back.

CHAPTER THIRTEEN
EMELYN

I lay on the floor of my cell until the door opened with a loud clank and Willow's murderer walked down the stairs. He had a tray in hand full of some type of food as he strolled up to the bars and slid the tray through the slot on my cell. The warm slop splattered against my already soiled clothes.

"Eat, dog." He snarled, and I didn't move. I waited until he left and locked the door again before I breathed. Although my stomach clenched with hunger, I didn't know what the soup-like liquid was, but it didn't look appealing. Especially not now that half of it was spread across the dirtied floor.

I didn't have the energy to care. I needed food. Or at least something edible. This would have to suffice. I grabbed the small bowl that was on its side still on the tray and I slurped up what little didn't get spilled on the ground. It tasted like watered down beans with mystery meat bobbing around in it. I assumed it was lunch. Luckily, it was bland and flavorless. But my mind betrayed me when it wandered back to the things floating in jars at Lyn's and I had to hold down a hurl.

I held it back. Laying on my side again, I gripped my moonstone pendant, and did my best to hold back the tears as I let the darkness of my cell swallow me whole.

"The great Peacebringer... You look like shit." Rhet said, crouching down on his haunches from the other side of the bars. I pried my tired eyes open to look at him.

"Fuck you," I said, sitting up with my back to the wall. "Let me out of this cage and I'll show you just how peaceful I can be."

"There she is... Save that energy for someone else." He unlocked the bars. "Come on." Once again, he gave me his back, and I followed him up the stairs. He took me down the halls, and to the deck where a crowd of soldiers were circling a large fighting ring on the large metal deck of the ship. Flames blazed from fists and kicks and I went for the bone shard that I had tucked in the waistband of my pants.

Rhet must have noticed my tense position because he spoke up next to me. "Easy, it's just the ring." He gestured to all the soldiers. "We bet on fighters, it helps soldiers stay up on practicing their bending while we're at sea. Whoever wins the fight, goes on to the next one, and whoever betted on the winner gets their coin."

I looked through the crowd, spotting the man who murdered Willow in the ring. He threw his arms in the air, victorious, as the other man he fought lay knocked unconscious on the floor. Suddenly, the crowd went quiet and I saw Kade walk in from a doorway off of the deck. He was shirtless. Golden, sun-kissed skin that matched Rhets layered with ripped muscle.

But something was different. Half of his chest and arm were burned, scars layered the uneven flesh. They looked old, but for scars to be so noticeable on a faes skin, the wound had to have been dire.

His presence demanded every faes' attention, including mine. The air changed, just like it did back in Esora. It gently coated my skin, fear prickling through me, and as quick as it was there, it was gone. I glanced back at the man parading around the ring.

"What's his name?" I asked Rhet, and he looked at the man I was referring to.

"That's Seth." He said as he chewed on his lip.

Seth continued to flail his arms around, yelling his victory before he noticed Kade and was the last person to quiet down.

"Sir." He bowed slightly as a few soldiers dragged the unconscious one out of the ring.

"Place your bets." Kade spoke, his voice smooth and lethal as he stepped into the large square fighting ring, and I saw Seth's eyes go wide with fear.

"What's happening?" I asked Rhet, and he nodded toward his brother.

"Kade's never lost in the ring, and the men he goes up against rarely leave breathing. He only gets in the ring if he's trying to prove a point." Rhet answered, and I looked back to the confrontation unfolding in front of me.

"Sir, what is the meaning of this?" Seth asked, trying to hide the tremble in his voice.

"What did I command you all to do the day we landed in Esora?" Kade asked, to no one in particular, as he glanced around at the crowd of his soldiers. His eyes found mine only for a moment before he went back to the matter at hand, looking back to Seth.

"To find the Chosen one and bring her back unharmed."

"Help me understand, Seth, how you took that command and then burned down an entire village, taking innocent life along with it?"

"It was just one old woman. She would have died soon anyway." He shrugged, glancing over his shoulder to where I stood, directing his poisonous words toward me.

Kade stepped up to him, toe to toe, and gripped his throat in one smooth motion before Seth had the chance to look back at him. Seth's eyes bugged out of his head.

"What the fuck? I did what you asked! She's here, unharmed." Seth choked out his words over Kades grip.

"A wound unseen is still a wound." He growled and threw Seth down on the metal floor. Kades arms lit up with flames as Seth scrambled to his feet, wiping at his mouth as he readied for the fight.

"Wait." I called out and Kade paused where he stood. Glancing over to me.

"He's mine," I said.

Kade flashed me a wicked grin. Seth went from looking terrified to being comfortable from my statement. He let out a laugh.

"You? Want to go against me in the ring?" He scoffed. "How much you wanna bet she'd be better in my bed than against me in any ring?" He shouted to the soldiers, only a handful of them getting riled up from the statement.

Kade's jaw ticked and his hands clenched at his sides, but he stepped back. There was a large throne looking seat perched to the side of the fighting ring where he went and sat down. Leaning his head against his forefinger, crossing an ankle over his knee, he took a steadying breath before he continued.

"My bets on the Peacebringer," Kade said, and I saw the smallest hint of a smile at me before he pulled out a sack of coins and tossed the whole thing into the betting bucket. "25 pieces... gold pieces." some soldiers went quiet, while others started placing their bets on the fight. My mouth had long gone dry. 25 gold pieces.

With money like that, I could rebuild the village, and live off the leftovers comfortably for a little while. Although, money had never been a priority in my life with how I was raised. Most fae of Esora were rich in their way of life, rather than having actual riches. But right now, I didn't care about the money. I wanted Seth dead at my feet.

I peered over at Rhet and he didn't look the least bit surprised I had just volunteered myself to kill this man. I was glad he knew I meant business. Seth bounced on his toes, hyping up the crowd as I stepped through it. I was weak and starving, those beans were a pitiful excuse for a meal, but neither of those things would get in the way of me ending this man.

I let my pull to the water course through my veins as I stepped into the fighting ring. I tugged it to me and it came effortlessly as it dripped and wrapped around my arms, cooling my skin and calming me after being without it in the cell.

I took a deep breath, getting into my stance, and waited. I knew Seth would make the first move. He was too cocky not too.

I was right. I dodged to the side when he jerked in my direction. Making him almost barrel right out of the ring. He came back around and started blasting whips of fire at me. My water sizzled against his flames with every throw of his fists.

"Show me all you got, dog." He spat as he came for me, his arms raised with red flames sheathing them, ready for close contact as he threw his first swing. Blocking it, I pushed him back, but quickly grabbed the short, dark hair at the nape of his neck and smashed his face into my knee. He grunted in pain as he stumbled back before quickly recovering.

I could have sworn I saw Kades fist grip the arm of his throne and spark a flame from the sidelines, but I couldn't be sure between dodging and weaving through Seth's blows. I made a mental note to keep my eye on him. If he wished it, he could step in and kill me in an instant, taking his money back for himself if he thought I'd lose.

I didn't know what his intentions were, but I didn't have time to think about them as Seth's fist connected to my face, making me see stars as I stumbled to the ground. My face felt like it had kissed a campfire. The crisp winter wind was the only balm against my raw skin.

The crowd roared with excitement. The clinking of coins in sacks from soldiers placing their bets echoed around the ring. I tried to bring my focus back to Seth as I got back to my feet. He threw his arm out for me again, tricking me. As I blocked it, he sidestepped and sent his other fist hurtling into my gut.

I gasped for breath and fell to my knees and he circled the ring, hyping up the crowd again, preparing for his victory.

Shifting in a crouch position, I swept my leg under his feet, knocking him to the floor. I jumped on top of him, straddling over his waist, and pulled the sharp bone shard from my waistband. I didn't give him time to think or move. I shoved the bone through the soft tissue of his neck and dragged the makeshift jagged blade across his flesh.

I leaned down as he choked on his own blood. "For Willow," I whispered in his ear as I pulled away and yanked the bone free. Warm crimson spurted, misting my face with my vengeance, and his eyes went wide with surprise. He gurgled on blood, desperately clinging to his throat, as if he could stop death from claiming him.

I stood, watching him, until he slowly stopped struggling and the light left his eyes. The soldiers had all gone quiet. I let the bone shard clammer to the floor, I only needed it for him. I stepped over his body. Walking toward Rhet, he watched me with a grin on his face. I looked over my shoulder, where his brother sat on his makeshift throne and his honey eyes met mine. His jaw ticked. I'd assumed he was angry since I'd just taken out one of his own. But at least he couldn't complain too much from the money he'd just won.

I didn't care, that man was evil. He deserved worse, his death was too quick.

I didn't wait for Rhet as I brushed past him and started walking back to my cell.

CHAPTER FOURTEEN
EMELYN

Stewing in my frustrations, I got turned around in the halls, but it didn't take long before my watchdog of a prince found me and guided me back down to the belly of the ship. The magic wards almost made my knees buckle as my fae abilities and my bending left me. I straightened my back. I wouldn't show weakness.

Rhet closed me in my cell. "Now you look even worse than before." He chuckled under his breath, and I grinned at him. I was glad to have Seth's blood on my hands. A knock sounded on the door.

"Wait here."

"Yeah, like I'm going anywhere." I murmured as he made haste up the stairs and through the door. A few moments later, he came back in with a large basin of water and a cloth. The steam billowed off the water almost made me beg for its soothing warmth. Almost.

"If I open the cell, you're not going to shank me with a bone shard, are you?" He teased with a playful grin.

"If you don't give me that water, I might." I quipped and he laughed opening my cage he handed it to me before closing me back in.

"I'll be back. Get cleaned up," Rhet spoke with care as he made his way toward the stairs and left.

I cupped the water in my hands and splashed the hot liquid against my face. My cheek stung from where Seth had hit me, burning me with his fire, but the burn wasn't bad enough for me to care. I undid my top and unstrapped my leathers, enough to get my arms and chest exposed without showing my breasts. I undid my pants and shimmied them off, wearing only my undergarments. I refused to strip completely down here.

I gathered up the towel and dried my face before dipping it into the clean water to wipe down my chest, arms, and legs. Once I scrubbed away all the crimson and grime from my limbs. I tried to get the crusted, dried blood out of my hair and off of my leathers the best I could. I discarded the basin and well-used water next to the cell door after putting my clothes back on.

I leaned against the back wall of my cell long enough to nod off to sleep when the door opened again. It wasn't the loud shrill of the metal opening that caught my attention first. No, it was the aroma.

Rhet sauntered down the stairs, and I scrambled over to the bars. My stomach grumbled with anticipation, and I swore internally that if this man was going to come down here only to eat his delicious dinner in front of me, I would shank him with a bone shard given the next opportunity.

Rhet stood in front of my cage with a tray full of food. Smoked venison, scalloped potatoes, with steamed vegetables. I knew I looked desperate, and when I met Rhets' eyes, they didn't carry a provoking strife like I thought they would. To my surprise, the food actually was for me. He opened the door and handed me a tray and I snatched it like a feral animal., A large glass of water almost tipped from my violent swipe, and a plump orange rolled around on the tray next to the plate of food.

I scurried back to the wall. Sitting down, I tore into the food and had to fight back a groan from how mouthwatering it was.

Instead of leaving like Rhet normally did, he sat on the other side of the bars with his back to me. I had just killed a man with a bone shard and he leaned back against the bars comfortably, as if he hadn't seen what happened in the ring.

I could reach my hands through the bars and snap his neck if I pleased.

It would be a shame. He seemed like a decent man, regardless of which side of the war he fought on. I learned long ago that I couldn't blame all Fire Fae for the emperor's choices. Those soldiers had wives and children, just as much as the rest of Osparia, but if they threatened my life, or Aces, or anyone I loved, it was us or them.

I'd choose us every time, no questions asked. They had made their bed, they would lie in it. I shoveled food into my mouth faster than I could swallow it.

"Hungry?" Rhet asked, sarcasm lacing his tone as he eyed me over his shoulder.

I had been starving. I would have taken the time to roll my eyes at his snark but I was too focused on stuffing my face. The thought of eating food after being showered in a man's blood didn't generally seem appetizing, but with that man being Seth, I could eat happily.

"What's your favorite color? Red?" He joked, giving me a mischievous grin over his shoulder before he turned to face me.

"I'm not interested in small talk, prince." I spat mid chew before I went in for the potatoes with my bare hands. I wouldn't have given me silverware either.

"Alright… So, a deeper conversation?" He paused, pondering on something to say. "Do you miss it?"

"Miss what?" I questioned, mumbling over the food in my mouth.

"The first thing you thought of when I asked that question."

I stopped eating. Surprised by the insightfulness of the question, I didn't think anything could have stopped my ravenous hunger, but I sat, frozen. "Yes."

"What was it–" He continued, but I cut him off.

"Blue… My favorite color is blue." I changed the subject back to his prior question. The things I missed, I didn't want to recollect at the moment. Didn't want to think about them. All I wanted was to finish my food and enjoy the small peace I had knowing Willows murderer was dead.

"That's a pretty color." He said, and seemed genuinely interested in miniscule things about me that didn't matter. I didn't understand it. Why?

I finished my food as the silence stretched between us. "What do you want, Rhet?" I finally asked, chugging my glass of water before grabbing my orange and sliding the empty tray to the door. I'd save the fruit for breakfast when I woke up tomorrow.

I lulled my head back against the cool metal. Resting my forearms on my knees, I accepted his presence. He obviously didn't plan on going anywhere.

"You're going to have to be more specific, Peacebringer."

"Don't call me that. I barely know what that entails. Why are you here?" I gestured to the prison I was in. I knew the weakness of the enchantments had to affect him too, so why would he stick around? Unless his blood was in the enchantments, or maybe his brothers was? Did the magic work for bloodlines or for only one person? I couldn't be sure.

"Oh, I just figured you would enjoy the company." A long pause made the silence awkward. He finally spoke up again after a few moments.

"Who's Willow?" He questioned, and my breath stalled. My blood ran cold.

"You really don't know how to catch a hint, do you?" I lifted my head to scowl at him.

"You whispered the name to him before you took his life. Was that the old woman Seth was talking about?" He continued without batting an eye at me.

"Yes... He took her in front of me and then left her at my feet." I didn't want to go into the details on how Seth had taken her from me. His searing blade, Willow's wide eyes.

I swallowed the lump in my throat and rubbed at my chest to try and relieve the ache there.

I'd keep that memory tucked away in the box in my mind where I kept everything I didn't want to forget, but also didn't want to remember.

Silence fell between us again.

"I'm sorry," he murmured. "That wasn't supposed to happen, Seth has–had— a way of taking control with his buddies when Kade wasn't around to keep them in check. These soldiers report to my father, not to Kade, so some of them feel they don't need to obey him."

"I'm sure Kade and his father agree on their ways of leading."

"Kade and our father have... A very different way of doing things." Rhet gave me a side eye.

"Never would have thought."

"Thought what?"

"That the princes of Ember regarded themselves as compassionate, as I sit a prisoner in the belly of their warship." I gestured to my cell. Regardless of the clean water and fancy food he brought me, I was still their prisoner.

"It's a fine line. I'd say we're morally gray." He gave me a wink, and I scoffed under my breath. Leaning my head back against the cool metal again, I closed my eyes.

"You put up a good fight tonight. I'll let you get to sleep, Peacebringer," Rhet said, giving the bars a tap before sauntering up the stairs and to the loud metal door. I didn't correct him, it wouldn't do me any good to try.

The screech of the door jolted me awake. I didn't know what time it was, but I assumed it was still night time because my eyes stung and my limbs were heavy with exhaustion. I couldn't tell if it was from the power of the room or from lack of sleep. But I assumed the latter, because my eyes felt like I had only shut them a few minutes, but maybe it had been hours. I couldn't tell being in this dark, windowless cell.

"Rhet, I'm not in the mood." I groaned out in the direction of the door, but there was no response. "Rhet... Is that you?" I spoke again.

"Isn't that cute, boys? She thinks the young prince is here to save her." A man mumbled through the lightly lit room, torches lined the wall. Multiple boots shuffled down the stairs. His mocking voice let me know they weren't here to play nice. I scooted myself against the bars of my cell, trying to reach through to grab a bone, something sharp, anything to defend myself from whatever was about to happen, but couldn't reach the next one through the bars. Before I'd walked away in the ring, I dropped my last bone shard. I regretted that decision now.

The door to my cell clanked as the man shoved it open and I saw his face. He was one of the same men that brought me on the ship with Seth. All of them were, they were his buddies. My mind went back to what Rhet had said about how Seth enjoyed taking actions into his own hands. I had a feeling these men were going to do the same.

"What do you want?" I questioned, trying to keep my breathing and voice steady.

"You." He growled through gritted teeth. Grabbing my ankles, he yanked me out of my cell. I tried to kick, punch, and scratch to get back to my feet, but there were six of them and only one of me. Two of them kicked me in my stomach, while one kicked at my back.

Pain rippled through me from every impact. I couldn't breathe. They had stolen the air from my lungs. Trying to catch my breath didn't slow me down, I continued flailing my limbs, grabbing and punching any of the men I could reach. I never stopped fighting, kicking and blocking with my arms as best I could while they continued their beating. My hips twisted relentlessly against their hold until one of my ankles slipped from the man that was holding them.

I heaved my foot back and slammed it back into his nose. Blood leaked from his nostrils as he released my other ankle so his hands could cradle his face.

I swiped out my leg, knocking one of them at my side to the ground. I crawled over him before the others could grab me, and I snapped his neck with one strong jerk of my hands. His body fell lifeless under me with the crunch of his bones. Looking up I could see the bottom of the stairs. I could escape. I readied to run.

"I'm tiring of you killing my friend's sweetheart, let's see how much fight you have in you after we take turns with ya." The same man who dragged me out of the cell said as he gripped my hair and roughly tugged me back into his chest. I could smell the tang of his blood from his nose dripping onto my shoulder. The other four still alive surrounded me, one of them gripped at the bulge in his pants.

"Me first, Aedion," he called to his buddy as he started walking up to me. I thrashed my head back into Aedion's already broken nose, making him stumble back with a guttural cry. I shot forward, trying to escape, but one man threw a fist into my gut. The pain was worse than a normal hit. I had spent the majority of my life training, taking more hits than not, this pain was different but still familiar. As he pulled away, I glanced down. The wrapped hilt of a dagger jutted out of my stomach. I yanked it out with a cough, trying to breathe through the pain of my wound.

"Iron, that should slow you down, bitch." He spat and I slumped to the floor, gasping for air. The enchantment on the prison had slowed everything about me down; my powers, my healing, my strength. I was so drained, and fighting these soldiers down here only made me weaker and weaker. With them adding iron into the mix, I wasn't sure I'd survive.

With the last of my strength, I quickly lurched from the ground and stabbed the man that had stabbed me in the thigh with his own dagger and he squealed as he stumbled back.

Another one of them kicked the back of my head with an angry grunt. I landed on my back, and bursts of light crowded my vision.

Aedion.

"Now lay there and be good for me." Aedion snapped as he fiddled with the belt around his waist. "She's mine first," he said, wiping at his sweaty face again. It was busted, bruised, and still bleeding. He looked awful, and a smile tugged at my lips even though I was preparing for the assault.

Tears burned behind my eyes, dark spots now flooding my vision as I looked away. I doubted I'd be conscious for much longer and I was glad about it. I didn't want to be awake for this.

An eerie silence fell over the room. Then screams. And fire. It took everything I had to pry my eyes open, they kept wanting to roll back into my head as I tried to focus on the room. I saw a man. I thought it was Rhet at first until the same familiar, looming feeling pressed over me and I got a better look.

It was Kade.

He held Aedion by the neck, crushing the life out of him as his hand lit up with flames. He was burning and strangling the man to death until his screams stopped and the only sound in the space was the sizzle of burning flesh. I glanced around the room, never lifting my head off the cold floor. I was so weak.

But I saw the other soldiers, laying on the ground in a pool of their own blood. One was still gasping for air. I didn't know how Kade got in here with no one noticing. I never heard the metal door open, or the thud of bodies hitting the floor as Aedion prepared to have his way with me.

I saw his dark figure approach before I felt his arms around me. One curled under my knees while the other rested on my back. He lifted me effortlessly, and I met his scent before I rested my head against his hard chest.

"Kade..?" I questioned weakly, barely able to get it out. My throat was dry. What was he doing here?

"Shhh, I've got you, Emelyn," he said, looking over my body. I heard him growl under his breath. "Fuck, you're bleeding."

Before I could even think to respond, the darkness finally caught up with me.

CHAPTER FIFTEEN
EMELYN

My heavy eyes fluttered open. I glanced around the room I was in. It wasn't the prison. The bed was enormous and had silk sheets, layered with the smell I now knew as Kade. Smoked amber hinted with vanilla. I couldn't remember the last time I laid on something so comfortable.

There was a desk lining a wall decorated with an assortment of swords. Maps were sprawled out over the large, dark wood. The work space was messy, as if Kade spent a lot of late nights there.

The slight sway over the waves, was the only knowing sign that I was still on the warship. There wasn't a window, only small bulbs of fire that looked like orbs attached to the ceiling. Small flames danced in them, creating a warm, relaxing glow to the room. There was a black furnace centered in the room against the wall, warming it from the frigid temperatures outside.

The details were beautiful. It looked like a dragon climbing down the wall, its tail coiled around the ceiling while its head looked out to the room, revealing its razor-sharp teeth. A small seating area sat in front of it on a dark fur rug, a single armchair pointed toward the heat

While I continued to come to, taking in my surroundings, I ran my hand over my wound, the dull pain throbbed through me. It was bandaged and healing. I could feel my strength slowly returning from being outside the prisons enchantments.

The bandage was clean, I noticed the rest of me was too. No trace of dried blood marked my skin. I wore my clothes, but they had been washed. I had been bathed, my hair was still damp and loosely braided, it smelled of lavender and citrus. I was no longer covered in three days' worth of sweat, blood, and tears.

The door swung open, and I snapped my eyes shut again. It felt good to close them. I was so tired, and my body still ached. I heard two voices and recognized them right away Kade and Rhet.

"You were supposed to be guarding her, Evereht!" Kade whisper-yelled at him.

"I know, I'm sorry. I went to go see him."

"I know where you went brother, he could have waited. They almost–" He didn't finish his sentence, I could feel his anger pulse through the air. His presence clouded me like a bloom of smoke dusting my skin. Gooseflesh pebbled my arms. Every nerve in me was hyper aware of Kades presence. My body was like a taut spring ready to be released.

"Did they..." Shame coated his words, he hesitated, "did they touch her?" He asked as though he may not have been ready for the answer.

"I don't think so. I didn't smell them on her, or her on them, but that didn't stop me from gutting them where they stood. I crushed Aedion's windpipe as he burned. His pants were undone, and his cock was out, but I don't think they had the chance." He fumbled over his last words. Emotion wrapped around them, as if he was trying to reassure himself that he killed them before they could go any further. Why would he care?

As the son of the emperor, Kade was heir to a legacy stained with bloodshed, tyranny, and unspeakable acts of cruelty. His father's reign was marked by oppression, ruthless control, and a disregard for the lives of those who stood in his way. The emperor's hands were tainted with the blood of countless innocents, his ambitions fueled by a thirst for power that knew no bounds.

Given this dark legacy, it was hard to fathom why Kade would care about my well-being, why he would take the time to save me rather than letting his soldiers deal with me. His father's ruthless nature suggested that he would have little regard for the life of a fae, especially the one who dared to defy his rule. Why did they want me alive?

"I'm sorry Kade, I—"

"Never leave your post again." He commanded, and Rhet went quiet. Something I didn't think he was capable of being. "You're dismissed," Kade said, and I heard the shuffle of boots as the door opened and closed again. I stayed still.

Kade was still in the room, my eyes didn't have to be open to know that. I heard the shuffle of papers, then footsteps, and then the sound of running water. I cracked an eye open to glance around the room. It was empty as steam floated from the open bathroom door.

I lifted off of the bed as stealthy as I could. My body begged me to stay down, but I couldn't. This was my only chance to gather information and run, but where would I go? We must be in the middle of Draynua, surrounded by deep waters filled with sea beasts that could swallow me whole if they so wished.

I padded lightly to the desk, looking over the marked up maps. The markings were familiar, and then I realized it was every place me and Ace had traveled to or been over the years. He had been keeping tabs on us. I tried to memorize anything I could before hurrying to the drawers; I needed a weapon. I ruffled through papers quietly, finding nothing, before I moved to the next drawer finding a dagger. I grabbed it, shoving it in the waistband of my pants before shutting it slowly.

Every hair on my neck stood on end. A presence appeared behind me from thin air. Kade. I never heard him take a step, but I could still hear the water running in the other room.

"What are you looking for?" He crooned in my ear.

"Does it matter?" I turned around to face him. He had pants on but was shirtless, the skin from his left peck up to his shoulder and then halfway down his left arm was covered in muscled marred skin—burns. Beads of water still dripped from his wet hair and down his chest. He was chiseled, tall, and disgustingly attractive as he bore into me with his honey eyes.

"You should be resting," he said, taking a step closer.

I didn't wait a moment more. I wrapped my hand around the hilt of the dagger in one swift motion, bringing it to his neck. He was faster. Grabbing my wrists, he twisted me around in his hold and held me firmly against his wet muscled chest pressing into my back. Turning the tables in his favor, he brought the dagger to my throat.

"Well, aren't you full of surprises." He grunted out in my ear, holding me through my struggle to get away.

"So are you, Do you tend to all of your prisoners?"

"Only you, Bunny." His warm whisper caressed my ear, sending a shiver down my spine, piquing my interest rather than making me want to run. I wanted to sink further into him.

"Bunny? Why Bunny?" I questioned.

"Because I'm the predator, and you're the prey." His tone didn't match the threat of his words.

And then I heard it, a whistle. The sound was like music to my ears. My best friend–my savior coming to my rescue.

Ace's wind blew against the warship. The metal groaned. Kade stumbled, but his hold stayed firm, keeping us both upright. The door to his room blasted off its hinges. Soldiers stirred awake. I could hear the shouts and commands of them as the sky shifted from black to dark blue of early morning. Men's screams rang out before they faded and then splashes hit the water.

From the open door frame, I watched the deck of the ship. Ace landed with a loud thud, denting the metal. The sound of it reverberated across the ship, his onyx wings outstretched around him, highlighted by the faint gleam of moonlight. One knee to the ground as he looked up to meet my gaze and then stood, showing all of his Sky Elf glory, proudly. His eyes darkened when he spotted me, and the blade to my throat.

Seeing him made something stir in my chest. Relief because I was being saved, but pride at seeing him reclaim his image. No longer hiding behind a cloak and my glamour, he was out in the open for everyone to see. The truth was out, and it had freed him.

Fire Fae soldiers surrounded him quickly, but whips of wind shot at the soldiers, causing them to blast off of the ship as they cried out. Any fire that hurled his way got immediately snuffed out.

"I love a good chase." Kades warm breath skittered over my neck, sending another shiver down my spine as his blade clamored to the floor and he released me from his hold.

"Run, Bunny."

I peered over my shoulder at him for a beat, only meeting the sly grin on his face with his hands in his pockets before I rushed to Ace. He grabbed me quickly, before any soldiers could get to us, and then spiraled into the sky. Fire balls launched at us, hurling toward us as we flew faster, and further away from the ship at a breakneck speed. I used my bending, creating a fog over the ocean to give us cover as we flew on.

I took one last look at the ship before it became clouded from vision. Their soldiers scrambled, but Kade stood on the deck staring out over the sea at me before the fog swallowed us up, the ship and the prince were left behind us.

"They were keeping tabs on us." I signed to him as he cradled me against him.

His eyes went wide. "Why?" he questioned

"I don't know. Either they knew you were a Sky Elf or maybe Ember knew the truth before the kappa revealed it."

He growled under his breath as I went on. "If they've been following us, they know who you are, they know we'll be together. I loved seeing you again like how we were when we were kids, and I'm sorry that we'll have to continue to hide because of me." I looked away, unable to hold back the tears blurring my vision, and the heavy winds didn't help to stop the tears from falling. His large wings flapped as he stopped his flight, keeping us hovering above the water below. He turned me in his hold and gripped my chin, forcing me to look into his azure eyes. He signed.

"Mai lao kahi." Forever as one.

I choked back my tears as my heart swelled from the sentiment of what that phrase meant to me—to us. Our people lived by it, together, as one, before Ember initiated the war, leaving nothing but ashes in the wind.

"Mai lao kahi," I said as I wrapped my arms around Aces broad shoulders, careful of his wings as he gripped me and flew us forward again. I wasn't sure where we were headed just yet. But I didn't care. I was glad to be free with my best friend again.

CHAPTER SIXTEEN
EMELYN

We arrived at the dock markets in Esora mid day, we flew through most of the morning. Fire Fae soldiers littered the place, and considering we had just escaped from the princes of Ember, we thought it best to stay on foot. They would look for Ace in the skies and me on the ground, and with the skies being clear and blue against the white snow, Ace's black wings would be an invitation to be shot down.

I pulled my hood over my head, tucking my cloak tighter around me. Ace stopped at Pricilla's for his when we made it back, it meant more to him now since Willow had made it for him. We had bought me a new one in the markets, along with the axe I now had strapped to my hip, with the last of the coin we had. They wrapped the handle in worn leather and it made me think of all the times my father and I would wake up before sunrise and practice for the day. Ace and I had continued to stay on top of our abilities, both close combat and bending, through the years, but I would always cherish the time I had with my Pada, father.

I was hungry after the trip back to Esora. I ran my hand over the wound still bandaged on my side, nearly healed now after I used my magic on it when we landed. My fatigue from the cell had waned now. Aces stomach grumbled softly in front of me, letting me know we both needed something after the flight.

"Come on." I motioned for him to follow me behind the small huts and shops. We could cut through to the docks and try our luck at catching some fish for lunch. The sun was high in the sky, it warmed my cheeks against the frigid winds. I had missed it. Even for the short time I was on the warship. I had missed the sun and the stars.

I tucked my cloak tighter around me again, pulling my hood down to cover more of my face. Fire Fae soldiers dealt with a lot of trades at the markets. Over the years, the Emperor had set up Fire Fae camps everywhere, near any small towns or villages, in order to gain more control of the people of Osparia out of fear of what they would do.

The soldiers carried no mercy. They were just as horrible as the Emperor himself most of the time. They had not overrun larger cities yet, but they definitely overstayed their welcome. I weaved through the people, although it was less crowded going through the back ways, there were still people back here. Ace was in front of me and he looked huge from this angle. His back looked broad from keeping his wings tucked in tight under his cloak.

"Hey," a man called to us, but we kept walking, acting like we hadn't heard him. "Hey, you." he called again, and I glanced over my shoulder. Three soldiers were a few paces behind us, one with a half burnt cigarette in his mouth. All of them looked rugged and dirty, as if they had been on patrol for a long while without a break. I looked ahead and kept moving.

By the time I faced forward again, my feet had started running, along with Ace.

"Hey! Get back here!" He yelled and Ace and I began full on sprinting.

"Go go go!" I whisper-yelled to him, urging him forward as we rushed back through the small alley of small shops and out into the open, bustling market, hoping to get lost among the busy crowd.

There were too many innocent lives at stake. We couldn't fight our way out of here without hurting people. I kept my head down, looking at my feet shuffling against the cobblestones, and only glanced ahead to be sure Ace was in front of me. I could feel his wind on my heels, pushing me forward, ensuring that I was near him.

Our walk was brisk for a few moments. I tried to settle my racing heart and ragged breathing, but then chaos broke out. I glanced over my shoulder where the soldiers swung whips of fire, trying to clear the market.

"Get out of here! Move it!" They called out to the people and creatures in their way. Women screamed, infants cried, the soldiers whipped their flames around at people's heels and legs with no regard. A few patrons fell to the ground, wailing in pain from the burns.

Ace yanked me behind a building. I almost squealed from the sudden jerk. He placed a finger over his lips. Shhh, he mimicked the sound. My hand entangled in the dead vines that had overtaken the side of the stone structure, the vines had grown over all the old buildings in the markets. I remained quiet as we peeked around the corner. Two men stood there in the middle of the now cleared path that ran down the center of the markets holding up posters of my and Aces faces on them.

Shit.

"Have any of you seen this woman? The Peacebringer? And her little bird friend." He scoffed out, as the other one hacked a spit ball to the ground. "Anyone?" The man questioned again. "If you harbor them, you'll be guilty of treason against Ember's emperor. The punishment will be death." He made the penalty clear for everyone.

A hand muffled my cry as a man wrapped his arm around my face and covered my mouth. Ace shot around. It was the other Fire Fae soldier. There had been three in their group. While the other two scanned the main market apparently he had been scouring the rest of the area, sweeping the side alleys. We should have been more alert.

"Hello Peacebringer. Oh how I'm going to enjoy the bounty I get for your head," he said.

It was only a moment between Ace and I—a look.

We could communicate without a single word spoken between us. He cocked his head to the side, and I did the same, moving my head out of the frame of his target. His dagger flew by the soldier's head.

"You missed elf–" he started, but didn't finish his statement. Warm blood splattered against my cheek and then the soldier's body thudded against the rough stone wall of the building before he slid to the ground. Aces dagger jutted out of the back of his head. He had bended it past the man's head, and then sent it back through his skull on the wind without a blink of an eye. It was a move we had used more than once over the years when we found ourselves in sticky situations. I guessed all the target practice against the trees when we were younger that Willow always got on to him about had come in handy.

The thought of Willow made pain ricochet through my chest. Ace and I still hadn't talked about what happened, but I knew it had to have been him who found her and sent her to her final rest. He wouldn't have allowed anyone else to do it. And I wouldn't have wanted anyone else to.

I went to grip my moonstone necklace draped around my neck, to center myself, but my chest was bare. It wasn't there. It was gone. My breath hitched. My eyes went wide.

"Eme, we have to go!" Ace signed with urgency, but I couldn't move. My moonstone was gone.

It was gone. It was gone. It was gone.

"Fucking Skies Above!" Ace signed his curse and threw me over his shoulder and started running for the open docks. Ships were coming and going, but my mind was spinning. Ships cost money to board, money we no longer had, but Ace kept going anyway, leaping off his feet using his air bending. He landed on the ship's beak. He crouched, peering around at the docks. Most of the ships were clear of people, all the crew members were in the markets, grabbing supplies and whatever else they may need before heading back out to sea. Ace walked down the beak's length, double taking across the deck space. Nothing, no one in sight.

He made haste across the rickety wooden planked floor of the ship and found the closest entrance under the deck. A hatched door nested in the wooden boards, and he went through it, using his wind to close it behind us as he kept moving with me still over his shoulder. I bobbed with every step, my heart still refusing to accept my loss.

Canons lined the small round openings down the length of the dark wooden ship. The floors looked slick with moss and sea debris, the air was stuffy, making it harder to breath. We were in the gun-port. We needed to get to the hull of the ship if we wanted a chance to hide away from any of the crew. That's where they would keep their merchandise and whatever else they were trading and delivering.

Ace placed my feet on the ground and tugged me along like a mindless puppy. It took everything in me to move, to keep myself together long enough to escape the Fire Fae soldiers. Ace moved me along. His wind on my heels brought me some comfort, knowing I wasn't alone, although my chest was empty.

The necklace that lightly hung around my neck, the weight of it being gone, felt like lead in my heels. I had to find it. I had to get it back. It was all I had left of what was once my home, my parents, a hope for a time when the world could be different.

"Eme." Ace crouched in front of me. "What happened? What's wrong?"

I peered around and it looked like we were in the ship's belly now. He had led us down here. I was so lost in my mind that I noticed nothing past the gun port.

"Its gone." I signed back, tears threatened to spill from my eyes.

"What's gone?" he asked, and as my hand went up to my neck, he understood, recognition glazed over his eyes. He pulled me into his solid frame.

"It's gone." My words muffled against his chest. "It's gone." I repeated on a sob. I couldn't hold in the tears any longer. Ace stroked my back in small circles, trying to soothe me as I broke apart.

"Everyone's gone." I pulled back to look at his face from my statement and his eyes softened. He knew I was referring to more than just our parents and the war. Willow was gone now, too. His lip slightly trembled, and I slammed myself into him again as I released all the pain. We had been carrying so much through the years. There was no need to put on a brave face for Ace. We had always been there together, through the battles of emotions, to the wars on the battlefield. We had always had each other.

Ace held me firmly, keeping me grounded just as the moonstone did, until my sobs ebbed. He didn't shed a tear. He didn't break. He was my calm in the storm.

Ace crouched in the corner with a wooden puke bucket. The man could fly between the land and the heavens at breakneck speeds, but the smallest rock and bobs of a ship had him hurling in a bucket.

"Ace, that's putrid," I whispered, wagging my head at him. The ship left the port a long while ago. We were deep at sea at this point. It was late afternoon. I could hear the shuffle of boots along the wooden slats above our heads. Orange light from the sun's last rays cast through the small openings. Loud shouts and commands of the crew rang through the air.

The waters were rough; the boat rocked in a lurching fashion from side to side. Wood creaked with every movement. It smelled of piss, musty air, and stout body odor from the crew. Peering around the room, they littered the space with large wooden crates of cargo, trinkets, and chests. The corners and baseboards of the ship lined with sea life, barnacles and algae coated the damp wood. This ship seemed old and in need of repair. Water leaked from a few places around the room.

Ace stumbled to his feet, wiping his mouth, and I huffed a laugh at him. He was pale, looking a little green, and rolling his eyes at me. he followed me around the room, if we were going to hideaway down here, might as well get a feel for the space. Every time the room tilted, Ace stumbled, covering his mouth, trying to hold back his sickness. I wasn't sure what else he could throw up at this point.

A wooden chest tumbled to the floor with a bang, all its contents pooling on the floor. It was coins, a mix of silver and copper. Ace leaned down, snatching a few of the pieces.

"What are you doing?" I asked, my eyes going wide.

"We're tired, starving, and we spent the last of our money on your cloak and weapon, and I doubt anyone's gonna be offering us a job with a bounty on our heads." He signed and then grabbed a coin pouch that was lying in the debris from the box and rammed a handful of coins into it before he shoved it into his pocket.

Pirates wouldn't notice a handful of silvers missing, would they? The boat shifted again with the waves of the ocean and all the coins clabbered and clanked against every slat of wood as they slid to the other end of the ship.

"Hey captain! You hear that?" A man called.

"Ay! Go check it out, Jones."

"Ay, Cap!" The man responded.

I practically pushed Ace over trying to get him to move on his wobbly sea legs to find a place to hide from the crew member, whom I assumed was Jones, coming down to the hull.

I heard heavy steps from above, then nothing. Then a loud thud from the man leaping down into the room rather than climbing down the rickety wooden ladder. He was whistling to himself some pirate folk song as he sauntered around the crates and narrow paths between all the merchandise. Finding the dumped chest, Jones gathered up its contents of riches and placed it back where it had been.

After he finished, instead of leaving, he paused, glancing around the room. His silhouette was large, but I couldn't see his features. I pushed myself back into Ace. I was sure the wall of the ship was digging into his wings under his heavy cloak, but I didn't have a choice. The crew member kept getting closer and closer. He smelt different. He wasn't fae. The sound of something dragged along the ground behind him.

I peered through the small opening between two stacks of wooden crates, trying to get a better look at him, and then I saw the side of his face. He had dark scales along his sharp angular cheek bones, with bright green snake eyes.

His tongue slipped out of his mouth, its forked end flicking through the air as if he could taste our fear of being caught.

A basilisk shifter. Part man, part beast. They were strong, could put you in a trance and pump you with poison before you had the chance to strike, and they loved wet environments. What better place for them to be than in the middle of the ocean on a pirate ship?

I held my breath through multiple beats of my heart before the snake-like man turned around, dragging his thick swishing tail behind him. Sweat beaded my brow and trailed down my back. I waited a reasonable amount of time before I moved, thinking Jones had retreated to the deck.

I stepped out from behind the large boxes, only to feel a slick, leathery appendage wrap around my ankle. I blew out the breath I had been holding. "Shit."

The man jerked my foot out from under me, sending me falling back onto the wet wood floor. My head thudded against the slats. He slithered over the top of me. His slick, cold skin made my stomach recoil and my flesh pebble.

"I can taste the magic in your veins, Peacebringer. You'll fetch plenty of coin for your bounty once we deliver you to Ember." Jones hissed a laugh.

A gust of wind slammed the serpent shifter into the wall across the room as Ace grabbed for me to run.

"Don't look him in the eyes." I signed as he helped me to my feet, darting for the exit. Ace flew through the door in the ceiling leading up to the gun-port with a death grip on my wrist before dragging me along to the next door. Ace had always been faster than me. Sky Elves were as fast as the wind, they had once said.

Ace's wind whipped at my heels, keeping me close to him as we moved through the ship. The rest of the crew were busy with work on the main deck.

The basilisk man lept onto Ace, coming from a different path than the one we had taken. He knocked him to the ground and wrapped him with his long snake-like tail. Constricting his middle and wrapping around his limbs, pinning him, his wings to the ground. He was unmoveable. Unable to use his abilities.

Jones hissed and Ace averted his gaze, knowing if he looked into his slanted green eyes, he'd be entranced.

Ace fought under the man's hold before looking at me with wide eyes and motioned for me to run for the door with a dip of his chin. I shook my head at him.

"I won't leave you." I growled out as I grabbed my axe and hurled it into the basilisk shifter. He cried out in pain and his grip loosened enough for Ace to break free of his hold. Water whipped around my arms. Before the snake man could regain himself, I wrapped it around his neck and slowly created a fish bowl around his head.

He gurgled, his body spasming and tail twisting and swirling around the room as he fought to be free–to breathe—until he didn't, and his body went limp. My water sloshed to the floor and Ace and I rushed to the door leading to the main floor of the ship.

Boots stomped around and voices boomed. Different crew members, all reptilian shifters of sorts with claws and scales whipped their heads in our direction.

"Who the fuck are you?!" One shouted.

"Stowaways!" Another yelled.

"Cap! Jones is dead!" Another emerged from below from a different door than the one we had used. This damn ship was full of secret passageways apparently. Ace wrapped me in his arms and didn't waste another moment as his wings outstretched and he launched into the skies.

"After them!" The captain's voice boomed before we disappeared into the sky.

CHAPTER SEVENTEEN
ACE

I glided above the clouds with Emelyn in my grasp, her back flush to my chest, my arms wrapped around her waist. Her body was tense.

"What's wrong?" I signed with one of my hands in front of her face.

"I'm just so tired. I didn't ask for any of this, neither of us did." She signed out, stretching her arms enough for me to see, and then she gave up and spoke instead. "I'm tired of running, I'm tired of hiding, tired of death, I want peace and now I'm the one responsible for delivering it to this world? I have no direction on how to do it. Where would I even begin? Everything is so wrong. The war has gone on for so long... How do I hold a chance against Ember? We've seen the destruction they cause wherever they go. Our fathers were stronger than I could ever be, and they fell. I won't stand a chance..." Her voice trailed off and her head hung and shoulders sagged.

"Hey, we'll figure it out. We always do." I signed, but she didn't respond. "You will bring peace to this world again Emelyn. I believe in you. Our fates were always destined to be more than water and wind, you were always the chosen one meant to bring peace to this world, and I will be by your side when you do."

She squeezed my forearm that wrapped around her midsection after my words of comfort. Her hands were stiff from the freezing air but I had hoped what I said had put her at ease as we flew back down through the dense clouds. The pressure of them lightly pushed against my skin, leaving me dewy from the water they harbored.

The pirate ship was out of sight now, and I didn't see any Ember warships sailing below. Their black barrels of smoke were like a beacon on the water when they sailed. The only thing below was the deep, dark waters rolling in large waves. Maybe another snow storm was coming. They seemed rougher than usual.

Suddenly, a voice called to me, beckoning me to follow the sound. It wasn't Eme. I glanced behind me and saw nothing before I looked back down at the stirring waves below. Nothing was there, but the voice became louder and louder, like a song I wanted to hear, wanted to get closer to.

"Ace." Emelyn's voice sounded muffled against the wind and the waves. The only thing I wanted to listen to was the alluring song of my name being sung in my ears, mixed with the low methodical hums that were in between.

"Ace, don't do it." Eme called again with a stern warning, but I didn't care. The music was beautiful, and all-consuming, and it was all I wanted, all I craved. Wind whipped at my face and through my hair as I plummeted towards it. The cresting waves became louder and so did the song.

"Damn the Mother!" She shouted, throwing her hands out in defeat, accepting our fate. Eme's cries were so distant, like an annoying background noise when all I wanted to hear was the lyrical melody made just for me. She flailed her arms around, trying to get my attention like an annoying bug buzzing in my ears. I swatted her away before the frigid waters of Draynua welcomed me into their icy depths.

It was silent for a moment. Bubbles swirled around my head as they made their way back to the water's surface. Suddenly, the song returned, louder and stronger than before. I didn't know where Emelyn was, and for some reason I didn't care—which was odd, and I knew it was, but then I saw her.

The most beautiful creature I had ever seen. Slow and meticulous, her tail swayed to and fro, moving her closer to me, her beautiful blue skin glistening like diamonds. She was glowing, calling me to her like a moth to a flame. I knew where I wanted to be. I stroked my arms and kicked my feet in her direction, wanting to be near her—needing to be near her.

Then everything changed. Her face morphed from something captivating to something terrifying. Her mouth opened abnormally wide, revealing rows and rows of jagged, razor-sharp teeth. The crunch of her bones shifting into her Siren form made a scream work its way up my throat. Her taloned hands reached for me as she tried to devour me whole. My wings flapped against the current, pushing me up and away from her.

My lungs burned for air. The water shifted, and then Emelyn was in front of me again. Her silver hair dancing in the water around my face as a burst of power shot out from her, she grabbed my arm as water swirled around us launching us into a whirlpool toward the surface. Sending the Siren in the opposite direction further into the deep waters away from us. The sirens tail swished against the current but she couldn't swim against Emelyns power.

We broke through the water's surface, gasping for breath. I quickly gathered Eme in my arms and sent us back into the skies with a few beats of my sopping wet wings. Her arms were crossed, and she had cocked an eyebrow at me.

"I told you not to do it." She scolded me, with a I told you so attitude.

"Well, when a pretty lady calls, I know how to answer." I signed, clutching her with one arm against my side, teasing with a wag of my brows and she rolled her emerald green eyes at me. I chuckled under my breath, holding her tighter against me. Her body was trembling, she was freezing. Sky Elves did better with cold temperatures, being raised in the tallest mountains in some of the most frigid temperatures in all of Osparia.

"I know they don't call often, so I guess I can't blame you." She playfully wounded me with her words. I gestured a knife plunging into my heart with a pained expression.

"Ouch," I signed and she couldn't hold back her laugh. "Thanks for coming to my rescue," I added.

"Next time, listen to me, and we won't fall to our deaths to be eaten by Sirens," she said.

"No promises." I smirked.

She rolled her eyes at me as the land came into view. Within a few minutes, I swooped down and landed on a beach, feeling the weight of the exhaustion settle into me as my shoulders relaxed. We needed food, and a break after the day we had. "Lets not have any more near-death experiences today," I signed with a tired sigh.

"No promises." Her words chattered through her teeth. We needed a fire. Fae had endless lives, but they weren't indestructible. Eme waved her hand, and the water fell from our clothes, leaving them dry, as if we had never taken a dip in the ocean.

"I'll be right back. I'm going to collect some firewood. Stay put." I signed, and she gave me a two-finger salute with her hand before she moved into the dense woods and sat down. Leaning back against one of the large trees, she wrapped her arms around her legs, resting her head against her knees.

I gathered as much wood as I could find. I wasn't worried about it being wet from the frosted ground, Eme could pull the moisture out of it so we could start the fire. I didn't venture far. We were treading along the edge of the Swamps of Illusion and Sirens Pass, both dangerous and deadly in different ways. Sirens Pass was self explanatory. The Sirens lure their prey, mostly men more than women, into the waters and then reveal themselves before trying to eat them.

The Swamps of Illusion knew how to manipulate all of your senses, convincing your mind that everything you saw, touched, tasted, smelled, and heard was real. Its smokey fog was its own magic, blanketing it at all times, waiting to enthrall its next victim to its mind games.

Walking through it would be like walking through a dense cloud of smoke. People who traveled through never came back out unless they could decipher what was real and what wasn't. It showed you illusions of things you wanted, feared, and things that were unknown.

I wasn't interested in finding out if it was as powerful as rumors had stated, so I steered clear of the boundary of smoke and stayed within the normal woods. Rescuing Eme from Ember, escaping serpent pirates, and Sirens Pass had been enough for today—maybe even a lifetime.

CHAPTER EIGHTEEN
EMELYN

I stayed put, rubbing my hands up and down my arms, trying to create the warmth my body desperately craved. I was so tired. My muscles ached, my eyes were heavy, and my stomach sent a pang of pain through me every so often to remind me of how it hadn't eaten today.

Ace would be back soon. I'd hoped he'd stay away from the treeline of the swamps. We were resting on the border of two of the most dangerous places in Osparia. If we had the energy, I would have suggested flying around the swamps entirely and finding an inn somewhere, but we had exhausted ourselves entirely. And flying over it was too big of a risk.

We needed to rest, to eat, and I desperately wanted to sleep without the weight of an enchanted cell draining every ounce of me. I walked the short distance to the beach and used my bending to sift through the water until I yanked a few fish from their home. I quickly skinned and gutted them on the shore before I took the fresh meat and skewed it, readying it for the fire for when Ace came back. I walked back to the same spot from before and waited.

I peered over my shoulder to my right and saw him walking through the dense trees. Hopefully, they would give us enough cover for a night to rest. We couldn't go any further into the woods than where we already were. I didn't want to risk getting any closer to the fog. Turning my head to look behind us, I could see the thick white sheet of it in the distance, lining the perimeter of where the swamps started.

I knew from stories that when you saw the white gloomy fog, that you needed to stay away. It would entice you if you got too close, beckoning you to come into it, similar to the way the siren sang Ace from the skies. I'd wondered if something connected their magic in some sick, twisted way, haunting this corner of the world. Hard to imagine, but the swamps were more deadly and could do more than just lure you in before feasting on your perception. Sirens couldn't make you lose your mind like the swamps could, or so they say.

Ace tossed the damp wood and brush on the ground in front of me and I flicked my wrist, pulling all the moisture out before he continued. He worked with his hands quickly to spark an ember before he blew on it, and a flame came to life. He tended to the small fire gently until it grew in size and in warmth.

I handed him a skewed fish. We cooked and devoured them. Having a full belly and a warm fire made it impossible to keep my eyes open. I laid down, and Ace climbed over me and nestled behind me. His back was to the large tree I had been perched against and the fire pranced in front of me, casting us both in a faint orange light. He wrapped me up in his muscled arms and cocooned us in his wings like a blanket. His familiar scent engulfed me. Blue ferns and citrus.

"I'll take first watch." He signed in front of my face. "Get some rest."

I was too spent to argue and in the next moment, I was sound asleep.

The nightmares were always the same.

I was on the battlefield with Ace. We were back to back in a whirlwind of fire, water, and wind, fighting for our lives. I sunk my blade into soldier after soldier. Fire sizzled and hissed against the rain and my water. I tasted the salt and iron from sweat and blood as it painted the wind. And then the world would go cold. A blinding bolt of light stretched across the plane as I screamed for my Pada. Then, as it always did, the darkness came. A calm fell over me as it beckoned to wake me up, letting me know I wasn't in that time—that place, anymore.

My breaths came and went, making my chest rise and fall fitfully. Sweat beaded my brow as I composed myself from the nightmare. The fire had dimmed to smoldering ash. Ace was sprawled out, his snores escaping quietly in his deep slumber.

So much for keeping watch, but I couldn't blame him after the day we had. I rose to my feet, careful not to wake him. My mind was awake and stirring and there wasn't anything I could do to ease it other than practice my bending and fight with my weapons until my body begged me to stop. Until my tense muscles were jelly, and my mind was quiet again.

It was something I did often while growing up. Any time I needed to relieve stress, anger, sadness, I would train until my body cried for reprieve and it made me feel better.

The moon loomed high in the sky above the canopy of trees as I walked far enough away to know I wouldn't disturb Ace's sleep. I wished I had makeshift dummies like the ones we had back home. Wooden posts jutted up from the ground with bags filled with straw for heads was what we used when we trained, but I guessed using a tree out here would have to do.

I unsheathed my battle axe from my hip and bended my water around me, pulling it from underground, its long tendrils waved around me like extra limbs, waiting for my command. I thrusted them all forward, lashing and whipping at the trees surrounding me, pretending they were enemies coming for me as I wielded my axe in fighting stances.

I repeated the sequence multiple times, and by the end, the trees looked like they had been mauled by beasts and my battle axe sat jutted out of one. I went to grab it, but I paused, thinking of all the times Ace had used his bending to call his weapons back to him with the wind.

I was the Peacebringer. I needed to learn the elements, needed to practice with more than what I was comfortable with. The peacebringer was supposed to be the balance of all the power Osparia was blessed with.

This was either a superb idea or a terrible one. I was going to do it or take my head off in the process of trying.

I thought back to the small lesson Ace had with me in the woods before we got to Bells. Taking a deep breath, feeling the chill of the night air against my skin, between my fingers, I envisioned every wisp of wind encircling my axe and sending it back to me. I tried, over and over and over again. Nothing happened.

Until it did. The axe flung itself from the tree and spun back to me. I slammed my eyes shut, fear of it taking off my hand rather than landing in my palm slithered through my gut, making me flinch when it finally reached me.

I looked at my fist, and I gripped its hilt in my palm. I had done it; I had bended the wind again. Leaping in place, a smile stretched across my cheeks, feeling joy for only a moment before a familiar voice found my ears. I lunged behind the closest tree.

"Find them. They couldn't have gotten far. They wouldn't risk the swamps." The captain from the pirate ship shouted commands to his crew of reptilian beasts. They were all lined up like a search party, sprawled out through the wood line. Every way I looked there was one of them. I had nowhere to run, or hide, other than behind this tree or into the swamps in front of me. Every step they took made my heart pound louder in my ears. I pushed my back harder into the tree, as if I could somehow hide within it.

Then the comforting darkness from my dreams encompassed me and I questioned if I was even awake.

I looked around, but saw nothing but black wispy shadows surrounding me, as if they suspended me within a room of nothing in my conscious mind.

A silhouette of a man stood in front of me, his irises glowed a faint gray as he peered down at me. He had a hood over his head and twin swords strapped to his back. Every part of him cloaked in different shades of night, but I could see the details of his features and his leathered armor.

I jerked away from him but his hands gripped my arms, holding me in place as he pushed me back against the tree before caging me with his arms. Our chests brushed with every breath we took.

"Shhh," he said as wood and foliage crunched and snapped next to us. The snake-like crew members slithered by and we both held our breaths. I could see them through the cocoon of shadows around me, but they couldn't see us, or at least, it didn't seem like they could.

This shadow man was concealing us within his darkness. One of the crew members stopped in his tracks, flicking his forked tongue multiple times in the surrounding area. The tension grew, the shadow man's smokey irises met mine, our chests heaved, and adrenaline pumped, preparing for whatever was about to happen.

The basilisk man turned in our direction and lunged for us.

"Shit." The shadow man cursed under his breath as he moved us through time and space, right to the front of the white veil that led to the Swamps of Illusion. "Run, I'll find you," he said, urging me into the fog.

"Wait! No, I–" I didn't have a choice as he pushed me into the white mist. The view of the woods disappeared, along with the mysterious man of shadows. My fate had been sealed.

I was within the Swamps of Illusion.

CHAPTER NINETEEN
ACE

The last thing I remembered was scouring the treeline and now my cheek laid pressed against the cold ground. I wiped the sleep from my eyes and the dried drool from my chin. I had slept hard.

Emelyn wasn't in my arms anymore and if we weren't in the situation we were in, it wouldn't have bothered me. I knew she had struggled with nightmares from the past. We both did, and she would clear her mind with practice before going back to bed. But with the circumstances now, it sent me into a panic.

I leapt to my feet, listening to the sounds of the woods. Something was happening. I knew what the sounds of battle were. I didn't walk. I ran toward it, feeling the guilt sink into my gut at the thought of something happening to Emelyn while I was asleep.

Skies Above. I cursed myself for it.

I pushed my legs further, my wind whipped at my heels, urging me to move faster. Crouching behind a tree, I peered around to assess the situation, but was unsure of what I was seeing.

The basilisk shifters from the pirate ship were here, but they were distracted. All of them were fighting themselves in the dead of night. What the fuck was going on? Was it possible I was still asleep? Or had I already wandered into the swamps, because the scene in front of me wasn't making any sense. The men bobbed and weaved between each other in the dark, and it seemed the darkness was fighting back.

The call of Emes' whistle came from the fog that billowed straight ahead, and I didn't know if it was real or an illusion. The thick blanket was cast so close to me and I knew it lured its victims inside. I wondered if the swamps had made the pirates go insane.

Why would Eme be in the swamps when she knew better? The call rang for me again and I didn't hesitate. If there was a chance Eme was in danger, I didn't have a choice. I had to go.

My wings expanded, and I sent myself into the skies. I soared over the swamps, thinking I might see her, but I couldn't see anything through the thick sheet of white other than the tips of the large sagging trees. I heard my name, but couldn't place where it was coming from.

"Ace." Emelyn's voice sounded as if it was coming from every direction, "Ace, I'm here." I looked frantically, my heartbeat growing rapid.

"Ace, Ace, I'm here, help." She kept calling to me, but I couldn't see her and every hair on my neck stood on end.

Fuck!

I decided before I had the chance to doubt it. I free fell into the blanket of white until I could no longer see the outside world. The night sky disappeared, and the white fog surrounded me. My boots landed with a thud into the muddy ground. My knees bent to absorb the impact of my landing. Looking around, I saw nothing but large sagging trees and their roots bulging out of the surrounding ground, making the landscape sloppy and uneven.

This place was eerily quiet. I could no longer hear my name, but I sensed a presence of something surrounding me. Was the fog a living thing? Gooseflesh trailed down my back and I jerked around at the sensation.

Golden flecks floating within hazel eyes met mine. The woman was inches from my face. I didn't move. Her beauty struck me. Short voluminous curls topped her head while the sides were edged shorter along her heart-shaped ears. She was an Earth Dryad. She had full pink lips that contrasted against her dark freckled skin.

"Ace, I was looking for you." She spoke calmly, trailing her dainty fingers up my arm. The touch was real–genuine.

What the fuck are the swamps truly capable of?

"Me? Who are you?" I signed, and she spoke back to me.

"We met at Bells, don't you remember?"

I thought back to where I had seen those eyes before. There was a woman I collided with on my way out, but I didn't know who she was.

"How do you know who I am? What do you want?" My spine stiffened and my feet remained loose, readying for an attack. These swamps were unpredictable, and I wouldn't let my guard down.

"I don't know. You called me here." Her smooth voice caressed my skin in a sensual whisper, one that threatened to disarm me.

"No..." I shook my head.

"Yes... You needed me Ace, you've carried so much on your shoulders."

"What are you talking about?" A puzzled look fell over my features. This was not the direction I expected this to go, and I felt even more unsteady on the uneven ground.

"Your father, Hallan. Kali, your mother. The entire race of your kind. Orion, Ivy, Willow, and so many others you've lost over the years." Her brows pinched together in pain as she placed a warm palm against my cheek, as if she could penetrate my emotions with her touch and feel my sorrows. "Including yourself, hiding who you are behind a cloak or glamor for so long... It's okay Ace, I'm here now, you can let it go."

Her words cut me, potentially more than the sharpest sword. I had no control over the hot tear that slipped down my face. She swiped it away, and I let her touch comfort me as it forced me to acknowledge every wound she ripped open from my past. My surroundings blurred with warm light, visions of memories played on repeat around me.

These swamps are fucked.

I did my best to actively not think about the losses over the years, but they always haunted the back of my mind. And with her, bringing them all to the forefront was my undoing. I would have rathered she'd punched me.

She tugged me into her warm embrace and let me fall apart. She became the glue keeping me together so I didn't have to do it myself. The surrounding air seemed heavy, but comforting. As I released the weight of my losses but gained another feeling, one of warmth and reassurance filled me, letting me know that one day, things would be different—better.

I just didn't know how or when.

I wanted to feel something more than the pain still radiating from my battered heart. I'd concealed every hurt for so long, that now the wave of all of it crashed over me, and I looked for something to keep me afloat. I didn't want to drown, I wanted to spread my wings and fly far away.

I met her gaze before glancing at her plump, soft pink lips, and she did the same to mine. Just the single look sped up my heartbeat. I waited for her, needing her permission before going for what my heart desired as I took in her flawless features.

I met her in the middle when she leaned into me, giving me the answer I needed. Our lips crashed against each other in a raw, fervent kiss. She wrapped her arms around my neck, and her legs wasted no time clamping around my waist. I pushed her up against a tree while we kissed with eager passion. Something hummed under my skin, begging to be free—to connect. This was an illusion, she wasn't real, this feeling wasn't real, but I couldn't pull out of it.

The swamp muddied my mind, making this feel right. I didn't want to search for Emelyn anymore. I didn't want to think about the things I had been through. She made me forget them all. Taking all of my pain as if it was her own.

Fuck.

She matched my pace and I couldn't help but wonder what things haunted her mind, soul, and body. What things did she keep harbored away to cry in the shadows about when no one else was around to see her moment of weakness?

Why did I care about such things from an illusion?

I almost pulled away to ask, but her hand slipped into the waistband of my pants and she stroked my cock, sending a growl up my throat.

Illusion or not, she would be my conquest.

CHAPTER TWENTY
EMELYN

I had whistled a few times for Ace, but I didn't know if the swamps would have swallowed my cries for help. Even if it didn't, he wouldn't be able to see me through the fog. My boots squelched against the muddy, wet ground with every step I took. I'd already lost my sense of direction. My nose wrinkled from the smell of marshy soil and decaying plants. The trees slumped and their roots were jagged, protruding through the soggy ground.

I peered over my shoulder every few steps, feeling uneasy about how quiet this place was. The sounds of the pirates in the woods had disappeared completely. No frogs croaked, no crickets chirped, only the sound of my shallow breaths and beating heart pounded in my ears.

"Hmmm." He growled, the sound low and husky, coming from everywhere and nowhere, reverberating through my body while his dominating presence coated my skin, making me want to run, letting me know exactly who was here with me.

I took off, weaving through the trees, the mud and the muck of the swamp made it harder to run. Water circled me, crawling up my limbs as I prepared to strike anything that moved. A figure shifted to my left, and I blasted my water towards it.

"That's not very nice." Kade crooned from the looming mist around me. I shuffled back against a tree, chest heaving. My eyes volleyed around the white fog and trees, but found nothing but his ominous presence.

"Found you, Bunny." Kade purred in my ear. His warm breath caressed my sticky neck from the humidity in the air, causing a shiver to skate down my spine. The cool metal from his dagger already pressed to my throat as he wrapped his other arm around my waist, jerking my back against his hard chest as he towered over me. The tree had vanished, leaving the prince behind me. "You've gotta be faster than that. Remember, I love the chase."

You're in the swamps, Eme.

He wasn't real, this wasn't real, but the warmth of him–his touch enthralled me at how true it felt. I turned around in his hold. I wouldn't run from an illusion.

"You're not here," I said, looking into those piercing amber eyes. He dragged the tip of the blade down my cheek, not enough force to draw blood.

"I am if you want me to be." He rasped as his hand came up my back and tangled into the hair at the nape of my neck, tugging my head to the side as he breathed me in. His nose skimmed across my delicate flesh. "Let your mind wander, Bunny. What is it you truly want?"

He's not real, he's not real, he's not real.

I ran my hand up his muscled chest, daring to touch him in a way I would never allow myself to. He was tangible–unimaginary. And everything in me wanted to keep touching him. To explore a world where he wasn't my enemy. A world without war. A place where we could just be. Maybe giving in would be a balm to my aching spirit. What was the harm in delving into something I knew was an illusion?

He leaned into me, the breath from his lips whispering against mine.

No Emelyn! It's the fucking swamps. Snap out of it.

I squeezed my eyes closed and focused on myself, doing my best to shut the fog of the swamps that clouded my brain. This wasn't real. He wasn't here.

"You're no fun." Kade crooned and his words faded and then the weight of his presence was gone.

I opened my eyes and found myself lying on the wet ground, alone in a foggy swamp, burning with desires I shouldn't have for a man I should hate. I swore I heard the swamp laughing at me.

I gathered my bearings and stood, walking through the swamps aimlessly, now coated in a layer of mud along my back. I didn't know where I was going or what things I would see next, but I needed to move. My body was buzzing and I couldn't stay still. The man masked in shadow said he would come for me, but there was no way he could find me in here. The fog would probably trick me, making him out to be an enemy so I'd run from him.

In the woods, he had moved without moving. Somehow, we traveled from one spot to another without ever taking a step. One moment we were behind a tree, the next we were on the border of the swamps.

Who was this man? I had heard stories during our time with Willow of a lineage of fae wielding light and shadows, but I didn't think they existed anymore. I had believed they had been killed off because of the abilities they wielded. Was that what he was? A legend from a bedtime story?

Grunts and groans pulled me from my thoughts. Peering to my right, I found Ace.

Damn the Mother.

Ace stood, one arm braced against a tree. His pants pooled around his ankles. His cock was hard and jutted out as he thrusted his hips, dry humping the empty air in front of him. I shook my head and looked away, turning to lean behind a nearby tree. Was this really happening?

I couldn't leave. If it was him, I didn't want to lose him to the swamps again. I could hear his movements quicken, followed by a growl, the smell of his arousal, and then heaving breaths.

I glanced back towards him and watched him as he came out of his illusion. The fog had lifted. He looked at the tree he was braced against, where his cum dripped down its trunk, before he peeked over his shoulder at me with eyes the size of saucers.

"The swamp got you to, huh?" I joked, but then wondered if what I was seeing was even real. Was this actually Ace or just another illusion?

"What the fuck." He signed the curse Definitely Ace. Fumbling, he grabbed for his pants, yanking them back up around his waist. After spending years together in a tiny home and traveling, it wasn't like we hadn't seen each other naked before, but we did our best to respect each other's privacy.

He tried to get himself back together again. Shifting, he looked around the area as if he was looking for someone more than me.

"She wasn't real, Ace. Whoever it showed you wasn't actually here." I signed, and his brow pinched together.

"How long have you been standing there?" He questioned.

"Long enough to know you finished while dry humping a tree." I huffed, and he wagged his head at me, a blush flushed his cheeks. A few moments passed before neither of us could suppress the laugh any longer.

We were both covered in mud and grime, bent at the waist, cackling like maniacs at how we had both been screwed by the swamps of illusion—one of us, quite literally.

And then a silhouette of shadow appeared in front of us.

CHAPTER TWENTY-ONE
CROW

Have they lost their minds to the swamp?

When I found them, they were cackling, covered in mud and peat, smelling of arousal and rotten eggs. As if they had fucked while rolling around on the marshy floor of the muggy swamp.

The thought sent anger rolling through me. Making my shadows flare and slip away from my body in large wispy tendrils. They had a mind of their own, especially when it came to my emotions. Even more so when it came to her.

Emelyn and Ace's scents weren't blended; they were unattached. It was the only thing keeping me calm, knowing that it may have been an illusion rather than a moment of intimacy between them.

Over the years, I had watched their relationship together from the shadows. I knew it was platonic, but the closeness of the friendship they shared always sent jealousy boiling through my veins. It was a closeness I couldn't have.

And now that she was here, in front of me, I didn't know how to keep my emotions in check. It was hard enough doing it from a distance, and now, keeping them masked within me was going to be my biggest challenge yet.

I had been hiding in the shadows for a century, for her, to keep her safe. But when I felt her so close and in danger I couldn't resist staying away any longer. The tug and pull from the bond was all consuming even from the space I had put between us, it was a living breathing thing. And now that she was here it was becoming unrelenting. Searing every part of her into my soul, assuring me of where I belonged.

Ace stood straighter upon seeing me, bending two of the daggers he had strapped across his chest at me before I had the chance to blink. He sent them flying on the wind, assuming I was a threat or another illusion.

"No, stop!" Emelyn shouted as I dodged the first one, but the second sunk into my shoulder making a hiss escape me as the first blade flew back around like a boomerang, its serrated edge stabbing into my side with enough force to take my breath away.

I fell to a knee, grabbing for the dagger that hit last. I fisted it and pulled it free from my gushing side with a grunt of pain. Emelyn rushed from Ace's side to grab for me. Her touch was gentle but firm as she placed her hand over the wound and applied pressure. My shadows whipped and whisked around her, grazing her hand.

"Control your shadows so I can see to help you." Emelyn said as her water slivered down her arms and glazed her palm, making her hand glow a faint blue against my side.

"They have a mind of their own," I replied with a roguish grin. "I think they like you."

She pushed harder against my wound, making me groan from the pain. She wasn't easily charmed, noted. I looked down at the dagger protruding from my shoulder. My clothes were damp with blood.

I withdrew the blade in one swift pull. "Fuck." I cursed, tossing it back to Ace. "I believe that's yours," I said with a bite to my tone. He looked at the scene in front of him with a puzzled expression.

"Who is he?" Ace signed to Emelyn while she tended to my side, the worst of my wounds. I recognized the language from the other Sky Elves back at camp. Only Maeve still chose to not speak aloud, but the others signed to her out of respect for their culture. Emelyn signed back, her hands stained with my blood.

"He saved me from the pirates." She hurried her hands back to my side. I could feel her healing pulsate through me, easing the pain as my bleeding slowed.

"Oh yeah, by throwing you into the veil of the swamp?" He scoffed as he swiped his bloody dagger over his trousers, cleaning the blade before sheathing it back to his chest.

"There wasn't anywhere else to go." She responded, her voice tinged with a mix of defensiveness and frustration.

Ace's eyes narrowed slightly, his gaze piercing as he countered,"he could've moved you anywhere but dropped you in the swamps. I don't trust him, Emelyn."

Emelyn sighed, shaking her head. "It was better than leaving me in the woods to fend for myself against a crew of basilisk shifters."

Ace's expression softened, guilt clouding his features as he signed, "I would've come for you, like always." His brow furrowed, the weight of his regret evident.

Emelyn shot him a wry look, her lips curling into a small, teasing smile. "You wouldn't have made it in time. You were asleep mister 'I'm going to keep watch'."

Ace's cheeks flushed with embarrassment, his eyes dropping momentarily before meeting hers again. "That's a low blow Em, you knew I was—"

Emelyn cut him off. "I'm not blaming you Ace, I know our journey has been hard and long, I'm just trying to say that we should be grateful that he showed up when he did, or I would've been captured yet again, or worse." She murmured the last bit under her breath as she returned her hands to my side.

"I–"

I cut off Ace before he had the chance to move his hands to communicate."Stop bickering, both of you." I stood with one arm cradling my side, my hand lay over Emelyn's. She didn't pull away as her power continued to faintly glow, her healing surging through me. Feeling her unyielding touch not lurch away from my umbra form, even though I was wounded, made my shadows writhe happily around me in long, uncontrollable tendrils.

She put her hand back to her side. It healed me enough. My body could do the rest on its own. I took a few steadying breaths before continuing. "We need to get out of here." I waved my free hand toward Ace, beckoning him to come to me. Emelyn was already close enough for me to Hollow us out of here.

"I'm happy where I am, thanks." He signed, and I rolled my eyes. In that moment, he realized I understood what he had signed to me. His eyes went wide and then I Hollowed, opening a hole of shadows between time and space toward him with Emelyn by my side. She gripped around my waist while I grabbed onto Ace's arm, my shadows pulling him along.

My side screamed in pain from Emelyn's grip, but the thought of her arms around me made me forget about the throbbing ache. I pushed them both through the gapping hole of blackness with me. For a brief moment, we were in complete emptiness. It's the quietest place there was. My shadows coiled and whipped around the darkness they craved. Then a breath of calm fell over me before all three of us were pushed through the other side.

Emelyn stood next to me, heaving a breath as she tried to regain her composure. I was drained, knees weak. I fell on one again, my side and shoulder thrummed in tandem with my heartbeat. I glanced over my shoulder at Ace bent at the waist, retching.

"Are you okay?" she asked, her voice soft as she bent down next to me.

"Aren't you going to check on him?" I said, nodding toward Ace.

"He'll be fine, he's always had a weak stomach. Are you alright?" she asked again.

"Yeah, I'll survive," I said, and she offered me a hand. I took it and my shadows threaded around her fingers and up her arm. "Sorry." I cleared my throat, pulling in my shade, and she let out a huffed laugh.

"It's alright," she said, flashing a small but illuminating smile at me.

Shit, this was going to be harder than I thought.

CHAPTER TWENTY-TWO
EMELYN

His shadows retracted down my arm. The tendrils were soft and delicate, like the lightest touch of fingers trailing gently over my skin, sending a shiver down my spine. They almost tickled. The feeling made it difficult to be weary of them—of him.

Ace's concerns had made me question why I was so willing to accept aid from this stranger. My guard should have been up, but it wasn't. I didn't carry fear or feel apprehension build in my chest when he was around.

It wasn't blind faith or naive trust. I was still cautious, still aware of the dangers that lurked around every corner.

But there was a comfort in his presence, a sense of safety and understanding that I hadn't felt in a long time... if ever.

Through the years, Ace and I had done well with reading a room, sensing danger had become a sixth sense. My instincts had never steered me wrong, and I hoped in this case they still wouldn't.

The shadow man got back to his feet. Ace continued to wretch behind us, jumping through the void must have triggered his motion sickness, trying to regain his composure, he signed to me.

"He understands my language." He wiped sweat from his brow before blowing out a breath from the nausea.

"What?" I questioned out loud, and the man looked at me. "Who are you?" I took a step back, putting some space between us.

"My name is Crow. I'm a part of the rebellion."

"What rebellion?" Ace and I asked in unison.

The mention of a rebellion sent a jolt of mixed emotions through me. It was a glimmer of hope that suggested we were not alone in our fight against the tyranny and oppression that had consumed our land. It was a sign that there were others out there, brave souls willing to stand up, to fight for freedom and justice.

But the war had left scars, both visible and invisible, that would never fully heal. It had stolen loved ones, shattered families, and left countless lives in ruins. And while the idea of joining a rebellion offered a glimmer of hope, it also carried with it the weight of responsibility and the knowledge that the path ahead would be fraught with danger and uncertainty.

"There's a lot you need to know, but right now, I think we all need some proper rest. A short nap and some fish aren't gonna cut it. We have a ways to travel" Crow said as he walked past both of us, sure of the direction he was going.

Ace launched at him, shoving him into a tree with a blade at his neck. Using his free hand to sign, he asked "How do you know?"

"Know what?" Crow growled, his shadows ready to strike.

"That we ate fish and slept before the pirates arrived. You weren't there." Ace signed, shoving Crow further into the tree.

I accepted it. My instincts were horrible.

"I'm a spy from the rebellion against Ember, I was sent to find the Peacebringer. The shadows showed me where you were. I would've come to you sooner, but then the pirates arrived, and then the swamps happened, and now we're here." He shoved Ace off of him as he straightened. "Now let's go."

"Where are we going?" I asked, and he looked over his shoulder.

"Hunting, then we'll find shelter for the day, and we'll travel through the night," he said, not stopping or waiting for us to catch up.

"Can't you just 'poof' us to this so-called rebellion you're talking about?" I asked, arching a brow, trying to keep up with him, and Crow let out a low chuckle. The timbre of it did something to my insides. His voice gravelled, as if he pulled it from his chest and sifted it through his shadows.

"It doesn't work like that, it's draining, and considering I 'poofed'." He made air quotes with his fingers as he continued, "around the pirates and then around the swamps looking for you, only to have your friend stab me, I don't have much left in me." He wagged his head. "And it's called Hollowing." He corrected.

"What is it exactly?" I asked curiously, watching his shadowed extensions move languidly.

"My shadows create an opening, or a hole between where I am and where I want to go, allowing me to move from one place to another."

"Does it work for long distances?" I couldn't stop the questions bubbling up in my throat.

"Yes, anywhere shadows exist, I can go, but the longer the distance, the more strenuous it becomes. Hence why I haven't Hollowed us to the rebellion, it's too far right now." Silence hung between us as I paused and thought about what Ace had said.

Crow kept walking. Ace and I shared glances before we both started after him.

"Wait, how do you know the signs of the Sky Elves?" I hollered from behind Crow as I quickly caught up to him again, with Ace on my heels.

"You'll find out soon enough," he said.

Ace shot into the sky and in a blink he landed in front of him. Dagger to throat once again. He was on edge.

"How?" He signed, his eyes piercing, as if he could see through Crow's darkness.

"I learned it from the rebellion, now move, I'm tiring of your shit, elf." Crow nudged the dagger away with the back of his hand before he pushed past Ace. His shadows seemed to cling to him tighter in his frustration, as if they were sticking to him waiting for his command to pounce. Their closeness revealed more of his muscled figure beneath.

Ace growled out a breath, pumping out his chest, and I lay my hand on his chest.

"Hey, cool it. He hasn't given us a reason not to trust him yet. He got us out of the swamps. Let's see where this leads," I said, trying to reassure him, but I could tell his outlook stayed the same.

He huffed under his breath before nudging past me in the direction Crow was heading, wherever that was. We caught up after a few moments. Crow had slowed, and his steps treaded lightly against the thin sheet of snow on the ground. He began weaving through the thick wood and I could tell was looking for our next meal. Twin sheathed swords hung from his back. His shadows clung so tightly against his figure I could see the outline of his clothes and other weapons he had attached to him. I wondered if it was because of how drained he was from Hollowing.

"Crow—"

"Shhh." He placed a finger over the outline of his full lips.

I was getting tired of this man shushing me. He pointed a single finger out to the left of him and I saw the stag in the distance. He took slow steps moving forward and then a gush of wind flew past my face.

Damn the Mother, Ace.

Ace went in for the kill, taking off into the sky as the stag jerked and looked in our direction. Crow vanished before my eyes, leaving nothing but the reminisce of smokey shadows in his wake. The stag saw me and ran. My heart thrummed in my ears as my feet hammered against the cold ground. Within a blink, the stag was on the ground, a sword jutted out of its chest. Crow leaned against the closest tree. Not a worry in the world bloomed on his face.

He had Hollowed in front of the stag, making it penetrate itself on his sword.

"Show off." I murmured under my breath as Crow sauntered past me with a smug grin. Moving over to the animal, he pulled the sword from its chest, cleaning it before sheathing it on his back again. He wasted no time as he grabbed the large animal and hauled it up and onto his shoulders effortlessly. He held it around his neck like a scarf, readying for the trek to wherever we were staying for the rest of the day. Why was everything about this man oddly attractive? I chalked it up to him being different, piquing my curiosity, and nothing more. I peered around, but didn't see Ace anywhere.

"Where's Ace?" I asked, and he paused.

"He'll be here in three... two... one." Crow nodded his head behind me.

I turned to look over my shoulder and watched as Ace appeared from the shadows. His hair and clothes were dripping; he was soaking wet. Swallowing down his nausea the best he could from the Hollow as he made long angry strides towards us.

"What the hell happened?" I asked him.

"Your boy here 'poofed' me into an icy lake while I was going for the stag." Ace rushed Crow, but before he could get to him, he stopped dead in his tracks. Looking paler than normal.

"Ace?" I looked at him, concerned, but he bent at the waist and blew chunks. I rubbed soothing circles on his back as I looked away. He got back to his feet and grabbed Crow by the chest, and pushed him against a tree. The dead animal thudded to the ground as Crow dissipated to nothing, leaving Ace's hands empty.

Ace peered around. I did the same, unable to see where Crow had gone. Suddenly, wisps of shadow appeared behind Ace and turned the tables. Crow pinned Ace to the same tree with his tendrils of shade, wrapping them around his waist and legs before he went back to doing what he was doing before. He hauled the animal back over his shoulders, leaving Ace pinned with shadows to the tree trunk, flailing his arms around in anger.

"Cheater." Ace signed with a scowl.

Crow took a contemplative moment before he replied, "Winner." His crooning voice added to the taunt between these two competitive males.

I couldn't stop the snicker that escaped me. Ace glared at me while Crow gave me a side eye and a charming smile. Shadows masked all of his features, but I could see the curve of his full lips, the outline of his tousled hair, and muscled arms as he gripped the heavy animal on his shoulders.

"Alright, enough, let him go, Crow." I commanded and his shadows fell away.

Ace sauntered close enough to him and ruffled his wings like a feral dog, spraying leftover water on Crow as he did. I thought they were about to go toe to toe again.

"Enough!" I shouted, my arm lurching in front of them. Snow shifted to water and moved up their legs before wrapping around their torsos. As if it would keep Crow in one place, but at least I knew Ace would stay put.

Ace calmed, and Crow gathered up his shadows before he started moving again. Ace and I followed him.

We walked for a few hours, only stopping to relieve ourselves or for me to bend some clean water into our skins. Crow and Ace played their cocky competitive games the whole journey. It all began when Crow and I played a game of kicking stones. Both of us tried to kick it further than the other. It was a simple gesture and something about how lighthearted it was made a small smile tug up on my lips.

We continued kicking it between each other. He would kick it and then when I came up to it again, I would. There wasn't any communication between us other than that stone, but it made something stir in me every time we passed it and he decided to kick it again rather than leaving it behind on the path. The last time Crow kicked the stone, it went the furthest it had during the journey and Ace viewed it as the perfect opportunity to join in.

Gathering his wind behind his heels when we all finally made it back to the stone again, Ace kicked it, launching it so far into the distance it would have been impossible to find again.

"Well, would you look at that," Ace signed, looking into the distance the stone was lost too.

I shook my head with a laugh.

"Cute trick." Crow shrugged it off, letting the act of dominance roll off his back as he kept walking. He shredded Ace with words instead. "If only you could've been that fast back in the woods with the stag, or with the pirates." I could tell Crow's jab made Ace's frustrations rise again. But Ace only huffed a breath and kept walking when I gave him a side eyed glance, telling him I'd kill him if they kept fighting.

Any chance they had to butt heads, they did.

I was surprised by the time we finally stopped at a cave for the rest of the day that they hadn't killed each other. Ace quickly started a fire with some twigs he found near our camp while Crow left to grab more firewood. I was left leaning against the stone wall at the caves mouth, arms crossed, with a shit-eating grin on my face watching these two grown men one up each other like childish preteen fae boys for hours.

"What?" Ace questioned as he glanced over at me, wondering what I was smiling about.

"Oh, nothing." I wagged my head, and he growled at me in frustration. His wings flared a little under his cloak, making it expand, giving the appearance of his already broad shoulders being wider and making him look more intimidating.

I arched a brow. "Your macho man is showing. I'm not the shadow man, Ace, you can unruffle your feathers." I watched his shoulders sag a little in relief for the first time all day.

Crow walked into the mouth of the cave with his arms full of large logs of wood. He walked past Ace's small fire of sticks and moved a few feet further into the cave. Throwing the wood down, he began building up his own fire pit with larger pieces of wood and shrubs.

You have to be fucking kidding me. With a few sparks of his iron, the fire was lit and burning bigger and brighter than Aces–considerably bigger.

I could feel the warmth of it from where I was perched against the wall. He tossed his large hunk of venison, sheathed on a stick, over the top of it and rolled it over the open fire, resting his elbows on his knees. He had already cleaned the animal while he was getting firewood. He looked up at Ace, giving him a cocky grin, and Ace snapped.

They lunged for each other. Foregoing bending all together, they moved straight to fists. They threw punches left and right. Ace got a good blow to Crow's jaw before Crow swiped his feet out from under him and leaped on top of him.

I bended a thin impenetrable wall of water between them, forcing them off each other from where I stood. Ace wiped his busted lip while Crow held his jaw as if he was trying to pop it back into place.

"I'm tired, I'm hungry, and I'm sick of your my dick is bigger game. We got our dinner. Now let's cook it, eat and get some rest." I released my water wall, and it pooled to the floor. "And I swear if one of you screws with the other again, I'll cut your balls off in your sleep."

They both got to their feet, trying to catch their breath as they straightened. Ace moved to sit by his fire, grabbing some skewed meat along the way. Crow did the same while they left me standing in the middle.

I hesitated a moment, and they both peered up at me, noticing my pause before I turned on my heel toward Ace's fire. I didn't know why I stopped to think about it. The choice should have been obvious. Ace had been my best friend my entire life, and this masked man of shadow I had only just met. But for whatever reason, I was drawn to him.

CHAPTER TWENTY-THREE
EMELYN

*A*ce growled under his breath.

"Stay with me, Eme," he signed to me, but his hand grew more foggy by the minute. Ace grunted as he tried to stand, and I thought it was from trying to lift me until he dropped me to the ground and turned toward an enemy. A dagger's hilt protruded out of his back, directly between his wings. The fae man ignited his arms in flames. He looked as if he were staggering, already injured, but that could have been my vision playing tricks on me, making the world feel like it was shifting.

A burst of air blasted from Ace, but it didn't harm me. The icy wind made my skin pebble against my soaked clothes. The *fae that attacked barreled away like a leaf falling away from the trees in autumn.*

I watched as Ace created a dome of wind around us. He turned back, cradling me quickly against his chest, before he launched us into the raging elements around us.

Fire, wind, and water came from all directions. Pouring rain pelted against my skin like shards of glass as my body drifted in and out of consciousness. Ace roared across the land, and as if his people knew the call, they took flight, but it was too late to retreat.

Bright light, red flames, and darkness consumed the sky as Ace's wings carried us through the devastation of Valla's wrath. Suddenly, we weren't in the storm of chaos anymore. The surrounding air stilled. The world had gone quiet, as if Ace had become an island of calm amid stormy seas.

I was falling into the depths of my despair. I had lived this again and again and I couldn't change the outcome no matter how hard I wanted to. The memories of one of my greatest losses haunted my dreams and pulled me under the weight of my sorrow, like the roaring waves against the shore.

Darkness surrounded me while I fought for every breath entering my lungs until I didn't have to. My mind went placid, my breathing returned to normal. Gentle caresses along either side of my arms centered me and lulled me from my panic.

My eyes opened, and I lurched up from where I was laying next to Ace. My clothes were damp from sweat, and the chill of the breeze blowing from the outside made my skin pebble. Our fire had gone out, leaving the glow of embers behind. The bones and leftovers of our dinner lay scattered along the cave floor. My eyes bounced around the space. It was dark out. Why hadn't Crow woken us up yet? I turned around to glance over at his camp. He wasn't there, but his fire was still alive, crackling and popping.

I got to my feet, and the movement made Ace stir awake.

"What's wrong?" He signed, groggy. He wiped the sleep from his eyes.

"Crow is gone." I signed back, and he jumped to his feet, quickly glancing to see for himself.

"I knew we shouldn't have trusted him. Who knows where he's taking us, Eme." He signed, but I could feel the reprimand rolling off of him as if he was saying I told you so.

I made my way to the opening of the cave and walked out, peering in both directions. I saw nothing but silhouettes of the surrounding forest against the night sky. When I glanced back to the right again, there he was. Crow walked towards us with more logs in hand.

"Where were you?" Ace signed as we both approached him, uneasiness bounced off of Ace and I, making the air tense. Although I didn't want to admit it, maybe Ace had been right to not trust him.

"I was getting more firewood, your fire went out." Crow nodded toward the cave before meeting my gaze. "I didn't want you to get cold."

Aces eyes volleyed between us as Crows' stare burned through mine. Ace scoffed, turning on his heel and I followed him, unable to handle how naked I felt under his gaze.

A few moments later, Crow's footsteps sounded behind me as we entered the cave and sat around the dead fire.

"I thought we were going to move at night?" I questioned, trying to take my mind off of what had happened.

"The nights are longer in the winter. I was going to let you both sleep a little longer," he said as he laid a log over the ash and sparked a flame with his iron within an instant. He blew on it, and in a few brief moments, the fire roared to life again.

"You woke me up," I said it out loud now that I had experienced the touch of his shadows. I was sure that was what had woken me, quieting my nightmares and drawing me from my restless sleep.

"Sorry, I tried to be quiet when I left." Crow spoke as if he hadn't grasped the meaning of my statement.

"No, your shadows pulled me from my dreams." I whispered loud enough for everyone to hear.

"What are you talking about, Eme?" Ace asked, and I continued.

"Who are you?" I asked Crow again, ignoring Ace entirely, keeping my focus on Crow.

His eyes were intent on me now as he sat on the opposite side of the flame.

"You know me. We've met before." Crow's voice was low and guttural as I tried to map together all the pieces in my mind of who he might be.

Ace stood next to me, gripping his dagger, preparing for whatever was about to happen. And then I remembered the dream, the war, a man in black that had saved us.

"It was you..." I murmured under my breath. "The stranger in the woods all those years ago." When Ace and I were wounded and dying a man cloaked in shadow had saved us during the war between Ember and Heavensreach. Ace pulled a dagger free and chimed in.

"So you were with Ember then."

"Yes, b—"

Ace didn't wait for his response as he lunged for him. Crow dissipated into shadows and appeared next to me as Ace stumbled into the stone wall of the cave.

"Stop, I want to hear what he has to say," I said without looking at Crow. I worried if I did, the tears burning behind my eyes would free fall. Recalling that period of my life was difficult. The only time the thoughts came to me was in my nightmares.

"I was with Ember... but I didn't agree with the war." Crow spoke as he moved back to his spot on the other side of the fire again.

"That changes nothing. You fought with them," Ace signed with a growl.

"Ember hired us to assist them. I was a part of an assassins group called the Western Wyverns. Ember had paid our leader a hefty price to send us to the shores of Esora. When we got there, the war had barely begun. My comrades took down the healers in the back while the princess of Ember attacked from the front. I stayed back, I didn't want any part of it and then when I saw you falling from the sky I..." Crow trailed off as he peered up and saw a single tear slip down my cheek.

Aces heavy hand graced my shoulder and I took comfort in it for a moment before my sadness turned to rage. I grabbed for my battle axe and sent it on the wind straight to Crow. He didn't move, didn't flinch, as if he was ready to take whatever wrath I gave him.

My axe stuck out of the stone within an inch of his head. I leaped for him. Water shot up my legs, encircling my arms, and became a tendril so thin it was like a blade jutting out of my arm as my forearm barricaded his neck against the stone. His long wisps of shadows danced around me, but they didn't attack, didn't defend.

"My mother…" I choked over my words, the pain of her loss still raw and palpable even after all this time. My chest tightened, a lump forming in my throat as I struggled to find the strength to continue. "Was one of those healers." I took a shuddering breath, the weight of my emotions threatening to overwhelm me.

"Eme, I–"

"Don't call me that. You don't get that right. Only the ones dearest to me call me that, and you're nothing more than a lying coward. You knew what Ember was doing was wrong, and you sat back and did nothing… All those people… The Sky Elves… My Pada." I lost it. Tears fell so fast I couldn't see anything but his darkness billowing around me.

Aces arm encircled my waist as he yanked me off of Crow, before he crowded me in his arms and I crumbled into his chest.

CHAPTER TWENTY-FOUR
EMELYN

I composed myself, wiping away the tears as I moved out of Ace's hold.

"Let's go," I said. Turning away, I rushed outside with Ace on my heels.

"Wait." Crow shouted from behind us. "There's nowhere for you to go. The only place left for you is the rebellion."

I didn't want to admit it, but he was right. No one would help us knowing who we were—what I was. Ember would destroy every home–every city, if they knew they harbored me. Crow continued reasoning with my back to him.

"We can work together, help you learn about your bending, your powers. You need to control them if you ever want this war to be over." His voice fell quiet. "I'm sorry about what happened back then, to your family, to both of your families... But they would want this war to end too."

I hated that everything he said made sense. I wanted to pummel him, leave and never return, but I couldn't. Not now, not when I was the Peacebringer and the only one able to restore this world, regardless if I didn't know how to. And the rebellion might be the help I'd need.

Ace looked at me, and I could see his hesitation too. It was as if he could hear my thoughts, having the same ones circulating through his mind.

"Please..." Crows voice was pleading, and it made my walls crumble. I loathed that the sound defused my anger.

A tense pause of contemplation stretched between all of us until I finally spoke up again.

"Fine..." I said, letting out a long breath. I turned and looked at him for the first time. "Lead the way..." I spat with a wave of my hand, and waited for him to lead us out of the cave and toward the rebellion.

I watched the ground, and every so often I glanced up to Crow's back in front of me. His shadows had been whipping wildly around him since we were back at the caves. The contrast between them and the night sky entranced me in a way I didn't understand. The different shades of blackness swirling around the other. I saw his fae ears peaking through his hair and the muscles in his back shifted with every step. I forced my stare back down to the ground when my eyes began wandering further down his body.

I wanted to be mad at him, but in all reality, he saved Ace and I all those years ago. I snapped about my mother before he had the chance to tell me anymore of his story. Guilt tugged at me, although it shouldn't have.

He was there, and not only that, he was there with Ember and did nothing to stop the war, or to fight back against what he knew was wrong. Instead, he sat on the sidelines because he said he hadn't wanted to be a part of it. People died because of that. My people. My family.

My mind replayed every moment back in the cave. His words repeated over and over again and it only made me have more questions. Why did he save us? And how had his shadows pulled me out of the worst of my nightmares? He hadn't even been in the cave. Did I make noise and my nightmares woke him up?

Every time I thought back to my dreams, one recurring thought kept trying to surface from the back of my mind. Waking up to the calm pull of darkness had been a regular occurrence through the years since the war, but the thought of them being Crows shadows made lead sink into my gut, and I didn't want to know if it was true.

Had it been him all these years? It was impossible, but the touch of his shadows had been so familiar.

Ace grabbed me and pulled me behind a large tree with him. I had been so lost in thought I didn't know what was happening. Crow was two trees in front of us hiding behind it as the small crowd of Fire Fae soldiers walked by. Some held heavy totes of gear, wrestling it further down the path, others sauntered nonchalantly while making jokes. I smelled pungent body odor and burning tobacco from all the men bustling through the trees to the large white square tents that were set up further in the distance.

A Fire Fae camp.

I had seen them before. Embers Emperor stationed them wherever he could to antagonize the smaller villages and towns of innocents around all of Osparia. He was slowly breaking down the spirit of the people in our world. The only places that hadn't been overrun yet were major cities, and although Ember hadn't won control over them yet, they still littered the surrounding areas like pests. Their camp blocked the direction we were heading. We'd need to get around them.

"Psst," Crow hissed nodding his head in his direction, wanting us to come to him. After the last few in the crowd walked by, we did, padding lightly one step at a time. We made it to where he was, his shadows wrapping around us in a welcoming embrace.

Serene.

Then the darkest umbra surrounded us. A rushing noise sounded in my ears before I suddenly felt the crunch of frozen foliage on the forest floor under my boots again. Ace bent at the waist, his face looked more ashen under the moonlit sky and the nausea rolling through him, same as last time. Crow stood leaning most of his body weight against a tree, his chest heaved and his shadows seemed more erratic than normal.

"Hey!" a gruff voice yelled from in front of us. It was a soldier buttoning his trousers. He had just relieved himself in the bushes. Realization flashed over his features as our eyes connected and he held our stare. He recognized who I was.

Damn, words spread fast.

"You're the... Hey... It's the Peacebrin!—" He waved and shouted toward the camp before Crow launched at him, cutting off his statement when they both dissipated into the dark. Frantic voices and heavy steps rang from behind us as the soldiers from the camp stirred.

"Run." Ace signed, and we darted forward through the trees. As we kept running, the forest became dense with trees, making the path harder to navigate. Aces wings kept catching against the trees, no matter how tightly he tried pinning them against his back under his cloak. At this point our paths diverged, but there wasn't time to stop. He launched himself into the sky, giving him an advantage. I hadn't been close enough to latch onto him.

My pace didn't slow, despite the icy winds whipping around my face, making my eyes tear. I kept catching glances of Ace's feathers and hearing the flap of his wings overhead. The second the trees cleared, I knew he'd swoop down for me.

My heart pounded and my lungs burned as I nimbly dodged and leapt over and around the crowding forest. Tree branches slashed at my face, but I didn't stop. My attention snapped back to Ace just as my foot caught on the uneven terrain and my body jerked before losing my balance completely.

I freely fell with nothing to find purchase on as I tumbled over the rocky, uneven hillside. Trying to catch myself, I threw my hands out in front of me. My palms grated against the sharp stones and thistles along the ravine. My eyes squeezed closed as my head collided with a thud against the cold ground before I finally stopped rolling.

I forced myself to move. My body burned and stung from all the cuts and scrapes on the way down. Getting back to my feet, Ace spotted me and spiraled down from the sky. Bending his knees to absorb the impact of his landing, he rushed to my side.

"Are you alright?" He signed, looking over what I was sure was my mangled clothes and skin.

"Fine, come on, we have to move." I spoke as a warm orange glow illuminated from the soldiers over the top of the ravine. The Fire Fae were on us. We had to keep moving.

I took the first step to run, but my body gave out from under me. I let out a groan from the pain shooting through my leg. Ace started for me, but in the next moment Crow appeared in front of him. His hands clenched into fists for a moment before he grabbed me, cradling me against his chest. Ace tried to intervene, but Crow snarled at him. This wasn't the time for petty bickering. I couldn't run, and we needed to move. I raised my hand to sign to Ace.

"It's fine."

Making Ace relax and step back again with an unsatisfied look on his face.

Crows shadows encompassed all three of us. I looked up to see his firm jaw tick as he peered over my injuries before he Hollowed us out of the ravine.

CHAPTER TWENTY-FIVE
CROW

Anytime Ace tried to undermine me I told him I would Hollow him on repeat every ten feet and the threat made his face go white with nausea. I would do it too, regardless of how weak I felt from all the Hollowing. After his first few failed attempts to have me release Emelyn, he finally accepted that I wasn't letting her out of my grasp.

We weaved through the enormous trees, their leaves bright oranges, reds, and browns reflected against the light of the moon. The trees of Woodhaven never died off in the winter like normal trees. Their limbs never went completely bare. They would change into different shades of beautiful colors throughout the seasons. My long strides carried me forward but considering it took multiple steps to get by one tree made it seem like I wasn't moving fast enough.

Seeing the strained expression on Emelyn's face as she tried to put on a brave one through the pain of her injuries made something in me crumble. It made me want to hold her closer, tend to every wound that marked her skin, and then kill all those that had put them there.

I could feel her distrust and frustration geared toward me from our earlier interaction. It pulsated through the air between us, striking me through the chest harder than any blow. I had to earn back her trust, even though we had only just begun forming it.

We had been close enough that I'd Hollowed the man to the rebellion so Atreya could question him. A Fire Fae camp had never come so close to the rebellion's base camp before. We had places set up through all the territories of Osparia in case we needed to sparse out, even in crevices of Ember. What better place to hide than right under our enemies nose? We never stayed in one place too long, usually never raising any suspicion.

The base camp was the only place that didn't move as often. It stayed hidden with magic all the time, so those who found it would turn away from the thrum of unease or fear they felt.

My shadows rescinded and clung to me as I Hollowed us through my void and pushed all of us out to the other side. We were close to the rebellion now.

My body was weak, my magic drained from all the Hollowing and masking I had been doing between Emelyn and I. I wanted to spill my guts to her, tell her everything from over the last century, but I knew it wasn't the time or place to do that–not yet.

I needed rest, and so did she in order for her injuries to heal. For now, the protection of the rebellion could give us that.

Time–we needed time.

Her body tensed in my hold when she attempted to wriggle free but I refused to put her down.

"Crow, put me down, I can walk." She commanded as she squirmed against my chest.

"No." I responded, keeping my eyes forward.

"What do you mean, no?" She huffed, still trying to get free.

"Exactly what I said, no." I repeated myself sternly before looking down at her and continuing, "your hurt, your leg is probably broken and if you won't take care of yourself, then I'll do it for you." My voice was low and guttural, even more so when it sifted through my shadows. She stopped fighting me and her body melted into mine, finally accepting that I refused to put her down.

My strides were long and determined. Ignoring my body's signals to stop, I began feeling the wards press against my skin, making gooseflesh rise over my neck. I could feel Emelyn shift in my arms as we walked through the barrier that kept this place hidden. The witches of the rebellion had done well with their spells to keep our hideouts as safe as they could be. It only took a moment for us to walk through the magical barrier. The pressure of it rose and dropped away from my skin.

Ace followed behind me, I glanced over at him. He peered around, his shoulders tense, his chest flared as if he was waiting for an ambush. An enormous bonfire smoked in the distance, the only evidence that'd make you question if the forest was empty. Ace signed to Emelyn and I.

"What is this Crow... You said you were taking us to the rebellion." I could tell by his body language that he was getting antsy. Frustration brewed under my skin. It was like treading over a shattered ice lake around them, hoping that the cracks would mend so they would trust me again.

"This is it," I said.

They both looked at me with puzzled expressions. I quickly weaved through a handful of trees, before I lowered Emelyn, making sure I held her body weight up against me so there wasn't any on her leg. Ace stepped up next to us as a precaution, but her arm stayed draped around my neck while she kept her balance. I moved a few large branches that were hiding a large rope pulley attached to the tree. I grabbed it and gave a few good tugs before gripping Emelyn's waist.

"Hold on to me," I said before I grabbed my dagger and slashed through the rope, sending a colossal weight down the tree and using it to pull Emelyn and I up the enormous trunk. She gripped onto me as we spun slowly up the length of the tree. I watched as she looked at the surroundings. The leaves were lightly falling from the tree limbs above from us jostling them, raining down different shades of red. A smile curved on her lips and it made a warmth pass through my chest, my own lips tilted in response to her happiness.

Her eyes met mine, and it would be so easy for me to drown in those pools of emerald. To show her exactly what we were to each other—but I couldn't, not yet. I wondered if she could feel even an inkling of the unrelenting tether trying to reach out from the depths of my soul because her smile faded, and her lips parted slightly. I held my breath, my heart fluttered behind my ribs.

My shadows flowed like fluid around us, wanting to caress every part of her flushed skin, I fought the urge, taking everything in me to keep them to myself. They never listened when I needed them to the most. A tendril of shade curled up from nowhere and moved a long, loose strand of her silver hair, tucking it behind her ear. Gently caressing her cheek before it fell away. Her eyes fluttered from the lightest touch and then her eyes met mine.

"You're—" The words fell out of my mouth before I could stop them. I didn't finish the sentiment.

Breathtaking, I waned to say, I wanted to tell her all of these things. How I could drown in her and it be the most exquisite kind of drowning, where you willingly lose yourself in the tides, consumed and yet strangely liberated. Just as water envelops and surrounds, she had filled every corner of my being, leaving no room for anything but the overwhelming sensation of being utterly and completely immersed in her. I had never seen someone so beautiful. Her gaze stayed locked on mine, until she ripped it away, severing our moment of connection. But the bond was there, lurking and waiting to finally be set free. I held it at bay.

Ace cleared his throat. Emelyn and I had stopped our ascent, leaving us standing on the rickety wooden path. I was still holding up her body weight against me. A tight rope bridge connected all the trees. The rebellion built large huts around their trunks, each used for different things. Most had rooms with beds, some of them had been made into permanent homes while others were used to house medical supplies and dried meats to keep the creatures that lurked at night away. What better place to hide than within the giant trees of Woodhaven?

Emelyn released her arm from around my neck, stumbling away from me. I grabbed her, but she nudged me off.

"Stop." Her voice was soft but demanding. An emotion I couldn't place hid within that one word. She nodded for Ace to help her, and he stepped up and swept her into his arms. And just as quickly as she had been in my hold, she wasn't. I tucked the emptiness that pooled in my gut behind the wall of sentiments I had internally built over the years. I hoped one day I could share them with her.

Small lanterns of fireflies lined every tree the bridge was attached to, leaving a faint glow so you could see where you were going. I walked in front of them, leading them to a room I knew would be empty. I had told Atreya in my hand off of the Fire Fae soldier that we would be coming so she would prepare. Most of the camp slept, with the exception of a few fae and dryads who kept watch, monitoring the perimeter. I was sure they knew we were here long before they saw us. They gave me a nod of their head or a wave in greeting as I walked past. I'd introduce Ace and Emelyn to everyone tomorrow. As of now, I needed to tend to Emelyn, and then we all needed to rest.

CHAPTER TWENTY-SIX
EMELYN

Crow led us to a room with the large tree jutting through the center of it with a newly made bed perched against the wall. A stack of fresh blankets sat folded at the end of it. The room reminded me of some sort of treehouse home. But I couldn't focus on anything else, other than the throbbing ache radiating from my leg through my entire body, even down to the tips of my fingers. I ground my molars. My adrenaline had worn off, and the pain had set in. Ace sat me down gently on the bed, being more cautious of my leg.

"I'm going to check out the perimeter. Will you be alright until I get back?" Ace signed and I could see the concern in his eyes.

"Yes," I signed, trying to give him a reassuring look, but I was sure my face was pinched as sweat beaded my brow. He hesitated until I shooed him away with my hand. "Go Ace, I'll be fine."

He huffed before turning on his heels and brushing past Crow, who waited leaning on the doorway.

"It's safe. You should get some rest." Crow said to Ace as he walked by, but Ace pretended he didn't hear him, going to do what he had planned anyway.

I struggled with the laces of my boots. My leg trembled with the strength I used to lift it and my fingers fumbled over themselves until Crow grabbed my wrists. He looked at me, asking silently for my permission to help.

I nodded, and he took over, gently untying the laces and pulling off the boot gently. I hissed in pain.

"Fucking hell, Emelyn." He cursed as he pulled off the sock, revealing my purple and blue ankle. The spot above it was bulged and had swelled to the size of a small ball.

"How bad is it?" I asked through clenched teeth, squeezing my eyes shut from the pain as he lifted it.

"It'll need to be realigned before you can start healing it or it'll heal wrong," he said, his voice deep but soft. When I opened my eyes, his shadows were caressing me soothingly, trying to quiet my racing heart. They darkened the room, making it almost impossible to see any details about it.

Shifting my focus to the pain and the silhouette of the man in front of me, "do it." I said through gritted teeth. My breath quickened as I fisted the bed sheets underneath me. Crow gently placed his hands on the lower half of my leg before his smokey irises met my gaze. I nodded to let him know I was ready, and then I heard the snap of my bone shifting back into place. I groaned in pain before grabbing my water skin with trembling hands. I bended the water over my palms, feeling the buzz of the magic as it glowed—preparing to heal.

I placed my hands over my leg, and the pulsating pain started to subside. Once it was bearable, I stopped. Healing usually had to be done in sessions. Not with everything, but considering how exhausted I was, I'd do more later, or just let my body heal the rest naturally. Fae healing was normally quick, only taking two or three days to heal a broken bone, sometimes only a few hours to heal a stab wound, depending on how bad it was.

Crows shadows drew back into his figure, leaving the space brighter with the large lanterns hanging off of the enormous tree trunk that grew through the center of the room. The walls of the large tree house were bare other than the small windows that sat aligned with each other from all the other sides. Dark red leaves scattered about the wooden planked floor as if this room hadn't been used in a while.

Crow moved the blankets and sat at the end of the bed, propping my leg on his lap as he wrapped it. "That's unnecessary," I said, but he didn't listen to me and continued to wrap it anyway. The cool breeze against my dewy skin made a chill run over my body. Crow stood, slipping my foot gently off his lap before walking to the other side of the tree trunk, where he knelt in front of a small closet. He grabbed a thicker blanket than the ones left next to the bed and walked it back over to me. "Thank you," I murmured, and he gave me a weak smile.

"No need to thank me." He climbed on to the end of the bed again. Sitting up, he leaned his back against the wall, craning his head against it, and closed his eyes. He pulled my leg onto his lap and cradled it against him, the motion so gentle I hardley felt it.

"What are you doing?" I questioned, trying to pull away, but he stopped me.

"You need sleep, you need to heal," he said, never opening his eyes to look at me.

I arched my brow at him. "Okay, neither of those things involves you being here." I snapped, still angry.

"I'll keep the nightmares away," he said as he lulled his head to the side to pierce me with his sleepy, unimpressed stare, as if my sass had no effect on him, before he turned away and resettled against the wood.

I couldn't remember the last time I went to sleep and didn't wake to the memories of my past coming back to haunt me. His shadows always stirred me awake. He had just confirmed it, but bits and pieces of the nightmares always made it through. I wondered with him physically here with me if my nightmares would find me at all?

Blowing out a breath of defeat, I flipped to my left side, which faced him. I wanted to turn the other way but my right leg still ached too badly to sleep facing away and I could've sworn I saw a small smile curve on the shadow mans lips, but I couldn't be certain with the lighting in here. I was about to open my mouth to say something, but Crow cut me off before I could.

"Go to sleep, mei wynsoara. I'll answer your questions tomorrow."

I huffed my frustrations again before I continued, "is that the old fae language? What's wynsoara?" I knew *mei* meant *my*, but that was as far as my knowledge of the old language went.

"It's not important." He murmured.

"How do you know old fae?" I prodded further.

"Tomorrow. Now rest."

"You're insufferable."

"So I've been told." He grinned.

"What is it with men and giving me nicknames?" I questioned, and his lips twitched in amusement. First the prince and now him.

"What does that mean?" he asked, peering over at me again.

"Not important." I huffed, and he let out a soft, low laugh. The rich sound of it made something flutter in my stomach in all the ways it shouldn't have.

I closed my eyes, no longer having the energy to keep them open, and sleep found me quickly.

CHAPTER TWENTY-SEVEN
ACE

I didn't trust Crow with my life, but I could feel something between Emelyn and him that I couldn't place. I knew he wouldn't hurt her, which was a comfort and a curse.

I paced down the rickety wooden bridges that connected the large round houses stacked, perched in the trees. I had to give it to them, it was an excellent place to hide rebels. If I would have stumbled through I wouldn't have taken a second glance. I found nothing out of the ordinary as I did a full lap around the uneven homes layered in the trees.

I spread my wings and soared down to the ground, walking through the woods, I found nothing that would suggest there was an entire army of people living here other than the large campfire that was now nothing with gray ash. They did well with covering their tracks.

I spreads my wings and flapped them once, twice, before I was flying above the trees. The icy winds cooled me down from my frustrations from earlier.

Crow had a way of getting under my skin. It wasn't jealousy, or at least, not in the romantic sense. I loved Emelyn, like the sister I never had–she was more than family to me.

The relationship we had ran deeper than the blood in our veins. But ever since Crow 'poofed' out of nowhere she seemed to side with him more than I'd like. Her guard was down around him, and Emelyn had never been one to let her guard down for anyone.

I let the cool wind blow the thoughts from my mind. I hadn't been able to get a moment in to clear my mind in weeks with everything that's happened, from being away and traveling to coming home and witnessing more destruction.

It never ended.

I saw a shift in some of the clouds from my peripherals, my brows knitted as I thought I saw a pair of feathered wings, not normal bird wings–Sky Elf wings.

I shifted my weight and changed course not believing my eyes as I plummeted into the clouds fog. Making it through to the other side only left me wet from the clouds gathered moisture, chilled in my disappointment as the air billowed through my wings. They were gone? Had my eyes played a trick on me?

I returned to my path but saw the black wings fluttering in the distance, two pairs of booted feet straightened behind them.

My eyes had definitely not played tricks on me. A smile stretched over my features at what I couldn't believe to be true. It was a Sky Elf, at least one from what I could see.

I barreled to where they were as they flew to the ground to land. My flight was strained, my wings flapped in tandem with my pounding heart. Needing to get to them, to see them, to be sure I was seeing what my head and my heart believed I was.

I ran into my landing, the frozen dew on the grass crunched against my every step. The male Sky Elf I had been following turned toward me, along with their companion, she didn't have wings but she had the same ears as a Sky Elf. They were always slightly longer than the fae's with a sharper point to them.

My eyes rounded in my shock, mouth parting, I could feel the sharp pang of emotion growing and twisting in my chest.

"Welcome home, brother." The man signed and spoke while he outstretched his arms with a wide smile. He spoke to me as if he had known me his whole life–two sides of the same coin.

The woman stepped back as he pulled me into a crushing hug, I pulled away and then the woman hugged me the same, she smelt of cinnamon and sweet flowers. Her long sandy blonde hair was braided down to the small of her back, and they both wore leathers. Loose strands framed her face, her smile dimpled her ivory cheeks meeting her warm brown eyes as she peered up at me.

"What's your name?" She signed to me as I paid attention to the resemblance between them, both had light brown eyes and blonde hair. The mans wings were black like mine, a stark contrast between his lighter complexion and hair. Sky Elf wings were aways black, sometimes a mix of dark gray, but usually black.

He had more of a complexion than who I assumed was his sister. His hair was tied in a knot at the base of his neck, a few feathers were weaved into a small braid dangling in front of one of his ears. I was so entranced seeing them that I hadn't realized the woman had asked me my name.

"Ace...My name is Ace." I fumbled over my hands, "and yours?"

"I'm Maeve, this is my brother Sedrin," She motioned toward him and he gave me a crooked grin with a nod, "did you come with Crow? He told Atreya he was bringing a few new people with him, but failed to mention one was a Sky Elf." She smiled up at me through her lashes.

"Yeah, we came with him, are there more of you. . . of us—Sky Elves?" My hands were barely working correctly as I tried to wrap my mind around not being the last of my kind.

"Yeah, a few." Sedrin signed and spoke at the same time, letting me know he stopped living by our peoples traditions of using only our mother tongue of signing. Not everyone did, it was considered an honor among our people to dedicate their lives to it. Not only did I continue because of my peoples traditions but also because I believed I was the last of my kind. I wanted to keep our culture alive in my own way.

It took perseverance, and after the war I made a vow to never give in and live by it for the rest of my life. Even my best friend had not been able to make me break it. I doubted anything would.

"Would you like to meet them?" Maeve signed, and interrupted my thoughts.

"Yes, of course." I signed, my palms grew clammy. I never thought I'd see another Sky Elf again other than when I looked in the mirror, and now I was walking alongside two of them, leading me to more. It made something stir in my chest that I hadn't felt in a really long time–hope.

Hope for our race.

Hope for the return of Heavensreach.

Sedrin took the lead while Maeve sauntered next to me, anytime she walked a step or two ahead of me, my eyes snagged on her back, no wings draped down her figure like mine and her brothers. I wondered if she was a half breed, but wings had always been a dominate trait, even among halflings, and she had our ears and sharper features. She glanced over her shoulder catching me gawking at her back.

"Curiosity got your hands in a twist?" She turned and signed to me, and a flush crept up my neck.

"Sorry, I didn't mean to–" She waved my statement away and replaced it with her own.

"Its alright, you wouldn't be the first to want to know what happened to them." She signed and the statement made my heart sink like lead.

Happened to them.

I couldn't fathom something happening to a Sky Elves wings bad enough to have to sever them, or them not growing back. I assumed it was a battle injury from the war but that didn't ease the nausea in my gut from the thought of what this woman went through that caused her wings to never return.

"That story requires a drink first." She signed and her brother chimed in from over his shoulder.

"More than one." He said as he walked through the opening in the trees that lead back to what looked like a large empty campsite from when we arrived.

"Which one is yours?" I asked both of them motioning toward all the makeshift homes lining the trees overhead, they were hidden from where we stood but I knew they sat just above our heads.

"I'm in that one," Maeve said, pointing to one of the trees on the outskirts of camp. I couldn't see it from the ground but after looking around earlier, I was sure I could find it. I was about to take flight when Sedrin chimed in.

"Come on, we all hang out at Nevara and Taryn's house, theirs is the biggest." Sedrin said as he kept moving forward, the names sounded familiar, like they were from a distant memory.

Maeve walked over to her brother and he wrapped an arm around her waist before spreading his black feathered wings and shot up into the trees. I followed as they landed and came to the front door of one of the tree houses, this one was larger. It was wider and taller, better for accommodating wings. I tucked my wings into my back, shielding them under my cloak as I walked into the warm home. This one had a small wood furnace that was lit and the space smelt of spicy cloves and smoked meats, and what was that I smelled–gin?

Sedrin outstretched his hand and pointed to every Sky Elf in the room as he introduced them

"That's Taryn and Nevara," He said, Nevara had shoulder length brown dreads laced with feathers, brown eyes, dark brown skin that was shadowed further against her high cheekbones, and a bright smile as she waved at me from where she sat with her legs draped over Taryn's lap, he had tousled red locks and a long beard that stopped at his chest. I assumed they were mates, I could almost feel the bond of fate, the closeness, the love between them. It was as if an unseen string tethered them together as one.

Taryn grinned and gave me a nod as Sedrin continued to introduce me, "that's Cyran."

Cyran lowered the book he was reading but his blue eyes never left the page. He lifted his glass of what I presumed was gin with his other hand in greeting, giving a smirk of his full lips before returning to what he was reading. His legs were criss-crossed at his ankle, leathered boots propped up on the table he was sitting at, his chair propped back.

He was masculine but held himself with an elegant grace in contrast to the gruffness of Taryn, Sedrin, and myself. Cyran's tunic was unbuttoned revealing the black hair that dusted his chest against his dark bronzed skin. His face was shaved and his hair was cut short against his scalp revealing his extended, pointed ears proudly as his wings draped lazily over the seat behind him.

"Nice to meet all of you," I signed, returning their warm greeting.

"Annnd, you've already met Sedrin and myself." Maeve signed cheerily with a wide smile on her face that made me warmer where I stood. I convinced myself it was the furnace and not my curiosity about her. She grabbed my hand and tugged me along over to the large table where Cyran was still reading.

"Want a drink?" She asked as she put her small hands on my tense shoulders and nudged me down into a seat. I obliged, sitting in front of Cyran only seeing the tread of his boots until he slid his feet off the table and sat up. The book thudded as he closed it with the hand it was in while he took another long drink. Setting the cup down with only the clink of ice in it before he signed to me

"You play Tile?" He asked with his voice as he pulled out the board.

"I haven't played in years." I signed.

"Well it's a good time to start." He grinned as he began setting up the game pieces.

"You don't need this, why are you still wearing it?" Maeve signed as she pulled my cloak off my shoulders and draped it onto the back of my chair before she grabbed us both a drink and took a seat herself.

Cool air ran over my onyx wings and broad shoulders and it made my chest heavy with emotion. As if someone shattered my chains and released me into the world again.

Before finding this place, I had kept my wings—my identity, under wraps for fear of Ember coming for Sky-Elves, and then once they were coming for Emelyn, I knew they'd search for me as well knowing we stayed together, we always had. A Sky Elf was easy to spot, And once she found out they had been keeping tabs on us, I knew I'd have to keep myself hidden, either under a cloak, or with the help of Emelyn's glamour.

"For protection, to keep myself hidden when traveling," I answered her question as she furrowed her brow at me.

"Why would you need to stay hidden while travling? Ember isn't after our kind anymore." She signed and I gave her a side eye.

"No, but they are after my companion, the Peacebringer." I signed and the room went quiet, I peered around the room to wide eyes and parted lips.

"The Peacebringer? Is here?" Maeve asked with a smile slowly creeping on to the curve of her lips.

"Yeah, she's the only family I have left." I signed.

Sedrin groaned, "ouch, I'm hurt, brother." He gave me a side eye as Taryn moved Nevara's legs off his lap, they both stood walking over to the table. Taryn pulled up two more wooden chairs, pulling out his mates first and letting her sit before he took the seat next to her.

Sedrin walked over from the other side of the room where I hadn't even noticed he'd moved to. He sauntered back over to the table with a glass for everyone balanced in his large hand and two bottles of what I assumed was gin in the other, the neck of the bottles were gripped between his fingers as he sat them on the table. He placed a cup in front of me, Maeve, Taryn, and Nevara, keeping one for himself while he poured everyone a hefty drink.

Cyran was the only one who sipped his while the others threw back their first drink like it was water–including Maeve. I took down the drink Maeve had made me before I downed the second as Sedrin began filling the glasses again.

"Anyone who has the blood of elves running through their veins is family of ours." Taryn said as matter-of-fact as he signed at the same time, giving me a wink before he raised his glass to all of us before he took down his second drink in one swig.

We followed the motion and did the same as we all took down our next drink, my shoulders began to sag and the warmth began to course through my viens from the alcohol.

"I'll play first with my mate, then we'll rotate, winners play winners." Taryn explained as Cyran moved to set up a game board in front of Nevara and her mate.

"We all already know I'll beat all of you." Cyran said with a grin.

"Not before I drink you under the table, boy." Taryn huffed out his words with a laugh and I couldn't hold back my grin as Nevara made the first move and Maeve sat next to me.

She told me about her story, what had happened to her wings. During the war a group of Fire Fae soldiers captured her and tortured her, cutting them completely out of her back to ensure they'd never come back. I didn't think I could hate the soldiers of Ember anymore than I already did–I was wrong.

I wasn't sure how we ended up measuring our wingspans in our drunken stupor but we did, and I couldn't lie about how smug I was when mine measured the largest, even Cyran huffed when mine ended up being half an inch larger than his. Until Nevara swooped in and her wings ended up being larger than everyones by a fourth of an inch. Taryn only beamed at her in pride while the rest of us stroked down our ego.

Before Sedrin passed out he had measured all of our wings in the house and afterwards Nevara and Maeve giggled together while enjoying their drinks.

Later on.

Somehow Maeve and I ended up shitfaced playing the last game of Tile against each other. Taryn and Nevara stayed awake cheering.

Taryn for me and Nevara for Maeve as the game was coming down to the wire.

There were only two moves left I could make and I knew one of them would win me the game but I wasn't worried about winning. Maeve wanted this win so badly, and I wanted to give it to her simply for the fact she could rub it in Cyrans face that not only did she beat me, but she had beat someone who had beat Cyran. Apparently he was undefeated, and had been for a long while.

Earlier when it came down to Cyran and myself, I had won, and the only winner left to play against me was Maeve. It had come down to the two of us and I wanted to give this to her. So I did.

I moved my Tile piece and within a beat she shoved hers into the spot that would earn her victory as she leapt from her chair with a holler and took down another shot of gin before giving me her bright smile.

Warmth swept over me, and it wasn't from the liquor.

Sedrin had long but passed out, while Cyran had moved to the side of the table to read a book, which now, was lying over his face as a light snore filtered through the pages. His feet propped up, just like before.

We all had way too much to drink...

Taryn smacked me on the back, too drunk to sign as he slurred over his words, "nice try my boy!"

His mannerisms reminded me so much of my own father's it made tears swell in my eyes at times when he would speak to me. I pushed them down.

Although I had only just met these people, I felt at home for the first time in a long time. The only other time I'd felt this way was when Emelyn and I visited Heavensreach together.

Nevara stood on wobbly legs from the table we had been gathered around all night and Taryn quickly shifted his attention from me to her as he wrapped a hand around her waist to steady her.

"We haven't had this much fun in a long while. We're glad to have you–both of you." Nevara signed and I knew she meant Emelyn even though she hadn't met her yet. I could see the hope shining in all of their eyes through the evening I spent with them, it was a reflection of my own.

Could we finally end this war once and for all?

My thought got interrupted as Maeve bent at the waist and retched up everything she had drank and ate. I staggered to my feet before too much of it splattered against my pants and made my way behind her to hold her long hair out of her face while running a soothing hand up and down her back.

"I'm so sorry," Her hands trembled as she raised from her hunched position, "Skies Above," she cursed, "it's on your trousers."

I glanced down at the splattered mess of my clothes and waved it away, "It's fine," I signed but she moved quickly to find a rag and did her best to rub it off of my trousers.

She was rubbing something else too.

She wiped a few more times as her body swayed drunkenly before she slowly stopped and her glazed eyes met mine, before they shifted to my lips and then back to my eyes again. I turned my head away from the tension of our stare and grabbed her waist and cradled her against my chest, she probably would've toppled over if I didn't.

"It's fine, I can walk…" Her signs were garbled, if I wasn't fluent I wouldn't have been able to understand her.

"Lets get you home," I signed as I pulled her into my arms, she didn't fight it as she lay her head against me. I tucked in my wings to walk out the door, giving her brother a look over. A sheen of drool drained from the corner of his lip as he snored before I walked out the door.

I navigated my way to her small home in the trees easily as she cuddled up against my chest. I landed gracefully in front of her place and walked her inside. She didn't try to get out of my hold.

I placed her feet gently on the ground keeping my arm around her waist.

"Can you stand?" I signed and she smiled and nodded her head before glancing to my lips and then back to my eyes. again. And then she went for it and moved in for a kiss.

Her lips were soft and claimed mine perfectly. I palmed her cheek pulling her closer to me to deepen the kiss. She hummed to my touch as my grip tightened around her waist. The warmth of the gin was still dancing under my skin, making this encounter hotter.

Her hands roamed over my abdomen before she tried to slip her hand into the waist of my pants. Stopping her, I grabbed her wrists, and pulled away. I cleared my throat.

"You've been drinking," I signed and she gave me a pouty look before trying to lean into me again.

"But I want you," She signed and tried again and I pulled back further.

"Then you'll have me when you have a sober mind." I signed and she groaned playfully.

"Fine." She rolled her eyes as she stumbled over to her bed, it looked larger than the bed in Emelyn's room, accommodating for Sky Elf wings. "But will you at least stay with me?" She asked as she sat down gesturing to the spot next to her. She gave me a look over with her beautiful brown eyes that I couldn't resist.

I walked over and chucked off my boots before I helped her with her own. She laid down and I gently pulled them off, setting them next to mine by the bed.

I laid down next to her and she wrapped an arm around my midsection and draped her leg over my thighs as she rested her head against my chest. A moment passed before her breathing was deep and slow with sleep. Soon, mine would be the same I thought to myself as I drifted off to sleep.

CHAPTER TWENTY-EIGHT

CROW

She slept peacefully. I paid attention to the small signs that nightmares were coming when her brows would knit together slightly. I would send my shadows to caress her through the bond that tied us.

I couldn't stop staring at her, admiring her every detail from her pillowy lips, down to the line of her jaw, the curve of her breasts, the shape of her hips, the thickness of her thighs as she slept half sprawled over me.

The swelling in her leg had gone down a lot through the night, leaving blue and purple bruises painted against her sun-kissed skin. The sight pissed me off. Made me want to kill every fae from that camp over the marks left from her fall in the woods. I was sure Atreya had already taken care of them.

I shook my head, reeling myself back in from my thoughts. Because although I had known she was my mate for a little over a century, she didn't know that. And that wasn't something I could exactly spill over lunch, so I'd wait, I'd be patient, I had already waited a century, I would wait until she was ready. Until our circumstances were different.

The truth hung around my neck like an albatross, the time couldn't have been worse. I'd wanted to find her, help from a distance, and then tell her the truth once peace was one with our world again and we could live a quiet life—if she accepted me.

I kept my distance all these years to keep her safe, but when the truth spread from her village, It made the choice for me. I couldn't stay away any longer. There was no getting around involving myself further.

The thought of her learning the truth with so many things standing between us being together made a knot form in my throat. I swallowed it down and gazed over at her one last time. The last of the winter wind billowed through the small windows surrounding the large tree house and I gathered up the thick, scratchy blanket laying over her legs and tucked it around Emelyn's shoulders making sure she was warm and resting peacefully before I lulled my head back and fell asleep.

My shadows loomed around the room, tugging on my consciousness until my eyes drifted open to a faint blue light, and fell to Emelyn's hands. They illuminated the space as she tried to heal her leg further. I knew mending bones back together again had to be painful, but when my stare raised to her face, she was focused. The only thing revealing to me that she was hurting was the way her leg slightly trembled against me in my lap. Tendrils of my shade caressed her shoulders.

I wanted to comfort her, but I didn't want to make her feel uncomfortable with the touch of my hand. Although I had control over my shadows, mostly, I didn't lie when I said they were fond of Emelyn. They seemed more erratic with anything involving her.

The glow of her hands faded, and she pulled her legs from my lap and, losing her touch against me, even in between the clothes and blankets, made a frown tug at my lips. She went to stand, and I pushed to my feet before she could do it alone and offered her a hand.

She took it and pulled herself up, not applying weight on her bad leg until she was balanced. She tested her weight on it a few times before she released my hand.

"I think it's better now," she said, taking a step forward and stumbling a little before she regained her footing. With every step she had a bit of a limp, but it was way better than the state she was in last night. At least she could walk. "I wonder where Ace has gone?" She questioned, glancing toward the door.

"He probably found the other Sky Elves," I said, offhandedly, but she looked at me in awe, her mouth parted and her eyes rounded in shock.

"What did you just say?" She whispered, taking a step toward me.

"The Sky Elves. He probably found them when he went out last night."

"Sky Elves? Here?" A smile slowly spread across her cheeks. "Where?" She rushed toward the door, practically galloping as she headed out of the narrow opening.

"Wait wynsoara."

"Will you stop calling me that." She tossed the words over her shoulder, trying to make haste toward the ropes that would bring her back down to the ground.

"No. You said I didn't have the right to call you Eme, so I'll call you mei wynsoara, from now on."

"At least tell me what it means before I agree to this."

"I'm sure you'll find out one day," I said, giving her a roguish grin as she faced me and rolled her eyes so far they must have touched the back of her head.

"Ugh." She groaned. "Fine, but only if you promise it doesn't mean anything disgusting or degrading." She squinted her eyes in a pointed warning.

"I promise." I took a single finger and made a criss cross impression over my heart. She flashed the faintest glimpse of a smile before she turned away and lept down, grabbing onto the rope mid-fall and climbing the rest of the way down. I watched her movements through my shadows as I Hollowed down to the ground beneath.

CHAPTER TWENTY-NINE
EMELYN

"Show off," I murmured to Crow as I finally got a good look at the bustling rebellion surrounding me. My eyes traveled over the place that was still and silent when we had arrived. Now full of people coming and going, doing their chores, pulling their weight, lines had gathered around the giant cauldron pot that was propped over the large fire pit for breakfast right in the center of everything. The sight of the pot sent a ping of pain through my chest, but I shoved it aside.

Shifter, fae, dryads, orcs, and all creatures of all shapes and sizes sauntered past. Some were even smiling and laughing. It was almost too good to be true. My green eyes went distant as I studied my surroundings, unable to comprehend having a reposeful place full of others like me that were all working together to grasp the same thing–peace.

Crowded trails lined between the enormous trees, big enough to house an entire city it seemed. I glanced back up to get a better look at the treehouse homes overhead in the light of day. All were different shapes and sizes, big and small, some were built around the gigantic trunks, there roofs looked like wooden mushroom tops. while others had their doors against the bark, being apart of the tree itself. Wooden rope bridges and planks were all mended together to create paths to get around through the winding trees blended into the brown branches and dark red leaves. The rebellion had built something beautiful.

Crows shadows caressed my shoulder, pulling my attention back to him.

"Amazing..." I whispered to myself, although I was sure he could hear me. "How long has this been building?"

"For as long as the war." He responded and suddenly everyone went still and paused what they were doing as two women walked in through the woods. The loud chatter had gone quiet. All the shuffling bodies of creatures went still. One woman had tan skin, long black hair with one side of it in a thick pretty braid close to her scalp and away from her face, and she wore full fighting leathers. The other woman wore the same leathers with dark bronzed skin. Coal lined her warm brown eyes, and small tight boxed braids draped down her front and back.

A man walked next to the woman with tight braids. He had dirty blonde hair and looked rugged with his stubbled facial hair, light skin and gray-blue eyes. There was a connection between them. You could feel it in the air as they approached. Mates.

When I was a kid, I never recognized the connection between two souls, other than my parents, but as I got older, it was easy to see the link between those who had found their mate.

Like Hink and Helena or my Ima and Pada, before they passed. The love they shared was so strong.

I rubbed at my chest from the thought and moved it to the side as the two women and the man approached Crow and I.

"As you were, and who is this?" The one with long black hair spoke with command in her voice, and judging by the way everyone mindfully returned to what they were doing before. I assumed she held authority over this place.

"Atreya, this is Emelyn," Crow continued, "Emelyn, this is Atreya, the leader of the Rebellion. And Shay and her husband, Baron, they are Atreya's right hand." He finished and Atreya cut in.

"I'm so glad you've finally found your way to us," she said, and I heard our surroundings go a little quieter. "We are glad to have you. You're welcome to stay, but everyone here has duties, even the Peacebringer. I'm sure Crow can get you acquainted, and then we can celebrate."

"Celebrate what, exactly?" I said, and she gave me a soft smile.

"You. With you finally with us, we have a chance of ending this war once and for all."

Uncertainty twisted in my gut. I'm only me, how was I supposed to help these people, this world? "I don't even know where to start with bringing peace to this world again."

"This is the start," she said matter-of-factly before she walked past Crow and me. "I'll see you at dinner." she called over her shoulder. Shay and Baron gave us a warm smile and nod as they walked past us and followed behind Atreya until they disappeared into the early morning crowd.

Crow grabbed for my hand. "Come on." He moved us along, guiding me through the busy morning. "Let's grab some breakfast. I'm sure you're hungry."

My stomach grumbled from the smell of food wafting through the large campground. The large fire pit that sat in the center of everything had a cauldron sitting over the small fire, flames licking up its sides.

A plump woman with dark brown skin stood behind it with her back to me, and then I recognized her scent as we approached.

"Helena?" I questioned.

She turned to me, revealing her large swollen belly, dark green eyes and heart-shaped ears. "Oh, hello dear!" She beamed with a smile at me. "I see you finally made it to the rebellion." She nodded to our surroundings.

"Did you know of this place the entire time?" My mouth dropped open from my surprise.

"Not the entire time, but yes, Hinky is over there helping with leathers and armor." She motioned toward where her husband was and he looked up to give us a smile and a wave.

"Why didn't you ever say anything?" My voice was quick from my rising frustration.

"We only got involved last winter, Eme—"

Hink cut her statement off by wrapping me up in his muscled embrace, giving me a bear hug before placing me back down on my feet.

"Eme! There's my girl. How have you been? Where's Ace?" he asked in his normal boisterous voice.

"I haven't seen him since last night. Crow assumed he found the Sky Elves."

He stood at my side as his shadows whisked around both of us. I looked to Hinky.

"I need answers. Why didn't either of you tell us about the Rebellion?" My eyes volleyed between them. Hink waved a hand to call someone over to keep serving breakfast. He pulled up a chair.

"Here darling, sit. You've been working hard this morning." He placed a gentle kiss atop Helena's head with a light touch on her pregnant belly before she sat down and he massaged her shoulders as he turned to us to speak. "We only got involved last winter whenever a fellow member of the rebellion came into Bells after being attacked by some Fire Fae. Turns out she was a scout looking for more recruits for Atreya. When we helped her and she saw that we had helped others, she told Atreya about us and then we started gathering recruits through Bells. We were going to tell you whenever you showed up, but then the Fire Fae came through the door and you and Ace were gone before we got the chance. I'm sorry about Willow. I had heard the news through guests at Bells. She was a lovely woman based on the stories you told us. I wished we could've got to you before the Prince did. Maybe it would have made a difference." His eyes were glassy and filled with genuine sorrow for our loss, making my heart heavy with the thought of her. Crows shadows swayed and bobbed gently around me, making a sense of calm envelope me before my mind pulled me under waves of grief.

Hink walked around the chair his wife sat in and placed a gentle hand on my shoulder before pulling me into another hug. But this one was gentle.

"Thank you." I whispered into his chest.

"I'm glad you're safe," Hink said as an Orc called out from where Hink was earlier mentioning something about his armor being too loose. Hink released me and gave me a nod of his head before he started walking away. "I'll see you later Eme, tell Ace to stop by and say hi at some point."

"Will do," I shouted back before he was gone. When I turned around, Helena was back on her feet helping a fae man that had walked over earlier serve food as a line of people waited for their bowls of thick oats. She turned to me with a large helping and a buttered sweet roll with a smile on her face before giving Crow one too and then shooing us along with the wave of her hand.

"Up there." Crow nodded up toward the trees.

"Our food will be cold by the time we–ahh" I squealed, not prepared to be encompassed by his shadows as he Hollowed us past the treetop homes. A few bedrolls and pillows were sitting up on a large wood patio above them as we watched the sunrise in the distance.

He sat and motioned for me to sit next to him as he shoveled a large spoon full of oats into his mouth. His shadows writhed happily around me, urging me to sit next to him.

"Alright, alright, geez, they're handsy today," I said as I sat down.

"I told you, they like you." He spoke with a grin before taking another large bite of oats.

"So tell me... Who are you? Or what are you? You said you'd answer all my questions in the morning. It's morning," I asked, glancing toward his figure of shadows while taking a bite of my food.

"I'm a Celestial Fae."

I searched my mind for stories from the origins of dark and light fae. But there wasn't much Willow or my mother were able to teach me about them. "So that's how you know the old fae language, from the fae of dark and light, but I thought Celestial Fae were extinct?" I asked.

My knowledge of them was little to none. My mother had taught me what she knew, which was that they were gone. Or so we thought. We only knew they could manipulate darkness and light, like Water Fae could with water, Earth Dryads with earth, Fire Fae with Fire, and Sky Elves with the wind. But I wondered what else he was capable of. I didn't know they could travel using their abilities. Hollowing was something I never knew was possible. And not to mention the way his darkness could touch my mind. What else could he do?

"We are, at least most of us. Long ago, celestial fae were slowly auctioned off to royal families, arranged in marriages to produce stronger offspring–bloodlines. Over time, people felt threatened by our lineage, our power, and hunted our kind down, killing most of us. Any who survived remained hidden."

His words struck me straight through the heart. "I'm sorry. I know what it's like to be sought after and hunted. I thought Ace and I had stayed hidden well, but the Prince of Ember has apparently been keeping tabs on our location this entire time." I took a few more bites of my food. The oats were thick, buttery, and sweet, the best thing I had eaten since leaving my village other than the one delicious meal I had on the warship. I did my best not to think about the kindness they showed me. This was the rebellion. Atreya might string me up and burn me at the stake for talking about being shown any sort of kindness from the enemy, even if I was the Peacebringer. They had built this place and survived this long without me. I'd keep it to myself.

"What makes you think that?" he asked before taking another bite.

"Before the pirates, I was captured as a prisoner on his ship. I saw his map. He had marked it with every place Ace and I had been." The thought of Kade made a shiver skate down my spine. The dread of that cell coming back to my mind, the weakness it made me feel, almost made the oats in my stomach want to come back up. Although the man had kept me locked away, he had saved me from Aedion and his friends, bathed me, and gave me my clothes back cleaned. I assumed it was because he wanted to be sure he could present me to his father like some prized trophy, but he let me escape.

"Atamai kanina," Crow whispered the unknown words to me.

I cocked a brow. "Enough with the old language," I said.

He gave me a wry smile. "You don't have to worry about the Prince." He tucked a strand of loose silver behind my ear and I leaned into his touch, the warmth of his palm against my cheek sent flutters through my gut. He gave me a reassuring grin before I turned out of his reach.

"I wish that were true, but I'm sure Ember is hunting for me now more than they were before, especially now that they know the truth of who the peacebringer really is. They know exactly who to look for now."

Crow gripped my chin and made my eyes meet his smokey irises.

"I'll kill anyone who tries to take you, wynsoara."

"But he's the prince of Ember you can't–" He cut me off.

"Anyone, Emelyn. Even princes will meet their end by my hand when it comes to you."

I didn't know what to say, but his words tugged on the deepest parts of my heart, drawing me closer to him. Our warm breath mingled in the small space between our lips.

I was supposed to be mad at him. I should've been mad, but every part of me wanted to be near him. I craved his closeness. The calm of his shadows surrounded me. It was as if they craved me too as they swayed and caressed my arms and the small of my back gently, almost like they were urging me forward to close the space between us. No matter how hard I wanted to be angry, how could I be when he saved Ace and I all those years ago? Regardless of him being there with Ember or not. He had saved us. And I was grateful.

I felt the feather light brush of his breath against my lips before he pulled back and released my chin as he cleared his throat and stood holding out his hand.

"Come on, I want to show you something."

"Now?" I glanced out into the distance where the sun had barely started peeking over the horizon.

"It's worth it, I promise." He spoke up again, and I sat down my now empty bowl of oats and took his hand as he helped me to my feet. I stumbled a little, my leg still ached. I was sure it would be completely healed by tomorrow. Crow took notice and wrapped an arm around my waist before hooking his other arm under my legs, hauling me up into his arms.

"I can walk Crow. Put me down." I squirmed, but he gripped me harder against him.

"I'll let you walk on your own when you're healed. Until then, get comfortable."

I rolled my eyes, but I sunk into the warmth of his embrace before I wrapped my arms around his neck as he leaned over and fell off the edge of the wooden patio that we had been sitting on. I had to hold back the scream that wanted to work its way up my throat before the quiet of his shadows surrounded us and we were within the darkness of his Hollow.

A moment passed, and my stomach settled from the free fall. The bend of Crow's legs jolted me slightly as he landed on the ground. I heard the crunch of his boots against the forest floor from the frozen early morning dew. The snow was gone now.

Light came through his shadows until they receded away from me and revealed the view completely. I was met with the white fog in the distance. The early morning light made it look iridescent, with different shades of oranges and pinks. This part of the forest was flooded before you met the white wall of the Swamps of Illusion. The water was mossy and littered with water lilies and lily pads floating along its smooth surface. Their pink and white blooms were beautiful.

Frogs croaked, and birdsong flowed through the trees. I turned around to face Crow, but he wasn't there. A wisp of one of his long tendrils of shade caressed my jawline to make me look in the direction he had gone. He stood further down, closer to the water, where the ground mixed between mush and water. He peered up at me and motioned for me to come down to him. The moment I went to take a step, I was within his darkness. And when it released me, I was standing directly in front of him. He had Hollowed me effortlessly. He really didn't want me walking on my bad leg.

My breath hitched in my lungs from the sudden move from one spot to another, making my chest brush against him. Our faces were mere inches from each other.

He didn't move. His tendrils of shadows swayed around us until he broke the eye contact and looked down at the small wooden boat that floated lazily on top of the murky water. He gripped my hand and helped me step into the boat. He released me once I was sitting comfortably.

The boat rocked a little as he got in and began paddling further out into the water. I couldn't stop my eyes from roaming over his muscled arms and shoulders with each roll of the paddles. Lily pads and flowers slowly shifted out of our way as Crow moved the boat further. The wooden paddles clinked together when he stopped and set them down against the bench seats in the small space. The sound pulled me out of my trance of admiring his physique.

"It's peaceful out here. You'd never think chaos lies just beyond the fog." I said, not meeting his gaze.

"Is that what you really want to talk about?" His question insinuated a deeper conversation, and I knew what he wanted to talk about. Or more so, what I wanted to ask. I didn't understand why he saved me–us, all those years ago. Out of everyone on the battlefield what made him come to our aid?

"Why?" I asked, keeping my voice steady.

"Why what?" he questioned, but I believed he already knew what I was asking.

"Why did you save me? Ember paid you to kill." I looked him over, and for the first time, I leaned away from him slightly.

"Are you afraid of me?" he asked with a somber expression on his face.

"No... Should I be?"

His silhouette darkened as his figure dissipated into his shadows before suddenly reappearing directly in front of me, as close as he was on the shoreline moments ago.

"Yes, but for reasons you don't understand..." His eyes trailed over my face before meeting mine again. His smokey irises drew me in further, as if a single glance from him could tug on my soul.

His hot breath brushed against my jawline. My line of sight went to his lips and lingered there a moment too long before I glanced back up at him. His shadows were writhing with a need to touch me, but they didn't, only coming within a hair of my skin before moving away again. They flared and slipped from his body in long, erratic tendrils, something I had noticed happens when his emotions stirred.

I wasn't afraid.

I closed the space between us. His lips were soft and gentle until he slowly deepened our kiss. I opened my mouth for him and he purred in response. Cupping my face with his rough hands, he pulled me into his embrace. I ran my hand along his jawline, then along the back of his neck, and up through his soft hair. A part of me wondered what color his hair and eyes would be if he weren't a Celestial Fae of shadows. The other part of me reveled in them and took comfort in their darkness—took comfort in him.

They drew me to him and the longer we kissed, it was as if the walls in my mind were crumbling and something as light as a feather brushed against my consciousness. It was his shadows. I pulled back from the sensation and from Crow, and he kept his eyes closed as his forehead rested against mine, as if he was replaying the moment in his mind again. He pulled back to look at me as he tenderly brushed his thumb over my bottom lip.

"Did I do something wrong?" His voice was graveled.

"No..." My brow pinched while my eyes trailed over his features and his shadows pooled within the small boat and fanned out around both of us. A few of the small tendrils experimented with the straps on my leathers. I ran my fingers through them, letting the tendrils of shade wrap and dance around and through my fingers, causing a smile to tug on the corners of my lips. "It's just... you touch the deepest parts of me with these."

A low chuckle escaped him. The sound was as soothing as when his lips were on mine. And I wanted them to be again.

He leaned back, resting his back on the boat as he looked me over with curious eyes. "We should get back," he said as he grabbed for the paddles.

"Allow me," I said with a wave of my hand. A current of water drifted us back to the shoreline.

He shook his head with a smile. "You couldn't have done that on the way out here?" He questioned.

I grinned and nibbled my bottom lip. "I enjoyed the view," I said, giving his body a look over.

The look in his eyes pinned me where I stood as his shadows flared, letting me know my words had got to him.

"Hmmm," he purred as he sat up in the boat in front of me, his face so close to mine. "You're going to be the death of me wynsoara." He tucked a loose strand of my hair away from my face again as his shadows surrounded us and then we were in the dark.

CHAPTER THIRTY
ACE

When I woke, Maeves petite figure was sprawled over me. I rubbed the sleep from my eyes and looked down at her sleeping peacefully on my chest and almost held my breath because I didn't want to disturb her.

She stirred awake a moment later and looked up at me with her warm brown eyes in the early morning light. A small smile dimpled her cheeks as she stretched and it made her thigh press over my very hard cock as it had always woken up with me in the mornings.

Shit.

She met my eyes again with a mischievous grin and an arch of her brow. After last night, I wasn't sure how she was going to feel about me once she woke up this morning.

"Did you mean what you said last night?" She signed with hooded eyes before she trailed a single finger down my chest and midsection.

"I said a lot of things last night. You will need to be more specific." I signed, and she stopped moving her finger.

"That I could have you with a sober mind?" She repeated my statement from last night and I held her gaze.

"Are you sure that's what you want?" I asked, and that wicked finger began trailing below my trousers where my pants had already pitched a tent, making my arousal very obvious. She brushed her fingers over my cock and it twitched in response. Wanting more than a light touch.

Maeve smiled and leaned in for a kiss. Her tongue found mine quickly as her kisses became more eager. Her hand wrapped around my cock and pumped.

I growled and turned over on top of her, pinning her to the bed, never breaking our passionate kisses. I slipped my hand into her pants and hesitated when her breath hitched. I pulled back to search her eyes for permission and she leaned forward, nipping at my lip.

Don't stop, she mouthed the words, and I dipped two fingers into her wet center and she groaned from my touch. It only made my cock throb for her. I massaged her sensitive bulb of nerves and listened to the sounds of her pleasure as I worked her closer to the edge. She nipped at my lip again as she squeezed and pumped me harder, making a growl crawl up my throat. Her chest was rapid as her breath quickened.

I undid my trousers. Getting to my feet, I shucked them off as she took off her own clothes, letting them pile in a heap on the floor and laying naked for me on the bed. I crawled over top of her, resting between her thighs, nudging my cock at her entrance.

She ran her hands down my back as she leaned up to kiss me again–this time it was slower, more gentle than before as she tangled her limbs around me.

I wanted to ravage her body, give her everything I could give, but I could tell that wasn't what she wanted right now. She was petite, soft, and tender against my powerful frame.

I thrusted my hips forward, sheathing myself inside her and she whimpered as she rolled her hips with mine.

We moved together until we were both panting and slicked with sweat. Her moans and breathing grew more erratic and wild, her walls clamped down around me as she went over the edge of her release. I thrusted one last time, hard, slow and deep as I growled out mine along with hers.

I wasn't sure what time it was or how long we had been asleep, or if she had even fallen back asleep after our slow-burning coitus earlier. When I woke, she was sitting on the edge of the bed. Her body lurched as she released the contents of her stomach into a large flower pot I assumed she had grabbed from outside.

I leaped to my feet, my pants loose and undone, draped around my waist from lazily throwing them back on earlier.

I moved to her side of the bed, sitting beside her, and held back her long blonde hair as she puked in the makeshift hangover bucket. I stroked circles along her back until she was done throwing up and heaving.

A few moments passed before she lifted her head with a pinched brow. She was paler than normal.

"I ruined that, didn't I?" she questioned with a sad look on her face as she rubbed at her head and I grinned at her.

"At least you didn't puke on me again, so no, I'd say you did better." I joked, and she groaned.

"I'm sorry. I hope you'll give me another chance. I had way too much to drink last night." She signed.

"Maeve, you did nothing wrong, nothing to apologize for." I stood and buttoned my pants and grabbed for my shirt, maneuvering my wings to slip through their designated holes as I pulled it down over my abdomen. No need to put on my leathers.

"What are you doing?" she asked as I pulled on my boots.

"I'm going to take care of you. I'll get you some breakfast and some water. It might help with the hangover." I finished lacing my boots, and I glanced over my shoulder at her as I walked toward the door. She gave me a weak smile.

"Thank you." She signed, and I returned the smile.

"Nothing to thank me for either." I winked, and she laid back down. "I'll be back soon." I signed before I walked out the door.

I outstretched my wings in the rays of the morning's sun for the first time in a century. The emotion of it weighed heavy on my chest for a moment before I stepped off the wooden ledge and let my wings glide me to the ground beneath.

My knees bent, absorbing the impact of my light landing as I made it to the center of everything. There were no lines at the large cauldron that sat in the center of camp for the food that they served, which let me know it was later in the morning.

I walked over to where two women were preparing the next meal. They were both fae. The one that had shoulder-length blonde hair and light blue eyes ignited her hand in flames as she lit the fire under the cauldron. It didn't surprise me that Fire Fae were a part of the rebellion. Plenty of people left their homelands when the emperor took the throne from his father all those years ago. He craved power, and he'd do whatever it took to get it. Anyone who didn't agree with his ways left or was too poor to leave Ember.

The other fae woman had light brown hair and brown eyes. She looked up at me as she bended water into the cauldron before she started chopping onions and potatoes that were scattered on the table in front of them.

"Lunch isn't for another hour." She said as the blonde wrapped her arms around her waist and kissed on her neck while she continued cutting the vegetables. I was sure everyone in this camp could smell their arousal for each other, I had to keep myself in check from how strong their need was.

They were like feral cats. Very happy feral cats.

"Do you understand sign?" I asked, but a woman came up from the side and answered for them since the two women were so lost in eachother I wasn't even sure they were paying attention to me anymore.

"Yes, most of us do." She said out loud as she hauled more bags of potatoes onto their table. "Don't mind them. They're newly mated and extremely obnoxious for each other right now. I'm sure it'll pass in the next few weeks." She finally looked up at me with her gold-flecked eyes and a smile that made me freeze where I stood.

It was her.

The woman I ran into at Bells.

The illusion of the woman that haunted me in the swamps.

My cock twitched from the memory and I had to take a steadying breath from the scent of arousal on the wind. On top of this goddess of a woman standing in front of me, smiling at me, waiting for me to respond.

Shit.

"Ace! I see you've met Luana." Hink stepped in and saved my ass from my stunned silence as he almost took me down with his heavy hand on my back.

What the hell was he doing here? Now I just had more questions than answers.

"Actually, we hadn't got to that part yet, Hink." She said before turning back to me. "Hi, I'm Luana. I believe we ran into each other at Bells not too long ago."

"I remember." I signed, and she gave me a small smile, "how do you both know each other? And Hink how are you here?" I signed and Luana continued.

"I'm a scout for the rebellion. Last winter, some Fire Fae soldiers attacked me in Esora while I was looking for new recruits." her statement made my blood boil, but I didn't interrupt. "Helena and Hink found me and tended to me. I saw how they took care of people while I stayed under their care and sought after them later on and they accepted the invitation." She said before Hinky chimed in.

"Helena and I were going to talk to you and Emelyn about it when we saw you two at Bells, but then the soldiers arrived and we didn't get the chance."

"I understand." I signed, glancing back over to the food table where the two women from before were no longer there.

"They probably ran off to get more privacy. Damn matting bond. That's the third time this week." Luana huffed her frustrations.

Hink chuckled under his breath, "ah, it's alright Lu, I'm sure it'll pass soon. I'll grab Dublin and Rory, they're hard working boys, I'm sure they can finish up the preparations for lunch and dinner."

"Thanks Hink," Luana replied before turning to me. "Was there anything I could help you with?" She asked and reminded me why I had come down here to begin with–Maeve.

"Could you point me toward some food and water? Maeve had a little too much to drink last night." Talking about Maeve to Luana made guilt twist my insides. I didn't do anything wrong, but it felt wrong.

"Here," she walked around the other side of the large well used table and grabbed a small basket of rolls that had been sitting on the ground behind it, along with a skin of water. "This was left over from breakfast. It should help." she handed them to me and my knuckles grazed her hand in the exchange, making her eyes meet mine. I stumbled over my signs.

"Thank you." I said with a head nod after we stared at each other for a moment too long. Something tugged at my gut, but I pulled back, ignoring what every instinct in me wanted me to do—to stay.

I turned myself away and out stretched my wings, being sure I flexed every muscle in my back before I took off and went back into the mass of tree homes without looking back.

When I made it back to Maeves home, she was lightly snoring, sound asleep, sprawled out on the bed. It made my lips curve into a smile. I set the basket of bread and the skin of water next to the bed. I brushed the hair away from her face and grabbed the large fur blanket that had fallen on the floor and laid it on top of her. The days were already getting warmer as winter would soon turn into spring, but the air still had a chill to it.

As I went back out the door, I made sure to not disturb her rest. I knew Maeve would wake up to some food and water, now I needed to check in with Emelyn. I hadn't seen her since last night.

I weaved through the trees, staying out of the open sky as I glided along the wind, glancing between the patrons below all going about their business until I saw Emelyn's silver locks of hair and Crow's shadows whipping freely around either side of them.

His palm rested on the small of her back as they walked through the crowd. Emelyn still had a slight limp to her walk, but I was sure she would be completely healed by tomorrow morning if she had another session with herself. I wondered how much badgering she had to do to get her boy to let her walk.

I landed softly in front of them gathering my wings behind me again and Eme gave me a bright smile as she leaped at me for a hug. I couldn't tell if it was from seeing me without the cloak or if someone had already told her about the Sky Elves, or both.

"Did you find them? The Sky-Elves?" She blurted the question into my neck, answering my question as she squeezed me. When she pulled away, I answered.

"Yes." I couldn't help the smile that stretched across my features. For so long, I had believed I was the last, that my people had been wiped from existence. The loneliness had been a constant companion, a storm cloud that followed me everywhere. I had Emelyn, I knew she would always be there. But knowing there were others still like me, changed everything. The discovery that my race still existed was like finding a missing piece of myself, a piece I had thought was lost forever.

"I'm so happy for you Ace." She signed and pulled me into another hug. Something was different about her and Crow, as if something had shifted between them.

It wasn't bad, but I couldn't detect what it was. But as long as Eme was safe and happy, that was all that mattered to me.

The ambience of the rebellion went quiet. I pulled away from Emelyn I glanced back at a woman dressed in fighting leathers with two other people at her side. Emelyn caught me up as they walked in our direction.

"That's the leader of the rebellion and her right hand." Eme signed before they approached us. Her steps were firm and lethal as she moved closer to us. I could tell this woman was well rehearsed with a weapon from how she presented herself alone. I felt bad for anyone who ever was on the opposite end of her blade.

"Ace, lovely to finally meet you, I'm Atreya, the leader of the rebellion and this is Shay and Baron, my seconds. We're glad to see more of your kind have found a place of refuge here." Her voice was smooth and kind, but her exterior was rugged and strong. Her dark hair braided on either side of her head away from her face while the top half was pulled back revealing her slightly pointed fae ears.

"Thank you for your generosity, but I have some questions," I glanced over at Emelyn. "I'm sure we both do."

"I'll answer any questions you have tomorrow night, when we celebrate. That is, if you still have any questions by then. Shay will tell you everything you need to know."

"What are we celebrating?" I chimed in and Atreya gave me a smile.

"Emelyn." She turned away and bellowed out her voice. "Tomorrow, we will feast. The Peacebringer has returned!" There was a beat of silence after her statement and then the roar of cheers. "Spread the news to our fellow men." Atreya finished and turned toward us again and I could see Emelyn's confliction on her face but I also knew that we hadn't been able to safely rest or find a place where we didn't have to hide who either of us were. The rebellion had food to fill our bellies, clean water to drink, and people who seemed to care about our well-being.

I had never been one to trust easily. I had always been the one who kept my guard up, even more so than Eme. But ever since Crow brought us here, they have welcomed us with open arms. Emelyn looked at me and I gave her a reassuring smile with a nod of my head before she smiled back.

"I can't wait." She spoke to Atreya before Atreya turned to Crow.

"We have business to tend to." She turned toward Emelyn and me again, "but anything you want to see, Shay can show you around while answering any questions you have." She motioned toward the darker woman with tight braids next to her, who I assumed was Shay, and she gave us a warm smile. "Come Crow." Atreya spoke directly to him and he gave Emelyn a kiss on the forehead.

"I'll be back." He said before walking next to Atreya. Both of them disappeared into his shadows, with Baron at their side.

"You and Crow, huh?" I signed to Emelyn, and she rolled her eyes at me, making a grin tug on my lips.

"So what do you two want to know?" Shay asked out loud and signed at the same time.

Emelyn changed the subject. "what exactly happens tomorrow at this celebration?"

"Well, there will be food and dancing, and a few other party games. The Sky Elves will probably want to night race," her eyes moved to Ace, "I'm excited to see how you do against Emeris." Shay smiled at me.

"What's a night race?" I asked.

"Occasionally, the Sky Elves will have a few friendly races at nightfall, since you're less likely to be seen in the dark. We don't do it often because it's a risk to the rebellions location but since the Peacebringer has returned, I'm sure Atreya will allow the races tonight."

"Who's Emeris?" I asked, and Shay smiled again.

"You'll have to wait and see." She winked at me before she lead us through the busy crowd, but continued to answer our questions.

"How has the rebellion remained hidden all these years?" Emelyn asked.

"I don't think we've remained hidden. Ember knows about us. Staying one step ahead is what we do. We move our camps regularly and do our best to stay on schedule. We have small pockets of people throughout all the continents of Osparia to help us keep track of where Fire Fae soldiers may make camps. We have scouts, and we have a handful of people who infiltrate Ember to gather intel, like Crow for example. Atreya sends him because of his shadows, it makes it easy for him to get in and out without being seen."

"What about food and supplies?" Emelyn asked, and Shay continued.

"We've made deals with the Capital City, and other small villages and sailors in the trading markets, like Iron Isle and Lintawa Bay. We keep our shipments disguised with Embers emblem flag. We should receive a shipment tomorrow *hopefully*." The last of her statement didn't sound sure, she sounded concerned.

"Do you fear it won't come?" I asked.

"We've been having trouble with our shipments lately, you'll learn more about it tomorrow, I'm sure Atreya will be taking you both to Westwell Harbor when we pick up the shipment tomorrow morning, before the celebration. She'll want you there to see how we run things."

"Do you and Atreya bend?" I asked, my curiosity getting the best of me.

"No, but I assure you, we don't need to." Her tone was even. And I believed her. To have survived this long without bending, I was sure they were both masters with any weapon.

"How did you end up in the Rebellion?" Emelyn asked, and Shay paused a moment.

"I promised myself that I would be there for the end of this war, so here I am."

"Where were you from?" I asked, and she looked over at me with glossy eyes, as if she hadn't talked about herself to someone in a very long time.

"The Espien Islands, before Ember took them over and renamed them the Islands Of Ash."

"I had heard about Ember coming for the Islands after they took Heavensreach." I signed and she nodded to me.

"I'm sorry for your loss," she said as she turned to me. "I know we all have lost a great deal from this war, but almost losing your entire race is something I could never understand. But you are not alone, and I'm glad you are here now. Both of you." she nodded to Emelyn as she ended her statement, placing a firm hand on both of our shoulders before turning away again. "Come on, we have a lot to see and discuss about how we do things around here."

She led the way as she showed us the ropes of our new home and what they would expect of us. Most of which were things we were already used to doing from growing up with Willow.

Everyone had their own chores or tasks throughout the day, while others took the night shift to keep watch around the perimeter of base camp. Twice a month there was a shipment at the docks of Westwell, and tomorrow we would accompany them on the quick journey there.

But my gut was telling me it would not go as smoothly as Shay had described.

286

CHAPTER THIRTY-ONE

ACE

Shay stopped at the training grounds, a vast expanse of hardened earth bordered by tall, ancient trees that rustled softly in the breeze. The air was filled with the scent of freshly turned soil and the subtle hint of oak from the surrounding forest. Training dummies stood at strategic intervals, scarred from countless battles, while weapons of all kinds were neatly arranged on racks along one side of the field.

As she touched base with some of her fellow men, their voices filled the air—laughter, banter, and the occasional shout as they sparred or practiced their drills. The sound of steel meeting steel echoed in the distance, punctuated by the occasional cheer or groan of effort.

Water blasted me in the face, and I scowled at Eme. The unexpected splash was a shock to my system, but the coolness was refreshing against my heated skin.

"Come on, that was a cheap shot," I signed, wiping water from my eyes as I got into a fighting stance. The ground beneath my feet was firm, providing a stable base as I squared off against Eme. We both kept our palms open, fingers poised for action, eyes locked in a silent challenge.

She moved. With a swift motion, Eme lunged forward, her movements fluid and controlled. She had been too eager to retaliate.

Tsk, should've been more patient, Em.

In one swift motion, I leaped into the air and twisted my body to avoid her attack before blasting her with my own. She barely lost her footing, but it was enough for me to get her down with another gust of wind. Instead of falling to her back like I thought she would, she did a back handspring landing on her feet with two large tendrils of water that looked as sharp as blades jutting from her back. They towered over her shoulders ready to move when she wielded them too.

I gave her a cocky smile before I lunged for her again, slashing sharp winds toward her, but then something shifted. My wind shifted. She was able to get her water tendrils through at fae speeds, wrapping them around my neck before I had the chance to block it. If I would've been the enemy, I would be laying decapitated on the ground at her feet.

She arched a brow with a shit-eating grin on her face and I looked at her with shock on mine as her water fell away. Leaving us both dry as the evening sun casted us in its golden light.

"You redirected my wind." I signed, still in disbelief.

Emelyn laughed at me before she responded, "well, did I do it right? I've practiced moving my feather a few times and my axe once in the woods, but that was my first time trying to move your wind."

I strode over to her and wrapped her in a tight hug before I pulled away. "That was the coolest shit you've ever done." My face lit up like a boy on a holiday. Seeing Emelyn bend the wind made my chest fill with pride, even more so knowing she had been practicing without me knowing about it. It was just one more way I felt closer to her than I already was. I didn't think that was possible. "Our fathers would be so proud." The words mixed the pride in my chest with sorrow, but I meant them. They would want us to remember the good.

Emelyn looked at me with a sad smile. She tried to hide her sorrow, but I could see it behind her eyes, in the way her smile didn't quite reach them. I knew she didn't like when I brought up our past, but she needed that reminder since having this weight placed on her shoulders. Her hand lingered on her neck where her moonstone used to be before it fell away to her side. That necklace meant the world to her, and if our circumstances had been different, I would have gone back to get it. She pulled me in for one more hug, trying to hide the tears that I knew were threatening to spill, when a voice I recognized made my body tense.

"Are you both alright?" Luana asked, as if she had appeared from thin air, I hadn't heard her approach. Eme tugged out of my embrace.

"Yeah, we were just finishing up." She said.

I chimed in, "come on, that was only one round."

"I'm sure," Emelyn glanced over to Luana, "I'm sorry. What was your name?" She asked.

"Luana," she gave her a curt nod, and Eme placed a gentle hand on her shoulder.

"I'm sure Luana, would love to take my place for the next round." Emelyn said Luana's name with a little sass to her tone, giving me a knowing grin before she sauntered away and I hung my head, trying to hide the blush creeping up my neck.

"She seems nice," Luana signed, getting into a good stance.

"Oh, yeah, she's just a peach." I signed, wagging my head as I watched Emelyn walk off toward the hot springs Shay had showed us before we came here.

I gathered myself, getting into position. If I was being honest, I hadn't had very many encounters with Earth Dryads over the years. Maybe a handful, when I was a little younger and let my frustrations get the best of me instead of walking away from a needless fight.

I kept my palms open; she was close enough that I could get a few jabs in from where I stood. But I didn't want to hit her. I wanted to toy with her with my wind. Show her what I could do.

"I won't be easy on you." I said smugly.

"I wouldn't dream of it." She quipped, and I paused for only a moment before I lunged for her. This woman didn't move–didn't even flinch. With the smallest motion of her body weight, the whole ground shifted out from under my feet and made my back slam into the ground.

The wind knocked out of me. Traitor, I cursed internally at the air I should have been in control of.

I desperately tried to suck it back in. The loud, wheezing gasps only made the burn in my lungs worse. If I wasn't blushed before, I was red now as my cheeks heated with embarrassment and the lack of air in my lungs.

So much for trying to show off for a pretty woman, Ace.

Luana giggled to herself over the absurd noises I was making in a desperate attempt to get the air back to my lungs. She kneeled down next to me. "What was that you said about taking it easy on me?" She signed as she arched a brow with the same smugness I carried before we started.

"Oh, you're mine." I signed, quickly recovering, leaping after her. I tackled her to the ground, and she squealed at my speed. She brought a dagger made of earth to my neck. She had formed it from soil, making a jagged blade of stone, and I did the same with the air, shooting winds from my fist. Both of us held elemental blades to each other's throats.

Every heaving breath made our chests touch.

Heat stirred in my gut as I thought of this woman in a deliciously dark way, being underneath me...

No Ace.

"Nice recovery," she said breathlessly, tossing her blade back to the earth, and it crumbled back into soil.

"You too." I signed, letting the wind slip out of my fist, the blade returning to the wind.

We shared eye contact a moment too long before I scrambled to my feet to help her up and cleared my throat. She stood but my hand lingered in hers and she didn't pull away. The tension was thick between us. If I stayed here a moment longer admiring this woman my lips were going to be on hers. What the fuck was wrong with me. Why did I want her so badly, and shit, Maeve. I shut down my thoughts and the moment.

"I'll see you around," I signed before abruptly turning away, walking in the same direction Eme had, not glancing back over my shoulder.

'I'll see you around,' what the fuck was that Ace?

I scrubbed a hand down my face as I thought about her, and every moment her body touched mine, the whole walk to the spring.

CHAPTER THIRTY-TWO
CROW

The drip of the man's blood made a tapping sound against the soil. I could tell Atreya had tried everything to get him to talk since I brought him yesterday. He bled from a recent wound on his head and was covered in bruises from his face down to his legs. I was certain he had broken bones.

She left him in iron chains, wearing nothing but his undergarments. She had even gone as far as pulling off his individual nails on his hands and feet. They had already begun healing and growing back.

"Has he said anything?" I asked.

Atreya came to me from the outskirts of the room. "No, which is why I brought you here. I wanted you to use your shadows."

"What is it you want to know?" I asked.

"Why was their camp so close to ours? What does Ember know and what does he know of our shipments, if anything?"

My shadows writhed and darkened the already dark room.

"I'm not scared of the dark, you stupid woman." The man spat out blood and snickered as he looked up at us with his swollen face. My shadows whipped around him and he started trembling as he watched with his blackened eyes.

"No, I'm sure you're not, but you will be terrified of what lurks within my darkness." I said. Atreya stepped back as my shadows took over the space surrounding us. The captive soldier screamed out a wailing cry. My shadows crept into the recesses of his mind, tugging on every painful memory while warping his greatest nightmares against him. Pain and terror consumed him. Tremors overtook his limbs as he tried to fight against the fear until he finally lost his resistance.

"Stop, I'll tell you all I know!" He yelled and my shadows paused and loomed quietly around us as Atreya stepped back up to us again and waited for his response. The man took a few steadying breaths before he continued, "What's coming is more terrifying than anything in your shadows," he taunted, letting out a low maniacal chuckle, he peered up at me with soulless eyes, and I realized it didn't matter what I put him through he wouldn't give us all the answers.

"What's more terrifying than that?" Atreya asked curiously.

"Valla." He said and Atreya and I gave each other a knowing look. "She's coming." He sounded wicked.

The Princess of Ember and a commander of their armies. She held no regard for anyone but herself. If she was scheming behind the scenes, we needed a plan.

"There's no escaping her, and now that you've taken me, you think I'm going to be welcomed back into the army with open arms?" He scoffed, "kill me, take me out of my misery, because if you don't, I don't know if I'll have the strength to do it to myself."

"Then why not tell us what we want to know? If you know, you're going to meet your end."

"I'd rather be killed as a captive than a snitch. And whatever you do to me is nothing compared to what she would do."

"I wouldn't be so sure." My shadows ensnared him in their darkness again. He screamed until his voice was hoarse and all that came out was a squeak on every loud, ragged exhale of breath. The smell of piss wafted around the room as his body shuddered in fear. Until it stopped and he died from the distress of my terror. I watched his chest rise and fall for the last time. "Hm, that's a shame I couldn't get anything more out of him. I'm sorry, Atreya."

"You did your best. I haven't seen you kill a man with fear in a long time."

"I wanted him to know that Valla isn't the only thing that's terrifying." I said, my anger simmered under my skin at how close Valla had come to our camp without me noticing.

Atreya grabbed a dirtied rag and cleaned off some of her weapons in the dark room. "You need to go back to Ember. We need to figure out what's happening. It seems Valla is doing whatever she wants, per usual, and you're the only one who can get in and figure out what's going on."

"But–"

"No buts Crow. There's more at stake than just Emelyn. I have spent my life building this rebellion in hope to one day regain peace for all of Osparia. If you ever want a life, a peaceful life without having to constantly look over your shoulder, we have to win this war once and for all."

"I know... we need to prepare to move the base camp. Ember is getting too close."

"I'll prepare. We won't leave today, but soon." Atreya said, and I nodded at her before I stormed away with my shadows writhing. "And Crow," she called, and I paused, "be ready for the trip to Westwell tomorrow morning."

I nodded and left the room where the remnants of the dead mans fear still lingered, making my shadows thick, whipping happily.

Baron was perched outside the door, he had taken watch when we arrived. I barley acknowledged him as I stormed by. My anger rose as my thoughts swirled. Ember being so close to camp and to Emelyn made me sick. The uncertainty of not knowing what Valla was up to only made it worse. Even though I needed to move soon to figure out what was going on, at least I had bought myself a little time.

I didn't have much, but I knew who I wanted to spend it with.

CHAPTER THIRTY-THREE
EMELYN

The loud knock on the door broke my solitude as I dried my hair before I wrapped my damp towel around my body. Shay had showed us the training grounds and the springs where we could bathe before she left us. Ace and I wasted no time on getting a bath in after the last few days we had. Of course, he showed up after he spared with Luana. I could tell from the moment her voice met his ears, he felt a certain way toward her.

"Come in," I called.

The door swung open with a gentle creak, revealing Crow, his silhouette framed by the dim light behind him. He looked to be carved out of the night itself, his presence both intimidating and alluring. I stood there, my breath catching at the sight of him. His eyes traveled over me, lingering just long enough to send a shiver down my spine. As they did, the shadows that clung to him like faithful companions stilled, as if holding their breath, before erupting into a frenzied dance around his body. My heart matched their wild rhythm, pounding erratically within the confines of my chest.

There was an intensity in his gaze that rooted me to the spot, a silent force that drew him forward. Each step he took was measured, deliberate, as though he struggled against invisible chains to approach me. The air between us crackled with unspoken desire, thickening with each moment that passed.

"May I?" His voice was a deep whisper, barely audible over the beating of my heart.

I found myself nodding, words failing me. His hand reached out, the shadows stretching forward from his fingertips, eager to bridge the gap between us. His touch was electric, sending sparks of anticipation through my veins.

"Is this alright?" Crow's voice was laced with need, yet tempered with an unexpected gentleness. His shadows seemed to pulse with the same question, awaiting my answer.

"Yes," I managed to whisper back, granting him the permission he sought.

Crow closed the distance between us. His lips met mine with a tenderness that belied the hunger I saw burning in his eyes. The kiss began as a soft exploration, a gentle assertion of his presence that promised more. But as our connection deepened, so did the fervor of his kiss. It grew more insistent, more demanding, echoing the chaos of his shadows that now swirled around us in a storm of darkness.

His mouth moved against mine with a growing urgency, the initial restraint giving way to a raw passion that bordered on possession. The shadows mirrored his intensity, their once gentle caress turning into a bold claim as they enveloped us.

In that moment, the world outside of Crow's kiss ceased to exist. There was only the fierce press of his lips, the taste of him that eclipsed all other sensations, the heat of his body melding with mine, and the dark embrace of his shadows that threatened to consume us whole.

The kiss detonated through me, obliterating all thought. Crow pressed me back against the wall with a force that was commanding yet careful, as if he were both claiming and cherishing. His hands explored with bold strokes, while his shade skimmed over me with an intimacy that left me yearning for more.

"Cro–" My attempt to speak was swallowed by the depth of his kisses. He devoured me with an intensity that felt like it could break the world apart, but in that moment, there was no world—there was only Crow.

The growl that vibrated from his chest was primal, resonant, sending a blaze through my veins that pooled into an ache of longing in my core.

"Wynsoara," he gasped against my lips, his voice gravelly with need and now tinged with a desperate plea. "Tell me to stop, or I'm going to take you where you stand."

Panting, the heat from our breath mingled in the space between us. I met Crow's dark gaze and saw the silent question flickering there. With deliberate slowness, I lifted a single eyebrow, daring him without words. My fingers brushed against the soft fabric of my towel, and with a flick of my wrist, it cascaded to the ground—a wordless consent that hung heavy in the air.

His eyes, those deep pools of night and starlight, flared with an insatiable hunger as they devoured the sight before him. The intensity in his stare was nearly tangible, a force that seared its way through my skin, igniting every nerve ending with anticipation. My fucking soul was on fire.

Without warning, he closed the distance, and his lips crashed into mine with a ferocity that left no room for doubt. Our tongues danced with a desperate urgency, teeth grazing.

As the shadows around Crow thickened, the room darkened, enveloping us in a world of our own making. One shadow, darker than the rest, reached out like a lover's caress, trailing up my inner thigh. Its touch was both a promise and a provocation, sending a shiver through me that forced a gasp to escape between our fervent kisses.

His shadows were everywhere, making gooseflesh pebble across my skin. Two tendrils pinned my wrists against the wall above my head while the one between my legs slithered over my center, making my legs tremble and spread wider to give it better access to me as I let out a moan. Crow trailed kisses down my neck. Before he rested his forehead against my chest, he breathed out the name he had given me. *Mei wynsoara.* As if he was begging.

Before he lifted his head, his lips finding mine again, his tendrils of shade shivered against my clit, coaxing and teasing me. I had never felt something so good. The vibrations made me desperate. My core pooled with the need for more. I ground against his shadows and moaned as I bit down on his bottom lip. Begging for more from him. He purred from my need but paused his movement and his tendrils released my wrists. I thought he was going to stop.

His brow furrowed with something akin to pain—or was it shame—regret maybe? I couldn't be sure.

I lunged for him, pulling him closer to me as I buckled down against his shadows again.

"Don't stop." I breathed. I wanted him. I wanted to let my walls fall away and let him have all of me.

"Don't move." He commanded as he pushed against me, wedging me between him and the wall again. I stayed still as every part of me buzzed with anticipation. His tendrils wrapped around my wrists and gently pinned them above my head again. "Good girl," he whispered in my ear before he ran his nose down my collar bone, breathing me in.

His shadows took over, relentlessly touching every part of me as one gently massaged my tight bundle of nerves while another sheathed itself inside me, pumping into me. I groaned out my ecstasy as I climbed closer and closer to the edge. Crow sucked and nipped at my peaked breasts as his shadows touched, vibrated, and fucked me against the wall. Finally his shadows released my wrists and I wrapped my hands in his hair, holding him there, my nails digging into his scalp. I grounded against him as I cried out through my orgasm, and he growled at the sound of it. My thighs were slick from my release.

"Look at you, dripping for me," His voice was almost inhuman, as if he had lost control of either himself or his shadows, "and I haven't even touched you yet."

My arms fell to my sides heavily with exhaustion already creeping into my bones. Crow swooped his arm under my legs while the other rested on my back as he carried me to the small bed. He laid me down and then crawled to the other side of the bed to lie next to me. I turned over and placed my head on his chest as his shadows calmed and swayed evenly around us. My hand trailed down his chest, to his abdomen, wanting to explore more of him, and then Crow caught my wrist with his hand. Knowing where my mind was going, he stopped me.

"The first time I have you, it won't be here, not like this." He gave me a grin as his other hand wrapped around me and swiped a lock of my silver hair out of my face. "Sleep now." And as if his words willed it to be, I closed my eyes and fell asleep to the sound of his beating heart.

CHAPTER
THIRTY-FOUR
KADE

My palms braced harshly against the edges of my desk, my shoulders taut as I leaned over, gazing at all the maps. The new door to my room shrieked as Rhet strode in.

"You wanted to see me?" He paused in front of my desk.

"Valla sent word to father," I began, the name of our sister leaving a bitter taste on my tongue. "She was bragging about how close she is to finding the Peacebringer since the rebels slaughtered her soldiers' camp in Woodhaven."

"We can't let her get the Peacebringer, father assigned that task to you, and if Valla brings her in, it won't be good." He said, looking down at the maps along with me.

"I had her in my grasp, Rhet." I murmured, my fists clenched against my desk while I blew out an uneasy breath. The thought of Valla reaching the Peacebringer first, of what she would do without hesitation or mercy, tightened my chest like a vice.

"I know, brother. You'll have her again." He said.

With the conviction of his words wrapping around me, I reached for the crystal bottle that held the amber liquid—a respite for weary souls like ours. My fingers curled around its cool neck, every facet glinting mocking promises under the dim light. The stopper gave way with a soft pop, breaking the silence that had begun to settle between us.

The liquid poured into two glasses, the sound a gentle rush against the quiet tension. It was a rich hue, a captured sunset that promised warmth but offered none. I lifted my glass, the weight familiar in my hand as if it were an extension of my resolve.

I tilted my glass and let the fiery liquid blaze a trail down my throat. Its burn was a fleeting escape from the chill of doubt that had taken residence within me. The glass clinked softly against the wood as I set it down, a hollow sound in the stillness.

Rhet watched me, a storm brewing in his eyes. He knew what was on the line. How hard this was for me. His hand was steady as he finally brought the rim to his lips, taking a measured sip as though savoring the taste of our shared determination. The light caught the edge of his drink and threw a golden glint across his face. His eyes held mine, an unspoken understanding passing between us.

"Father wants the Peacebringer alive. She can't be trusted with that task. Our dear sister is too enthralled with blood. She'd be sure no one was left breathing. Tell the men we're changing course. We need to get to Woodhaven before Valla does."

CHAPTER THIRTY-FIVE
ACE

My hair was still dripping as I wandered back to Maeves. The springs had been nice to get a bath in after not bathing for a few days. I tossed my dirty clothes in a bag with my weapons, they reeked from days of sweat and grime, I gripped them in my fist as I walked completely naked through the rebellion's base camp with nothing but a towel draped around my waist. I had stayed at the springs with Eme for a while, we got caught up talking about the trip for tomorrow and I gave her shit for what she pulled with Luana but she only laughed at me and told me about her own emotional situation with Crow. It was nice to unwind, and talk about our issues. It reminded me of all the times we would sit on the ledge of Heavensreach through the years and release all our problems to each other over tea or gin, depending on the topics we were discussing.

Now that it was late, I wasn't worried about anyone seeing me. The only light was the fire fly lanterns flickering and lighting the pathways between the enormous trees.

A clanking sound startled me and I realized who it was immediately. Luana struggled with the pots and pans from the days meals. She huffed with frustration but even with a scowl on her face, she was beautiful. Her dark skin was illuminated by the moonlight and when she looked up at me with those green, golden flecked eyes, I paused, I could stare into them all night. Then I realized I was almost naked and she was the only woman I wouldn't want to see when I'm only wearing a towel wrapped around my waist.

Not because I don't want to see her, but because of the unbearable desire I have to always want to be around her. Everything about her drew me closer.

I leaned down and picked up one of the larger pots she had dropped on the ground. I could tell she was a hard worker for the rebellion. Earlier, as Emelyn and I were walking to the springs, we overheard Atreya and Luana planning for the trip tomorrow. Atreya had pulled us into the conversation, letting us in on what was going to happen. Atreya had a stern exterior and I couldn't get a read on her, but Luana seemed worried. It was almost like I could feel it from her.

Every time I saw Luana, she was doing something. Whether it be scouting, cooking, or planning the rebellion's next task. She stayed busy helping others. The thought tugged at my heart. It seemed she didn't leave any time left for herself. She picked up the last of the pots and pans on the ground.

"Thank y–" Her voice cut off when she glanced down and saw what I was wearing. Her eyes lingered over my body before she finally met my gaze again. "Thank you, Ace" she said as she cleared her throat, I could hear the spike in her heartbeat.

"Anytime, Lu," I signed, shortening her name. She gave me a small smile before she steadied herself and moved past me with her hands full. She looked over at me when I tapped her on the shoulder. I shouldn't do what I was about to do, but I also couldn't stop my hands from moving as I continued, "want some help?" I asked, and she looked up at me through her thick lashes.

"You want to help me in a bath towel?" She glanced down and I could only imagine how ridiculous I must have looked asking, but I didn't want the moment to end yet. I blew out a low chuckle and nodded at her and she handed me some pots and pans with a shake of her head and a fresh blush on her cheeks. She turned from me and I followed her to one of the large trees that had a pulley system attached to it to get up the tree. I was about to grab her and fly her up. The thought of having her in my arms made something stir in my chest.

But then the ground shifted beneath my feet, making me almost fall over as we began rising up the tree. We stood on the cylinder of earth that she controlled until it stopped at the ledge of the wooden walking platforms. She continued to her destination as gracefully as ever. The large piece of earth sunk back into the ground as if it had never moved.

I made haste toward her rather than growing further behind by admiring her bending. Within a few short paces, we were at one of the tree houses. They used a few of them for other purposes. Like washing the pots after mealtimes, or the infirmary to care for those who are injured or ill. Shay had said they kept the infirmary in the trees to help keep the injured safer, but I was sure it made it more difficult to get them here.

She walked in and sat down the pots and pans on one of the two tables that sat next to each other in the small room, wincing when they clanked against the wood. She tried to be quiet since we were close to the small homes where others were surely sleeping. I followed suit and sat down the few I was holding on the table next to where she sat hers. Large basins of water were perched at the ends of the tables for washing.

I glanced behind me, seeing her staring at my naked back and wings.

"they're beautiful," her voice was soft, reminding me of the illusion in the swamp, and it warmed something in me.

I turned around and our eyes met again. It was like there was a tether binding something between us. Everything was more heightened about her. I wanted to be closer to her. I needed to be closer.

Stepping around the table, my feet carried me without thinking about my movements. I was a breath away from her, but then she turned her head away.

"I better get going. We have a long day tomorrow to Westwell, and with the celebration. Besides, I'm sure someone is waiting for you." She put emphasises on the someone, letting me know she knew about Maeve, or at least enough to know that there was someone else. "You can put your laundry with all the others. Hink will get to it in the morning before we head out."

I found my words a moment later. "yes, of course, I'll see you tomorrow," I signed as she walked out the door. I stood there a moment thinking of what I had almost done and wanted to punch myself in the gut for not thinking about Maeve. If Luana wouldn't have cut me off, I would have kissed her. And if she would have wanted me, I would've laid her on the table and played out all the fantasies in my mind about her—about us.

Shit.

I blew out a heavy breath and reeled in my thoughts. I needed to talk to Maeve. I didn't want to hurt her, but I knew she deserved to know that there was something between Luana and I that I couldn't shake. Something deeper than just physical attraction–something more that I didn't understand. Not yet, but I was determined to figure it out.

I tossed my laundry in the bin with all the others and walked out the door Luana had walked out moments before, yet she was nowhere to be seen. I'd hoped she was actually going to get some rest for tomorrow. She would need it, we all would.

I flew down from the wooden platform and held my now dry towel in place as I landed. I made my way back to my quarters, where I had some spare clothes and a few other essentials waiting for me. I threw on something quickly and headed directly for Maeve's place.

I landed quietly before I knocked lightly against her door. There was no answer. I pushed the door open and peeked inside and found her sleeping soundly on her bed. I didn't want to disturb her, so I turned away and went back to my quarters.

Once I laid in bed, I stared up at the tree-carved ceiling, and my mind wouldn't stop racing. The last thing I thought of was Luana before my eyes grew heavy and my mind slipped away as I fell asleep.

CHAPTER THIRTY-SIX
EMELYN

When I woke, Crow was leaning up on his side with his elbow, watching me. His shadows bobbed and writhed gently around his muscled silhouette, and for the first time since I'd met him, he seemed a little relaxed.

"Good morning," he said, and I smiled sheepishly as I rubbed the sleep from my eyes. His shadows wrapped around me like a hug as one tried to push the loose strands of hair away from my face. Crow shooed them away from me with his hand.

"It's alright, I like them too." I said more to the tendrils of shade than to Crow, and he released a light chuckle as his shadows swarmed me again. A wide smile stretched across my face and I noticed Crow watching me from the corner of my eye and I turned my head to glance over at him.

"Is something wrong?" I asked, and he pulled out of his dazed state.

"Nothing at all, mei wynsoara," he said as he leaned over to brush his lips gently against mine. Something tugged on my navel, beckoning me to him, like a puppet on a string, and then it was gone as soon as his lips fell away from mine. "We have to get going. Atreya is waiting."

I looked out of one of the small windows to see it bright with the early morning sun and quickly lurched to my feet to.

"Why didn't you wake me?!" I scolded and grabbed for my leathers, shimmying in my pants before putting on my top and strapping on my leather boots.

"You were sleeping peacefully, I didn't want to wake you, besides Westwell Harbor isn't too far from here, we should make it there before lunch, and back in time to celebrate tonight." he said as he made it to his feet and sheathed his twin blades on his back and a dagger on his hip. I watched as his weapons became one with his shadows.

I did the same; I placed my axe on my hip, and a dagger in my boot. Glancing around the room to be sure I hadn't forgotten anything, Crow handed me a skin already full of water before he placed his own against his hip.

"Thank you," I said, and he placed a gentle kiss against my forehead before he reached for the door and opened it for me.

"Let's go, wynsoara."

I smiled even though I still had no idea what his nickname for me meant.

"You can call me Eme." I said and his face went slack as he gave me a relieved smile, like I had rewarded him by telling him he could use my name.

"I think I like mei wynsoara better," He said it with a wink as we walked out the door.

The trip to Westwell Harbor went smoothly, just as Crow had said. Until we stumbled upon the havock Ember had left behind in one of the small villages along the trail in our journey. Homes were left in piles of ash, smoke still barreled into the skies. my boots crunched on something brittle. I didn't need to look down, the sound was all too familiar.

Bodies of Ember soldiers were jutted out of the earth from Earth Dryads fighting back, now nothing but skeletal remains as their own fire seared the meat off their bones. Regardless that they had fought back but the village had been outnumbered. The dirtied faces of children cried, running into the arms of their mothers. A pang of guilt twisted in my gut—another battle fought, another home razed, while I had been absent.

My gaze lingered on a little girl, no more than five, clutching a singed ribbon—the kind used to adorn hair on festival days. Her tear-filled eyes met mine, and in them, I saw the same realization that had dawned on me countless times: War spared no one. It creeps into every corner, into every smile, casting long shadows that stretch out across lives—generations.

Death. So much death. It brought me back to reality. Being with the rebellion and catching some what of a break had been nice. But this was what war looked like. Even when you didn't see it, it was there.

I watched Atreya walk over to some of the survivors, talking to them for a moment while we waited. I glanced over to Ace and Maeve, they seemed distant from each other but I assumed it was because Sedrin and Maeve had come together. When I looked back to Atreya, a black bird was perched on her arm, tucking a note with it. She sent it off before walking over to me.

"This is why I created the rebellion all those years ago." She said with a somber tone. I could tell the pain of these people made her distraught. She wore the exterior of a warrior but the raging emotions behind her eyes for these people, for our world, told me everything. I recognized it, because I felt the same.

"Shouldn't we stay and help?" I asked.

She shook her head, "no, there's nothing we can do here now, the fights already over. Besides, they were probably looking for you." She placed a heavy hand on my shoulder. "I sent a bird to camp, a group will come and help them, for now we need to keep moving." She assured me before walking back to the front next to Shay. The thought of Ember destroying this place because of me made my chest hurt. I swallowed down my grief., I would figure out how to fix this world, I promised myself.

All eight of us traveled alongside the large flat bed wagon in sets of two.

Maeve and Sedrin took the back behind us as we moved along the terrain, Ace and Luana took the tail end of the wagon while Atreya and Shay took the front.

Crow and I stayed behind them.

Westwell was beautiful, so different from Lintawa Bay. This place was charming and alluring, with picturesque scenery. Eye-catching flowers and thick vines grew along the stunning stone buildings. Fae, dryads, and creatures of all sorts dressed in their finest walked through the markets with their families. While Lintawa Bay was run down and no longer in the former glory from before the war started, Fire Fae had taken over the dock markets back home after the battle all those years ago. But this place seemed like they hadn't been a part of the war.

The feeling I got when talking to Shay about how they had trouble with shipments recently made my stomach twist into knots.

"Westwell is owned by the Capital City of Woodhaven." Crow whispered loud enough for me to hear under his breath as we passed a small group of dryad and Orc soldiers wearing the crest of Woodhaven stamped into their leathers on their chests, it was a large tree with intertwining roots that also connected to the top.

Some gave us a nod of their heads in recognition, while others continued their afternoon chatter. Aster, the king of Woodhaven, used being able to bend the earth to his advantage. Over the years I had learned about Embers' efforts to take over Woodhaven by taking down the Capital City, but they were always unsuccessful. Any intruder was sucked under the earth, never to be seen again. But Ember seemed to think it was worth the loss of life if it meant they could one day rule all of Osparia.

"It is part of the reason the base camp of the rebellion has remained hidden for so long. Woodhaven wants Ember to be stopped just as much as Atreya does. So they let us use their docks for trade, among other things."

"I see," I said, looking past Crow on the other side of the wagon before checking my surroundings again.

"Where's Mo?" Atreya asked a large scary looking man that was at the entrance of the docks. Her voice was smooth and steady. The man kept the gates open for us to pass.

"Oh, he took the day off. He'll be back for the next pickup." The mans voice seemed strained although he tried to hide it.

I kept my hands loose at my sides, ready for anything that may come. I glanced back at Ace. His features were stiff, his jaw jutted, shoulders wound tight. We both were feeling wary. My steps slowed and so did Crows.

"Something's wrong." Crow whispered and Atreya raised her hand, commanding us to stop before we went past the gates to the docks down the narrow cobblestone path.

Pedestrians passed us, leaving a distance between us, so we had plenty of room to keep going.

"Is that so?" Atreya responded with a lethal tone to her voice before she grabbed for her sword and sliced it through the large fae mans neck before he ever got the chance to fight against her. The man clawed at his neck as his blood spilled over his fingers, eyes rounded in fear of what would soon come—death.

"Mo... Is a woman." Was all Atreya said as she kicked the man over and turned toward us. "Run!" She yelled, but it was too late.

A sudden silence draped over the marketplace like a suffocating blanket before pandemonium erupted. The once harmonious hum of bartering voices and children's innocent giggles splintered into chaos—loud and hectic. The soft chatter disappeared as soon as the man's blood poured out over the stones. Parents and children's screams echoed around us. I didn't see any fire fae, but I saw a wave of gleaming light hurling in our direction. A wave of arrows were flying towards us at rapid speeds, catching us all off guard.

I saw Ace out of the corner of my eye leap for Luana, while Sedrin took off into the skies with Maeve wrapped up in his arms, and then darkness fluttered at the edges of my vision when I tried to look for Crow, a figure appeared in font of me–his figure, he had hollowed.

He wrapped his arms around me, shielding me from the wave of arrows. His pained grunt was the only indication that they had hit him, his shadows more concerned about saving me than shielding him, before he hollowed us under the wooden wagon.

I fought to calm my racing heart and ragged breathing as the darkness dissipated around me. Crow lifted his body off of me enough to glance down at my face. "are you hurt?" he asked, worry and pain twisted his brow as he looked at me. Not for himself—*for me.*

"Crow," I whispered his name, staring up at him in shock and disbelief that he would willingly sacrifice his life for mine.

"I asked, are you hurt, Emelyn?" His eyes roved over me, searching for any sign of an injury.

"N-no." I stuttered over my words, trying to swallow the swollen lump of emotion forming in my throat. He released a heavy breath of relief, bringing his forehead down to mine.

"Good." He whispered, his warm breath danced across my jawline. "We have to go."

We crawled out from under the wagon and ran for the woods we had traveled through to get here. I looked around for a moment and didn't see Ace. My heart began pounding harder behind my ribs and I paused. Searching the skies for him. I got the faintest glimpse of Sedrin and Maeve. Atreya and Shay had already made it to the treeline.

But where was Ace? Where was Luana? Panic made bile rise in my throat. I couldn't lose him. I wouldn't. Fire Fae began storming from the opposite side of the woods. There was no time...

"Emelyn!" Crow roared, making my feet move, and then I saw it. The earth shifted and Ace flew out of the hole made in the ground like an angel rising from the dead.

Relief flooded my senses. I sucked in a breath and tried to let go of the fear that was strangling my chest only a few moments ago.

Crow grabbed for me and pulled me along with him until we had all made it into the woods. My lungs burned, my legs ached. The wagon had been long left behind. I wasn't sure how far we ran, but I could no longer hear the rolling waves of the waters of Draynua, or smell the salt of the sea. The screams had all but gone silent. And the only sound was the sound of our boots pounding into the soil as we ran.

I looked to the soil, focusing on my footing along the uneven ground, and tried to make myself keep going. I bended the blood in my veins to pump faster into my legs to keep me moving. And then I noticed stains along the ground in front of me.

I glanced up at Crow and gasped at how this man was still standing, let alone moving. His shadows had all but stopped, his tendrils were no longer there to greet me, they had dissipated and he was nothing but a dark silhouette running. Now that his shadows weren't writhing, I could see the arrows jutted out of his back as his blood dribbled to the ground in front of me.

"Crow," I called to him and grabbed for his shoulder, hauling him to a stop. He turned to me with wild irises. "Stop, you're going to bleed out." I said, and the only sound between us was Crow's shuddering breaths. I watched as the adrenaline left his body and his shoulders sagged. His body leaned on the closest tree to support his weight. I wrapped my arm around his waist and turned him so he was facing the large tree.

"Do it." His voice was weak and hoarse. I used my bending to weave water around the head of the arrow to make it dull as I fished the arrow heads out of his back. One by one, I broke the backs of them off and pulled them free. Crow flinched with a growl on the last one. It had been the deepest, I bended the last of the water from my skin around the palms of my hands and they began glowing a faint blue as I laid both hands over two of his six wounds, he let out a breath of relief as my touch took some of the pain away.

"We need to go," He said as he moved away from my touch and began stumbling in the direction Atreya and Shay had gone.

"Crow, you can't travel like this. Stop."

He kept moving,

"please," I begged, and his steps faltered. He glanced at me over his shoulder and that's when I knew he was about to fall over.

"Eme–," He murmured on a shallow breath before his body slumped against the tree closest to him. I could tell it was taking the little strength he had left to hold up his weight.

"Crow," I rushed to him with my healing hands, and blew out a whistle, my call to Ace.

A few moments passed, and I was able to get the bleeding to stop by the time Ace landed gracefully a few yards away and rushed to my aid.

"We have to get him back to camp," I signed with bloody hands to Ace right when Crow's eyes began to flutter and small shadows began moving. "Can you get him there?" Ace glanced from me to Crow and then nodded before grasping Crow in his arms and taking off into the skies.

I watched Ace fly off into the distance before I stood and made my feet pound as fast as my racing heart against the soil to get back to the base camp.

CHAPTER THIRTY-SEVEN
EMELYN

After I had gotten back to base camp, I found everyone waiting in the infirmary. My emotions were overwhelming, pushing me over the edge as tears pricked and fell from my eyes. I was breathing hard when I rushed through the door. All conversations stopped as everyone's attention fell upon me. My chest ached. Ace was the first one I saw, and by the look on his face, he shared the same feelings I did.

We were scared in Westwell.

I wasn't scared of dying or getting hurt. It wasn't those things that I feared. For the smallest inkling of a moment, I'd thought he was gone. I thought I had lost him. And that was what I feared more than anything in this life, this world–losing those who meant everything to me.

Ace left Luanas' side, taking long strides toward me. I slammed into his chest, wrapping my arms tightly around him. I let out a sob of relief. He held me in his powerful arms, one of the few places I had found comfort.

Until recently...

He tugged me back, gripping my shoulders before swiping a tear from my cheek. "I'm here, Eme. I'm okay, we're okay," he signed. It only made the bolder of emotion in my throat swell. I did my best to swallow it down as he released my shoulders and gave me a reassuring smile before returning to Luana. Maeve looked away before she walked out of the room with her brother on her heels. I could feel the tension growing between Maeve and Ace, just like I had on the trip to Westwell. Luana glanced at Ace before she followed suit.

"I have some things to tend to. I'm glad you're okay, Crow," Luana said as she walked toward the door. Ace's eyes followed her every move as she strode across the threshold and out of sight. He caught me staring.

"What?" He signed.

I nodded toward the door, giving him the signal to go after her. Apparently he needed the push, but agreed as he smiled before moving toward the door.

"You shouldn't have tried to fight, Shay. Especially *not right now*. You should have followed me sooner than you did." Atreya reprimanded Shay while she bandaged her arm, where I assumed an arrow had hit her.

"Now is not the time or place," Shay whispered back as Baron came barreling through the door. He moved quickly to face his mate, cupping her face in his hands as he looked over her intently before kissing her lips gently and pulling her into a hug.

"I was so worried," Baron murmured into the crook of her neck.

"I know, I was too," Shay responded. The love they shared was palpable in the room.

"I should have been there," he said as he pulled back. Shay only shook her head.

"No, we needed you at camp to train the rebellion's troops, my love. Do not blame yourself," she spoke, but his eyes only focused on the bandage wrapped around her arm. "It'll be healed within a day, Baron. I'm okay," she reassured him. He expelled a sigh of relief as he grabbed her hand and ushered her toward the door.

"I'm going next time," he said toward Atreya.

She simply nodded in understanding. Forcing mates to be apart when they didn't choose it would be worse than death.

"Crow. Emelyn." Baron nodded toward us in farewell before they walked out the door together.

"I'll give you two some privacy," Atreya said as she started toward the door. "I'll need you to report to me soon, Crow, but until then..." She gave Crow's hand a light squeeze as she passed his bed. "Rest." She left, shutting the door behind her.

I looked at Crow for the first time since I'd watched Ace carry him away. I could feel the tightness in my throat again as the emotions bubbled up in my chest. A few quick steps brought me to where he sat up on the side of the bed. The shadows rolling off of him were small, probably from the overexertion of trying to escape.

I was about to speak, but he did first.

"I'm sorry." His words took me by surprise. What made this man think I needed an apology?

"For what?" I asked.

"I should've gotten you back to camp. You shouldn't have been left alone after what happened back there."

"Stop," I said, moving to the other side of the bed to get better access to his mangled back. His leathers were still on, I could see the outline of them under his shadows. "Take this off," I said, motioning to his shirt.

He obliged.

I helped him lift it up and over his head, letting it fall to the floor. His shadows clung to every curve, revealing every taut muscle, along with the six jagged holes that lined across his back unevenly. They had already stopped bleeding, leaving gaping wounds and swollen skin behind. I was sure if he had a skin tone under his shadows, his back would be covered in blue and purple bruises.

"It's not as bad as it looks. I'll heal," he said as I bended water from a small bucket next to his bed. My hands glowed, and I focused on his injuries for as long as I could before my hands trembled. Healing always took a lot of energy. Even bending could drain us if we used too much at a time. It was why my father had always kept me up on my training.

"Emelyn," Crow said softly as he turned around and grabbed my hands. I would have kept going until the darkness swept me under if that's what it would take. He took these arrows for me... The glow faded as the water slithered back to its bucket. His wounds were closed and almost gone now. "I'm okay," he said.

Ace wasn't the only one I had been scared to lose today.

"Do not apologize for giving the biggest piece of yourself to me," I said, finally getting some control over my emotions.

"What piece is that?" he asked.

"Your life–for mine."

"I'd give it every time."

There was not even a glimmer of hesitation in his voice. He spoke so sure of himself, and I didn't doubt he meant it. I guessed being the Peacebringer was the only reason he'd save me, but a part of me wanted it to be more than that. Over the last few days, the feelings I had for him had grown immensely, and I didn't know what to do with them. I had never felt this way for someone before, but I refused to admit it out loud. Not now, not yet—maybe never.

He closed the distance between us. My heart stuttered as he placed a gentle kiss against my lips. He then, wrapped his arms around me as he pulled me onto his lap. With my legs straddled around him, I ran my hands over his back softly, memorizing for myself every spot the arrows had hit him. Every sacrifice he had made for me. His eagerness to do it was what tugged on my heart the most.

I poured all of that into the kiss I gave him. His enormous length hardened against my inner thigh. My hips rolled against him with a primal call. The growl he let out went straight to my core. He stood, lifting me with him as he pulled away from the kiss.

"Wynsoara," he said breathlessly. I let my feet fall to the ground and stood before him.

Crow's eyes, dark and fathomless, searched my face, as if seeking answers to questions even he didn't know. His hands, firm yet gentle, found their way to my cheeks, cupping my face, steadying me beneath his hold. The tension in the room seemed to thicken as his head fell, his eyes looking to his feet as he sat down, the mattress dipping beneath his weight.

"What's wrong?" Concern coated my voice, the earlier rush of adrenaline still thrumming through my veins. "What do you need?"

He didn't answer immediately. His gaze met mine again with an intensity that sent a shiver down my spine. Then, with one fluid motion, he pulled me into his chest. His arms encircled me, drawing me into his warm embrace.

"You," he whispered against my hair. "I just need you."

It wasn't a request; it was an admission. The weight of his words settled heavily in the space between us. The air seemed to thicken—charge. I could feel the heat of his breath against my hair, the sincerity in his voice leaving an indelible impression on my heart.

I eased onto the bed beside him, the warmth of his body a stark contrast to the cool air of the room. I lay against him. He held me as if I was the most precious thing to him.

A thought skimmed across the surface of my mind like a stone across still water. How fragile life was, how the precious beat of a heart could so easily be stilled. I nestled closer, burrowing into the protective circle of his arms, letting the heat of his body seep into my cold bones.

I drew in a deep breath, my lungs filling with the scent of him, and earth, and sweat, all mingled with the iron tang of dried blood—a reminder of how perilously close I had come to exist in a world without him. Tears stung my eyes, and I gripped him tighter

"Emelyn," he murmured, his voice a soft rumble beneath my cheek. "I'm okay, I'm okay," he assured me again, running his hand gently through my hair and up and down my back. Relief, fierce and overwhelming, surged through my veins. I had almost lost him and Ace today. The reminder almost made me tremble. I couldn't lose anyone else.

"Shhh, I'm right here, Mei Wynsoara."

Moments of comfortable quiet passed as I breathed him in. The shadows in the room gathered around us, confirmation that he was gaining his strength back already. My head lifted slightly as I watched, transfixed, as little shadow crows emerged above our heads. Their silhouettes were delicate and fluid, twirling above us in a smokey dance.

"When I was a child, my mother used to make the shadow crows dance when I was scared," he said. "She used to call me her *little crow*, and it stuck."

The thought warmed my heart, imagining what he would have been like as a child.

"Crows have always been a sign of new beginnings," he continued, a note of wistfulness threading his tone. "She used to tell me I would make a difference in this world."

"Your mother was right," I whispered, my voice breaking the silence. "You have."

Crow shifted beneath me, his fingers tracing soothing patterns on my back. His voice, when he spoke, carried a heaviness that I didn't quite understand. "It doesn't feel that way at times. I've done a lot of bad over the years. Unforgivable things..."

"Maybe so," I said softly, "but it is not the sum of our past that defines us. It's what we do with the time that follows." My hand found his and I threaded my fingers through his. "You've made a difference in my world. I wouldn't have made it here without you."

The shadow crows paused mid-flight.

"You've given hope to this rebellion. To the world. To me." My voice cracked slightly, emotion lacing the simple truth. There was a raw honesty in acknowledging the depth of what he had done for me—for us all. It seemed he was always putting himself on the line. I just hoped and prayed that it would never take him from me.

We lay in silent acceptance and shared understanding that we were both pieces of something greater than ourselves. Despite the daunting call of our futures, I was glad to have him by my side.

Crow's arms tightened around me. "I do not deserve you," he murmured as the crows resumed their flying.

CHAPTER THIRTY-EIGHT
ACE

I followed Luana through the bustling crowd of the rebellion, scrambling to get ready for the celebrations tonight. She bobbed and weaved through them. I knew she was avoiding me.

Then she spun around, stopping like a small mountain in front of me. Unmoveable once she got past the busyness and into a small opening in between the crowd and the trees. Her small frame stood tall in front of me. She held her chin high, her height barely hitting my chest. She glared at me. I stopped, both of our chests were heaving heavy breaths, almost touching on every inhale.

"Stop this Ace." She said instead of signed.

"Stop what?" I questioned.

"This, finding me, being around me, following me." She said with a desperate tone to her voice.

"Why?" I asked, and she shook her head.

"Because I know you have something going on with Maeve. And she's a dear friend, and a sweetheart. I refuse to have any part in hurting her, and besides, I want nothing to do with whatever this is." She motioned with her hands between us.

This is.

"So you feel it too?" I asked, and she couldn't meet my eyes. I cupped her face with one of my large hands and asked again. "Do you feel it too?" I asked, my signs more certain, direct and desperate for her answer. She let her hazel, golden flecked eyes find mine again, staring deep into my very soul and I watched as all the dots connected in her mind. All the threads that connected between us.

"No..." she murmured, but I could hear the deception in her tone.

"Liar... I'll talk to Maeve." I signed and she quickly witted back.

"No, don't do that for me."

"Tell me you don't want me too." She couldn't meet my stare as she pulled her face away from my palm. I let my hand fall back down to my side. "That's what I thought."

"Hey guys." *Skies Above, speak of the devil.* Maeve signed as she appeared from behind me. Based on the worried expression pasted on her face, I had hoped she hadn't heard our conversation. I wanted to talk to her alone, but with the celebration happening so soon, I wasn't sure I'd be able to and I didn't want to ruin tonight.

Luana gave her a smile before walking in the direction Maeve had just come from. Maeve pulled me into a hug and my eyes watched Luana as she sauntered away. She glanced at me over her shoulder and shook her head, signaling to me she didn't want me to mention it to Maeve at all. At least not right now.

A part of me saw it as her being selfless. Feeling and knowing there is something between us and being willing to stay back to spare another woman's feelings because she cared for her. The thought just made me care for Luana more. Did the woman ever put herself first?

"Come on, let's get ready!" Maeve signed enthusiastically, and I did my best to put on a face for her. "I can't wait to show you what dress I'll be wearing." She grabbed my hand and tugged me along, before I pulled her into my arms and launched into the ever-growing trees of Woodhaven to prepare for the party.

"I'm not wearing that." I signed as Maeve and the seamstress circled around me like a pack of wolves ready to attack.

"It'll look amazing on you." The seamstress said as she laid out suits for me to wear, they accommodated for my wings. I couldn't remember the last time I wore a suit. And now that I was thinking about it... I had never worn one.

"Com'on, do it for Emelyn. I'm sure she'd love to see you dress up with her tonight."

"What makes you think Eme, my Eme, the same woman who keeps daggers in places you can't see, is going to wear a dress?" I asked, and Maeve and the seamstress shared a knowing look. "What don't I know?" I asked, and they both smiled.

"You'll have to trust us." Maeve signed before she winked at me and I smiled back at her. Luana was right, Maeve was a sweetheart, too sweet, especially for me. She was gentle and kind, and everything about me was the opposite of that. But I didn't want to hurt her and I couldn't help this connection to Luana that overpowered everything else when I was around her. As if the world deemed it so from the moment I ran into her at Bell's. She haunted my consciousness in every way.

The seamstress poked me with one of her needles, pulling me from my thoughts as I scowled at her.

"Oh, what are you, a baby? That didn't hurt." She mumbled her words over the needles she held between her lips. I looked ahead in the trifold mirror that lay in front of me. I mouthed the words 'did too' and Maeve chuckled back at me in the reflection. She looked absolutely beautiful, as another seamstress was working on her for the celebration. She wore a peachy colored dress that was long and fit snug to her small figure. I admired her for a moment, and although Maeve was beautiful and kind.

She wasn't Luana.

I looked away and my lips tugged into a frown as the seamstress finished and when I looked back up in the mirror, I looked fit for royalty.

The black collared tunic had a v neckline that showed off my muscled chest with cuffed sleeves that fit snuggly around my arms with a fit pair of dress pants that made me feel like I didn't belong in them. The top accommodated my wings comfortably. And the shoes they had put me in weren't war boots, so I wasn't sure how to feel about them.

Emelyn and I had dressed up for festivals and such while we were growing up, but never like this, and then when the war hit, we never really got the opportunity to.

"You look as handsome as ever." A loud familiar voice spoke up from the doorway and when I turned, it was Hinky. He was wearing a white tunic and trousers that both looked to be a few sizes too big, like something you'd wear to bed.

"You're not coming tonight?" I signed as my brow pinched and he went on.

"No, Helena hasn't been feeling well, so I told her we could stay in together and get some rest after all the preparations for today. But I wanted to stop by and see you and Eme beforehand and wow," he paused, "you clean up well for a winged brute," he joked with a heavy hand on my back and a loud chuckle.

I breathed out a chuckle and pulled him in for a hug.

"Thanks Hink," I signed, "tell Helena hi for me,"

"Will do, have fun tonight," his tone grew more serious, "you and Emelyn both, you deserve it." he spoke with soft eyes before walking out the door.

"You ready?" Maeve signed to me with a kind smile before wrapping her arm around mine and guiding us toward the door.

Bulbs of fire fly lights hung in uneven rows from the tree limbs and bridges of the Rebellions base camp, casting a dim glow over the party. Food and drinks sat at tables while men and women made haste on their rounds of appetizers and drinks. The forest floor had been cleared of its red leaves and debris. Instead, the bright reds and browns decorated the tables and the sidelines of the dance area. The Earth Dryads had smoothed the ground, creating a space for dancing in the center of everything. I could've sworn they had moved even some trees around–shifted just enough to create a wide open space. Maeve took me by the hand,

"care to dance," she said, tugging me along to the dance floor.

"I can't dance," I responded honestly, and now that I was out in the open, a part of me wanted to melt away, back into the crowd.

"Don't think about it. I'll show you. We can practice." She grabbed one of my hands and placed it on her lower back while taking the other one and holding it up to the side in front of us. She swayed gently to the music, and my eyes kept trailing down to my feet to watch where my next step was going. Maeve gently tugged me closer to her, causing my eyes to meet hers as she scowled at me.

"Look up here," she signed with one hand before taking the next step to the sound of the music. After a few more tries, I got it down and moved gracefully alongside her until the music slowed to a stop and then a new song began. This one was slower and more romantic. Maeve leaned into me and rested her cheek against my chest for a brief moment, as if she was searing it into her mind before she leaned back and stopped dancing.

"Now go do that with her," her signs caught me by surprise.

"What?" I questioned

"Luana," she nodded to where Luana stood, "go dance with her."

"Maeve I–I've been needing to talk to you about that."

"Theres no need, Ace," she wagged her head with an amiable smile, "I see the way you look at her, and the way she looks at you." She glanced down. "You've never looked at me like that."

"Maeve–"

"No, really, Ace, it's alright, the Mother designed someone for everyone, and I'm sure I'll find someone that looks at me the way you look at Lu." She huffed out a small laugh, "I'm happy for you, truly I am, for both of you." Her brown eyes met mine. "In the world we live in and the lives we've all had, life is too short to not be with the ones you truly love."

"I don't know if love is the right word—"

"It is," she said with a wink as her brother, Sedrin, came up from behind me.

"May I have this dance, dear sister?" He asked with a large overdramatic bow at the waist, while he flared his wings with a wide smile stretched across his features.

"Absolutely, dear brother," they both put emphasis on their words using their hands before he held out his arm with a laugh and was about to tug her away when she turned and signed. "There's who you're looking for." she narrowed her eyes into the distance before she gave me one last nudge and a lighthearted smile before Sedrin whisked her away on to the full dance floor.

My eyes found the woman I desperately desired. Her sage green dress made her dark skin glow in the soft light. She was devastatingly breathtaking. Her tight, short curls sat atop her head, revealing her taut jawline. The front of the dress hung loosely over her breasts while the rest of it hugged her body tightly. I had to force myself to blink.

When she saw me, she looked away, as if she had been staring too long to. I forced my legs to make haste toward her, placing a single finger to her chin and lifting her gaze back to mine.

"May I have this dance?" I asked with sweaty palms as she gave me a worried look.

"But what about?–"

"I have already handled it." I signed gripping her fingers and pulling her into me on the dance floor. "She understands." I signed, and Luana sighed in relief.

I followed the steps Maeve had walked me through, placing my callused hand on the small of Luanas back only to realize that the back of her dress was bare. My rough hand caressed her skin gently, making heat pass through me. She paused for a moment before running one of her petite hands up my chest and laid her head there as we swayed gently to the music.

"Do you know what this is?" Luana whispered, and I only shook my head, because I refused to release her from my hold. Her scent wafted around me. She smelt like midnight and jasmine. Something about it made gooseflesh trail down my neck. I was aware of every place our skin touched. My insides turned to mush. I wrapped both arms around her and I felt her body relax into mine, and my thoughts wondered by to if she had ever taken care of herself.

Every part of me wanted to take care of her, just like she had for everyone else. I ran one finger up and down the center of her spine, and the way her body tingled for me made a naughty grin appear on my face.

"Don't do that," she murmured.

"Do what?" I asked as my eyes roamed over her again.

"Look at me like that,"

"Like what?" I played dumb as her eyes narrowed in on me.

"Like I'm a treasure, or something." she rolled her eyes, and I gripped her chin and pulled her tightly against me so she couldn't look away.

"Never think of yourself as anything less than priceless." I signed and her lips parted slightly as she gazed up at me like she had never been viewed as anything of high importance. I glanced down to her full lips before the hand I was using to sign cupped her face, while the other caressed her back and pushed her further into me until her lips were a breath away from mine. I waited, ever so impatiently, for her permission.

And when she leaned in and her eyes fluttered closed, I kissed her with the force of the winds and the gentleness of calm seas. My tongue found hers as our lips rolled together as one, deepening our kiss together. Nothing existed outside of us. No one was dancing. The music faded as the world spun around us.

My body hummed with hers, perfectly in tune with one another. As if the light of the sun encircled us and twined our souls together in this moment.

She stopped and her brow knitted as she pulled away.

"I'm sorry," she whispered it almost to herself, a mix of uncertainty and awe painted her features. Her posture stiffened. "I'm sorry, I have to go..." She back stepped away from me and when I went to follow her, she stopped me. "No, stay. Please, I just need a minute." Her tone sounded desperate. I paused, giving her a nod of my head before she turned on her heels and walked away from me and into the crowd of people.

did I do something wrong?

CHAPTER THIRTY-NINE
EMELYN

Hinky had found me as I walked down to the party in his night clothes, wishing me well for tonight's celebrations.

I hadn't seen crow since he had met me at the Springs when Ace left. Afterwards he dropped me off at my room so I could prepare for tonight. Which I was already late for my own party. We had a little too much fun at the springs. I could taste his kiss on my lips. I bit at my bottom lip from the thought and looked over to the bed, where a burgundy dress lay.

It was long and had a satin shimmer to it, with delicate straps to go over my shoulders and the slit looked to go all the way up to my hip. It was a beautiful dress, but something I'd never pick for myself. A note lay on top of it.

For *mei wynsoara*, was written in thick ink and it made a smile tug on the corners of my mouth. This man had been in my every thought, had infected my mind like a plague and I didn't know how to get him out of my head, or if I even wanted to.

I put on the dress, shimmying it down over my hips. A small, heeled, golden pair of shoes sat next to the bed. The long laces intertwined up my calves. I had to practice walking in them around my room for a solid half hour. The heel was small, but I had only ever worn boots made for battle or travel. Never something as elegant as this.

After I could walk as close to normal as I could get I left my room and traveled the short trip to where the ropes we normally travelled down to the ground with and I found that some of the Earth Dryads had lifted the earth from below to make a staircase climbing up through the trees. I guessed women in dresses and heels going down a rope didn't sound too appealing to most. The thought made a light chuckle escape me.

I took easy steps down the stairs, passing through all the strands of fire fly bulbs with the small bugs dancing and glowing inside. The ground below was smooth and servers moved freely through the crowd of light chatter, dancing, and drinks. A small band of what looked to be dwarfs played lutes and other instruments while a beautiful woman sang, her voice was soft and velvety and flowed well with the tunes.

Tables lined the open space, which I assumed was now the dance floor. On the other side of the large tables of food were small tables and chairs for people to sit and drink. I glanced around and found Ace swaying slowly on the dance floor with Luana. He was practically glowing and the sight of him, happy, made tears swell in my eyes. As I walked out and into the open, multiple people found me, asked me questions, gave me hugs, thanked me, some even cried.

All the attention made my mind swirl with all the endless possibilities of failure. What if I couldn't bring peace back to Osparia? My chest felt overwhelmingly heavy, and I needed to move past the enormous crowd that had gathered around me and get some air before I broke into a million pieces where I stood.

Excuse me, excuse me, excuse me...

I kept murmuring under my breath as I moved through the sea of people that wanted to show me their smiles, their gratitude, their hope.

Hope that I had given them, or at least the Peacebringer had given them, and I didn't know how to handle it. I was nothing more than a fae from a small village who lost just as much as the next in this raging war.

I was nothing more than them, but they believed I was the answer to everything.

I pushed on past the crowd toward the darkened parts of the woods, leaving behind the muggy space full of people, and I breathed in the crisp night air. I took deep, steadying breaths, trying to calm my racing heart.

"There you are," Crow's voice crooned from the shadows. I stumbled by the surprise of him appearing from nothing. "What's wrong?" He asked, placing a gentle hand on my arm.

"It's just all too much," I whispered, not looking him in the eyes.

"What is?" He asked, and I fell apart.

"Everything. This party, this war, me... I don't know who I am anymore or what I'm supposed to be, or become, and so many people are counting on me to restore a world I had no dealing with destroying. How do I bring peace if I've never known it?" I croaked out and Crow wrapped his shadows around me, like a calm dark ocean. The sound and the light drowned out in the background. It was nothing but us, in his darkness, as if suspended above a vastness of nothing.

"Close your eyes." He palmed my cheeks while gently placing his thumbs over my eyes. "Now, take a deep breath." He whispered. As he did what he was instructing me to do. "Now again," He muttered, and I obliged.

"Crow what is the–"

"Shhh," He quieted me and I huffed a breath and did my best to listen to him.

"Only think about this moment,"

"Crow I can't–"

"Ah, ah." He tsked, and I groaned, "try again," he whispered and I did. I took a breath, and then another, and another, and waited for his next command.

"This is the only moment you need to concern yourself with," He trailed his lips down my jawline before placing a gentle kiss on my exposed collarbone, "Not the past, nor the future," his words were like velvet against my skin as his warm breath skittered over my neck.

"You're precisely where you are supposed to be," he kissed back up my neck until his lips brushed against my own, "right here, with me. Looking devastatingly beautiful in that dress." I leaned into him and kissed him, letting my mind only explore all the thoughts of him and I and nothing beyond that, for just this moment. He pulled back, trailing his nose against mine, "better?" he asked and a smile curved my lips.

"Better." I said, and he grabbed my fingers gently and tugged my hand to his lips, placing another kiss on my hot skin.

"Can I have this dance?" he took a step back towards the party and I didn't move.

"I don't think I'm ready to go back just yet." I said, enjoying the quiet of the night.

"I have a better idea." he said and instead of tugging me back to the party, he went in the opposite direction.

"Where are we going?" I asked, and he paused and turned toward me.

"Close your eyes again." He said, and I did. His light footsteps crunching against the ground sounded around me as he tugged me along. After a few moments, the warmth of his hands covered my eyes from behind me and he continued, "okay... now open." He took his hands away and multiple shadow looking men and women were dancing around one another in between the trees.

"Crow, what is this?" I asked, smiling, before he grabbed my hand and pulled me into his chest.

"You can't hide in the shadows at your own party, but you can invite them to dance." He said, offering me his hand again, and I took it as he swayed me to the sounds of the crickets chirping and the soft music from the party in the distance.

I wasn't sure how long we had danced, but if I had to guess, I'd say at least three songs before we found a wide opening in between two trees and laid on the ground together. Fire flies swirled around us, flickering their bright orange beams of light in tandem as we gazed up at the stars twinkling in the sky. My head lay on Crow's chest as his hand played with my hair, running his fingers and tendrils of shade through the soft curls of silver.

He leaned up on his elbow to look down at me silently.

"I thought we were supposed to be admiring the stars?" I whispered sarcastically when he didn't stop peering down at me.

"I wished you could see how even in the dark, you shine brighter than any star." His words tugged on the deepest parts of my soul, making tears prick behind my eyes that someone could find me bright in some of my darkest times. Crow's hands slid into my hair, gripping my nape softly as he kissed me. And his kiss—it made the world go quiet and still, if I was bright before, I had to be glowing now.

Tendrils of shadows and light intertwined around us, or maybe it was all in my head as he deepened our kiss. I pulled back. I wanted him to see the awe in my eyes and then the sound of a whistle rang on the wind, my call from Ace.

"We better get back." Crow cleared his throat as he got to his feet and offered me his hand. It rendered me speechless, the feel of his kiss, as he lead both of us back to the party.

Crow and I walked in from the dark woods. Howls and hoots came from some men in the party and made a blush creep over my cheeks, although we hadn't done more than kiss.

Ace and Luana stood side by side with Sedrin, Maeve, and the rest of the Sky Elves. Ace seemed stiff, but I assumed it was because neither of us were used to gatherings like this. Everyone gathered around and that was when I saw Atreya part from the crowd. She wore a dress fit for a queen, she knew how to throw a party fit for royalty too. It was red and sleek, small sparkling jewels were weaved into her up do. She wore sandals instead of heels and it was something I believed she could easily fight in if she needed too. I was sure she could fight in anything.

She raised her glass and looked at Crow and I.

"To finding peace again," she nodded her head toward me with a smile before she took back the whole drink and let a moment of silence stretch over the crowd before she continued, "Now, time for the races," she grinned and so did Shay as she stood next to her, Shay wasn't wearing a gown like the rest of us, she was in her normal fighting leathers.

"Who are they racing? Each other?" I murmured to Crow.

He smiled with a wag of his head. "You'll find out in a second."

Shay lifted her head and whistled loudly toward the tops of the trees. A beat passed before the dirt spread from heavy winds and a roar echoed in response from the treetops. A black scaled winged beast fell from the sky and landed next to Shay. Her bright yellow eyes glowed in the night as she stood behind her like an immoveable statue of protection. She snarled at those who seemed to be too close to Shay.

"Easy Ris," Shay spoke softly as she ran her hand along the chest of the wild dragon behind her. A real dragon.

I had seen them before in the far distance soaring through the skies, but never this close. I had always been told they were mild beasts who stuck with their own kind, but it had seemed this one had a close connection with Shay.

She ran a hand down her snout and I could see the dragons demeanor shift into something calming as she blew out a bloom of smoke that smelt of roses and ash. The smoke rained down over Shay before it pooled to the ground and spread around everyone's feet, and then it faded to nothing. As if the dragon was marking her somehow. Baron ran a hand down the dragons side as he walked along the length of her body.

"You seem stressed Emeris, is everything alright?" He asked, giving her a gentle pat, and the dragon nudged him with her head as if letting him know she was fine.

"You ready for a race?" Shay asked with a cocky grin on her face and Emeris spread her enormous wings, casting a shade over the crowd with a beastly screech of excitement.

"We're racing a dragon..." Ace's signs fell away as his shocked expression shifted to something of excitement. He glanced at Sedrin, and they smiled devilishly at eachother.

"Let the race begin," Atreya shouted as she raised her glass again to the crowd that was enthralled with anticipation.

CHAPTER FORTY
ACE

Sedrin tugged off his dress jacket, getting it off his wings easily, and tossed it over his sister's shoulders.

"Ready," he said toward Emeris, and the dragon huffed a loud sigh.

"Alright, line up," Atreya said as Luana created a starting line in the earth for everyone to stand on.

"Cyran, are you not going to join?" Sedrin asked him as he readied himself at the starting line.

"Fine, I suppose I will." He said on an exhale as he sauntered to the starting line and undid the cuffs on his nice dress shirt. I did the same, loosening my taut clothes. Luana and Maeve stood next to eachother, and I admired Maeve for her kind heart before I glanced at Luana and she gave me a warm smile. But she was hiding something behind it, and I didn't know what. She had been with me most of the night, but after our moment earlier, she seemed distant.

Emelyn watched me with emotion swimming in her eyes, and I understood. I felt the same as I watched Crow wrap his arms around her waist from behind her. All my life I always imagined it would be only us until the end of time. Emelyn was my best friend, my sister. She was more than blood to me. I never thought we would find a happily ever after, and this–this was far from it. But it was a step toward where I'd like us to be. Both happy, both falling in love, both at peace.

"Forever, as one." I signed to her, and she released a shuttering breath with a bright smile before I spread my wings and got into position in line next to the black scaled dragon.

"How do we know where to go?" I signed to Sedrin, and he responded.

"You'll see it once you're up there."

"Ready... Set..." The tension of the silence before the next word made adrenaline shoot through me. "Go!" Shay shouted. Emeris and the rest of us launched into the skies. A whip of fire that was like a speck in the distance twirled through the air from the tops of one tree—a finish line flag.

I darted for it. I pushed my wind faster, harder, than I had in a long while. Magic pushed against my skin and fell away as I passed the rebellions barrier. The dragon soared by, but Cyran stayed ahead of her and Sedrin and I were neck and neck as we twisted around the flame and shot back the other direction to get back to where we started. The wind whipped through my feathers and softly stung against my chilled skin. For a moment, fear coated me.

Something made me want to turn away—the barrier I remembered it was meant to turn intruders away. I powered through the awful, gut wrenching sensation and it faded away to nothing as I pushed on and landed in front of the rebellion party goers.

Cyran had apparently beaten Emeris, as he prowled around the crowd, giving high fives and bowing at the ovation he was getting. Emeris had already forgotten about the race, I supposed, as she wrapped her tail around Shay and lay down next to where she and her mate Baron stood. Both were in their leathers. Emeris nudged at Shay's waist for attention. The bond they had to the beast was amazing. I could see how much the three of them all cared for eachother from watching them.

Sedrin landed shortly after I had.

"Apologies," He spoke lazily, "there at the end I was rather enjoying the flight more than the competition," he said as he moved over to where Maeve was standing, taking the drink in her hand as his own and finishing the liquid in the glass before setting it down. He was definitely tipsy.

Who could blame him? Any of us really, how long had it been since we had hope of a better future? I turned and saw Emelyn and Crow on the sidelines. Eme was still eyeballing the dragon that now rested next to Shay. Maeve was right, Emelyn looked beautiful tonight.

"Crow," Atreya walked over to them, "a word," her voice was stern and the moment of peace I had reveled in fell like lead in my gut. Crow gave her a nod and kissed Emelyn atop the head before he released her waist and walked away with his leader. I watched as Emelyn beamed at him as he walked away and seeing her smile heated my chest like the winter coming to spring. I hadn't seen a genuine one from her in so many years. And I was sure she felt the same for me when she witnessed Luana and I together. I promised myself then that I'd let myself just feel for the rest of the night, and save my troubles for another day.

FORTY-ONE
CROW

I followed Atreya to the same small room, the one we had interrogated the soldier in before. She paced the length of the room, her dress swished with every step, before she turned to me.

"Something is happening," Atreya said, "The scouts have been hearing bits and pieces of information–rumors, from Ember's soldiers but nothing solid, they reported to me during the race and something doesn't feel right, ever since we interrogated that soldier and found that village in shambles I feel as though Valla is on the move and up to something. And with it being her, it can't be anything good." I slumped in the chair at the small interrogation table and released a heavy, tired breath. My shadows dissipated to nearly nothing.

"You can't keep this up, Crow, you have to get your shit together, I need you to be ready to go tonight, the longer you stay because of Emelyn, the weaker you'll be, why can't you just tell the girl the truth."

"I can't, not yet, please, just give me a little more time."

"We're out of time. You have till tomorrow morning." I go to stand and lean against the table during a moment of weakness as I prepare to put up the glamour again before I head back to where Emelyn is waiting for me.

It's painful at this point. Before I stayed as far away from her as I could and loved her from the distance, but now that she was around me every waking moment trying to keep my love, our connection at bay has been excruciating.

Day by day I get weaker and weaker, trying to keep her from feeling the bond at it's full strength. I'm sure she's felt small instances of it from moments I couldn't keep control. If she did, I wondered if she knew what it was? What I am to her? I tucked the thought into the back of my mind and steadied myself. My body was tired of keeping our fate's design under wraps. But I couldn't let it slip, not yet.

"And Crow," Atreya said from behind me.

"Yes,"

"Don't be late."

I didn't respond. I walked out the door and headed toward the only place I wanted to be, the only person I wanted to be with.

Upon returning to Emelyn's room, I saw her laying comfortably on the bed. Under the thin sheet, I could see the outline of her hips and ass. Everything about this woman set me on fire.

"Hi," she whispered, the seductive hiss from where she lay before she tossed the cover back and revealed her naked flesh and nothing more. My cock sprung to life in my pants, pushing against my trousers.

I growled at the sight of her, drinking her in.

"Emelyn–" She cut me off

"I've been waiting for you," she said as she sat up on the bed and revealed her plump taut breasts begging for my mouth to be on them. My shadows writhed, wanting to caress every bare inch of her.

Fuck it.

I couldn't hold back any longer. I wouldn't. I'd have to beg for her forgiveness later.

CHAPTER FORTY-TWO
EMELYN

Crow got to me in three long strides, wrapped his arms and shadows around me, and kissed me deeply. The kiss was devastating, full of teeth and tongue. I couldn't catch my breath. As he lay on top of me, I hummed with need. I ripped off his jacket and shirt before I moved to his trousers, the belt and buttons taking longer than I'd liked before he shucked them off to the floor.

He trailed soft kisses down my body, making my breath hitch when he sucked in one of my taut breasts, sucking and nipping at it before moving to the other one. I cried out when one of his tendrils of shade rubbed along my taut bulb of nerves. My pussy was slick and ready for him. He moved further down my body and placed gentle kisses against my naval before he breathed me in. I trembled with need as he dipped his head between my thighs and devoured me with his tongue. My hips thrusted against his mouth and he placed his hand on my belly, shoving me back down onto the bed and holding me still with his strength as his shadows caressed all my bare flesh, making every touch feel that much more intense.

My movements become rabid as I gripped my fingers in his hair and rode his face until I was screaming his name. My orgasm shuddered through me and he lapped every drop until my hips gave out and my breathing bated.

He moved slowly, so so slowly, up my body.

He bracketed me within his arms. His full lips hovered just above mine, glimmering with my release. I could feel his throbbing cock nudging at my entrance.

"Mei wynsoara," He breathed before he kissed me with such a gentleness tears pricked behind my eyes and then he thrusted into me. Filling me so perfectly, so fully, I never wanted him to leave.

He groaned from the feel of me and golden rays of light and tendrils of shade intertwined through us, *light and shadows.* Suddenly, my chest fell open like a cavern. Emotions stormed around me—raged inside me. My brow pinched from pleasure and pain as I panted between our kisses.

Happiness, hope, fear, the strongest of them all, love...

He kissed me again, deeper this time, as he moved his hips harder and rougher against mine, keeping the same rhythm. Soon I was bubbling close to the edge again as dark and light threads intertwined our very souls. Pressure built in my chest and in the surrounding air. I screamed out as I fell over the edge again and he roared out his release along with me.

As fast as the tether of emotions was there, they went, falling away as my body trembled from the weight of my release leaving me.

I wasn't sure how long Crow stayed sheathed inside of me, rolling his hips tepidly in tandem with mine, while kissing me softly and whispering sweet nothings in my ear.

I lost track of how many orgasms this man gave me. The last thing I remembered was him looking at me as if I was the most precious thing he had ever laid eyes on.

"Remember this Emelyn, know that it was real." he whispered to me before I drifted peacefully to sleep.

My dreams weren't filled with the demons of my past. They were filled with dreams, beautiful dreams.

CHAPTER FORTY-THREE

EMELYN

When I woke, the spot next to me was cold.

And I was empty. Which made little sense to me after the remarkable night I had had with Crow. But I felt empty...

All the emotions I had, it was as if they had all been ripped from my chest and it left behind an open wound. The pain of it made tears swell in my eyes and I had to choke down the lump in my throat.

What the fuck is wrong with me?

I didn't know, but whatever had happened between when Crow was with me last night to when I woke up without him had made excruciating pain fill me to the brim of almost breaking into a million pieces. It wasn't physical pain, but overwhelming emotional pain.

I shoved it all down, swallowing back the tears as I got to my feet on wobbly legs after the night I had. It surprised me I could even stand.

I made my way to the small closet off to the side of the room that had been filled with a few sets of clothes my size from the seamstress. I tossed on something quickly, just wanting to get to the hot springs to relax and wash away the horrible feeling thrumming under my skin. It was like my body was reaching out for something that wasn't there.

I reached at my neck desperate to grip on to my moonstone necklace to focus on it, to steady me, but it was gone and I knew it was gone but my body still looked for it, after all the years I wore it, I was surprised its mark wasn't permanently etched around my neck.

Thinking about it being gone forever made this feeling lurking in my chest worse. It was like a living thing, as if my soul was clawing at my chest, demanding to be let free to search for whatever was missing. But I pushed forward and kept telling myself a hot bath before breakfast would make it all better.

I didn't see Crow as I strode down the narrow path to where the springs were. I hadn't seen him all morning, and it made whatever hole within me writhe and ache more and more.

What the fuck was this?

My mind wandered for a moment about what it might be before I slammed my thoughts down.

No, absolutely not. I wasn't going there.

Get it together, Eme.

No matter how many times I repeated that to myself and tried to push down the emotions in me, I knew I couldn't. Something happened, something changed last night. It was as if Crow had released an overflowing dam on me all at once as soon as his cock filled me. I remembered bits and pieces of it like some fluid, wet dream. As the tendrils of shadows were warring with the golden rays of light between us, until I orgasmed. Again, and again...

I chewed on my lip as I remembered last night, shucking my pants to the ground as I pulled off my shirt. No one was at the spring, probably because breakfast had already started being served. The smells of the sweet sausage and breads wafted into my nose the whole walk down here. I dipped my toe in to the warm water, wishing it was hotter but there weren't any Fire Fae here to make it hotter for me with food being served. This would have to do.

I took the first few steps in, the water stopping at my waist before I found the rocky ledge and sat down. Sinking all the way down to my chin and taking deep breaths to clear my mind before fully submerging myself under the water. I appreciated the silence under there. Enjoying the little bit of solemn peace it gave me before coming up and taking a breath of crisp morning air.

I scrubbed myself down the best I could, washing off my night of passion with Crow, and something feral in me didn't like that, but I knew I needed a bath. After I was finished, I dried off, put my clothes back on and began walking to where that lovely smell was coming from so I could fill myself until I couldn't breathe. The bath did little to help, but I hoped the food would make me feel better after the way I had woke up feeling this morning.

My stomach rumbled happily from the thought alone. Walking through the pitched uneven rows of tables, I stumbled across Hinky and Helena eating breakfast with two large bags packed and I knew it meant they were preparing to leave.

"Oh, don't give us that sad face Eme, you'll see us again soon." Hink spoke up as he stood and tugged me into a strong one-armed hug while Helena did the same on the other side of me. Being between them brought a smile to my face. Their antics never seemed to not tug a smile on my lips. Hink towered over me while Helena barely reached my shoulder. They were adorable in every way and I loved them.

They were two of the closest people I had left after the war all those years ago. And now that my village had ousted me, and with Willow being gone, Ace, Hinky, and Helena might be the only ones I have left from my past. I knew Atreya wanted me to feel at home here, and considered all of us a family, but all of those things come with a history, a past, and as of now, Ace, Hink, and Helena were the ones that fit that bill. Crow too, even though I had only known him personally for a short while, he had been around all those years ago. And now I found myself feeling hollow without him.

"Where are you both headed off to?" I asked as they pulled away, tossing their empty plates in the trash bin closest to us before continuing.

"Back to Bells. Helena will have our son soon and we have already been away too long." Hink said as he tossed both of the packs on himself like they weren't heavy at all.

"Besides, Tulgan is probably losing his mind already with having to run Bells. It'll be good for us to be back home for a little while, scouting for new recruits when we can." Helena said as she ran soothing circles over her swollen belly.

"Son, huh?" I said, giving Hink a warm smile, and he nodded, looking down at Helena as if she had hung the moon.

"It's only a gut feeling, but we're both thinking it's a boy." Helena said with a smile.

"I'm hoping she'll finally let me have a Jr." Hinky said with a wink at her and she shoved at his chest.

"I'm not naming our son Hinkleton, I refuse, who the heck names their son Hinkleton," she sneers the last bit at me and I can't hold back my chuckle.

"Hey, it's a family name, not like I had the choice," Hinky shrugs with a grin. I was sure he was used to people talking about his name.

"Tulgan got your middle and last, and that's the closest you'll get to your Jr. And after this one, the gates are permanently closed." She said it, but Hink just tugged her against him and gave her a soft kiss, as if he doubted she could ever resist him. And it made another warm smile tug on my lips. They gave me one last quick hug before they strode hand in hand over to Atreya and Shay, bidding them farewell before walking through the protective barriers on the camp and disappearing through the trees.

I hadn't noticed I had been watching them the entire time with tears swelling in my eyes until I looked away and I wiped them. Once I finally glanced back around at my surroundings again, I saw Ace and Luana sitting at a table together, enjoying their morning breakfast and cheerful chatter between them. Ace was happy, and it showed. I turned and walked toward the servers, who were still serving food to the stragglers who had yet to eat, and grabbed a plate of fresh eggs, a large buttered roll, and some sausage.

I strode over to a table and sat by myself, not wanting to ruin Ace's breakfast with Luana. It had been so long since I had seen Ace glowing with happiness, and I didn't want my sour mood to ruin it for him. Or whatever this thing was that was happening to me.

I didn't get two bites into my meal before the two lovebirds were flopping down in the two seats in front of me. I didn't look up from my plate. I knew it was Ace. Over the years of being with him, I could sense him anytime he was close enough to me. Smell his scent—blue ferns and citrus. I'd recognize it anywhere.

A small breeze made me lift my chin in his direction, I knew it was him coaxing me to look at him with his wind, he gave me a stern look, one that said 'did you really think, I'd ditch you and leave you all alone now that I've fallen in love with this beautiful brown-skinned goddess sitting next to me.'

Okay, maybe I didn't pick up that much information from it, but I think I was close to the mark.

"What's wrong?" Ace signed, and I shook my head and blew out a breath.

"Nothing, I'm fine, really." I signed back, plastering a tight smile on my face that Ace didn't believe for one second before I glanced over at Luana. It's not that I didn't trust her, but I had never been one to speak about my emotions openly to anyone other than Ace. And until recently, Crow. The small thought of him curled the emotions in my chest.

Luana picked up on the tension between me and Ace as she glanced between us before she went to stand. "I'll give you two some time." She signed with a warm smile before leaning into Ace but she stopped herself. She straightened, seeming tense and uncertain. Redness bloomed on her cheeks before she turned to walk away and all I could do was grin at my best friend practically glowing just from a glance at her.

When her back was to us, I signed to him again, "you are definitely in love, brother." He glanced back over his shoulder to be sure she wasn't looking over at us when I said that as if it was some big secret.

"Is that even possible? We've only just met, but I feel like I've known her for as long as I've known you." He blows out a breath. "Enough about me. What's wrong Eme?"

"Nothing." I repeated, and he scowled at me before getting to his feet, rushing to me in three long strides around the table, lurching me up in his arms before shooting off into the skies at breakneck speeds.

"What the hell, Ace!?" I shout over the sound of the roaring wind whipping past my face, making my skin pebble from the early morning chill. Soon it would be muggy and warm, with spring coming.

Ace didn't answer me as he leveled out and moved between the gigantic trees of Woodhaven before finding a mountainside with a ledge that overlooked the large rebellion beneath us. It reminded me of Heavensreach.

If only rocks could hear, the Heavensreach cliff side would know the emotional turmoil on slaught of everything that Ace and I are and had been through.

He landed gracefully before he tucked his wings in behind his back and I huffed from the disruption of my breakfast. My stomach was still growling from hunger. I hoped no one cleared my table and cleaned it while I was away because I might just fight Ace over not eating.

"Now," Ace signed, giving me a smug look, "what's wrong?"

I rolled my eyes, but a part of me enjoyed knowing that even though he was very much in love with Luana, it had changed nothing about our friendship.

"I told you already, nothing."

"I'm going to assume it has something to do with your boy, considering you reek of him." He said with a lift of his nose and my cheeks heated, thinking back to all the things we had done only hours before.

"Have you seen him?" I moved to sit next to him on the cliff side, letting our feet dangle as we sat on the edge of death. I glanced down to the Rebellion below. They were like ants coming and going during their morning chores.

"No, I haven't seen him since the party yesterday." He ran a hand through his long locks. It had gotten longer during the winter. Usually I was the one to cut it and it could use a trim, but since we had found the rebellion, it hadn't been on the top of my priority list.

"Well, last night we had earth shattering sex, and then when I woke up this morning he was gone, not sure why, but it stirred something in me, something more than just a normal rejection, and it's been effecting me all morning." I had never sugar-coated anything when talking to Ace. He had always been my person, my best friend, more than that. So I wasn't worried about his judgement when he looked over at me, his eyes were raging, and I knew it wasn't directed at me, but toward Crow, because what kind of ass sleeps with you just to leave your bed cold the next morning unless it was only a screw? When I knew it wasn't just that, what I had with him was more. Or was it? Had I read everything so wrong? My mind began spiraling as Ace pulled me into the crook of his arm.

Or maybe something bad had happened?

"I don't think Crow only saw you as a hole to put his dick in, it's more than that, and I know that because although the man has endless voids for eyes, I've seen the way he is around you," he signed, letting his words hang between us a moment before he continued, "have you talked to Atreya? I'm assuming she would know where her spy is."

"No, I haven't. Do you think something bad has happened to him?" The weight in my chest lurched from the thought alone and I had to rub at it to get it to settle down.

"No, Crow can definitely handle himself." Ace assured me, but it still didn't make me feel better. Why would he leave without even saying goodbye?

"Enough about me and my feelings, what's new with you?" I signed as he rubbed the sticks together to spark a flame in the brush to warm the pojo waiting for us.

I bended some water from the small amount leaking from and glazing the side of the mountain when Ace had left for a minute to get the last of the tea leaves we had picked from Heavensreach earlier this winter.

The tea had become more of a comfort drink that we would sit and sip together when we were all in our feelings just like we did back whenever we were teenagers sitting on the side of Heavensreach.

"I don't smell Luana all over you yet, so I'm going to assume you haven't gotten any action." I signed with a smile and he chuckled under his breath at me.

"No, I haven't, there is definitely something between us. But I feel like she's hiding something from me."

"Care to elaborate?" I said with a wave of my hand, wanting to know more, keeping my mind off of my own emotions.

"I can't describe it. I'm drawn to her in a way I've never been drawn to someone else. But she pulls back when we have these moments together." He signed before blowing on his embers and the fire burst to life and danced in his eyes when he looked back up at me.

"See it's different with you and Luana, when I'm around Crow there are only moments when I'm overrun with a draw to him and then it dissipates, like it only brushes against me for a moment, barley stirring under my skin, it's infuriating, because I don't understand it."

"Maybe he's your—" I cut him off before he had the chance to sign it, or even think it.

"Impossible, a mate, by what I've read, is someone who, once found, you're completely and utterly obsessed with, it's something you just know, something that snaps into place, and after mating, both are practically feral, especially after the two mates accepted the mating bond between each other." I glanced at Ace, who was now sipping his tea, looking down at the Rebellion below as if he could catch a glance at the woman who he's been spending every waking moment with. A few moments passed as we sipped our teas and took a reprieve in the silence before I spoke again.

"Maybe she's your mate." I whispered, and he looked over at me with an awestruck facial expression, as if the idea was new to him.

"No..." His hand trailed off as he looked back down at the people below, as if he could find her amongst the crowd. "If she was, why would she pull away from me? I'm constantly wanting to be around her, but I don't think she feels the same. At least, not yet. But then again, I don't know how the whole mating thing works, I never thought either of us would get a happy ending like that, no matter how many times I'd hoped we would, I never thought there would be a chance of it becoming our reality." His eyes glanced back to mine, and I gave him a kind smile.

"Well, you never know. What are we waiting for? Let's go." I said, setting my cup down as I let my ass slip off the cliff and free fall down the side of the mountain. Ace leaped, throwing his tea and nose diving straight for me, before wrapping me in his embrace.

When we landed below, he signed, "you're just as fucking crazy now as you were when we were kids." He huffs out a breath in relief.

"No, probably more so now, but what would be the fun if I got boring?" He rolled his eyes before I turned away to go look for Atreya or Shay. "Go get your girl, brother." I said out loud with a grin and he didn't need me to say anything more as he took off into the trees.

CHAPTER FORTY-FOUR
EMELYN

I searched for Atreya and Shay with no luck around base camp. A few scouts had told me they had left but wouldn't give me anymore details. I thought being the Peacebringer would've given me some leeway, but I guessed wrong. Which I assumed was a good thing. Even Atreya was more respected than the Chosen, and that spoke volumes to me.

I wasn't sure how long Atreya and Shay were going to be gone, so I sat and wallowed in my feelings all afternoon, stuffing myself to the rim with comfort foods until I couldn't handle the clawing under my skin anymore. I thought I was going to lose my mind. The sun had set, and I decided to get out of my room and try to get this feeling out of my chest.

I made my way through base camp to where I knew Baron trained the rebellions men and women. Shay had shown it to us when we had first been introduced to the rebellion.

Baron wasn't a bender, which was surprising to me that Atreya had non benders as not only her second hand, but as the ones who trained everyone in the rebellion to not only fight but to use their bending. And then I remembered, as far as I knew, she wasn't a bender either.

Who would've thought that a non bender would have built a rebellion against the most ruthless Fire Fae of all time. Her determination amazed me.

Once I made it to the open ground of where Baron trained, I noticed Luana was here, training with the evening class on stances and stretches before they would move on to something more difficult.

"Where's Ace?" I asked, and she looked over at me with a smile.

"He just left. I told him I'd meet him after the evening training, but he insisted on practicing with me. He said he was going back to his room to change before coming back. Are you going to train with all of us?" She asked, and I glanced around the space, there was a good mix of everything here, a few Orcs, some Fire Fae, Earth Dryads, non benders and even some Brownies but I wasn't sure if they were here for practice or to clean profusely afterwards when the space would be covered in sweat and blood from the one-on-one combat training. Which was ridiculous to think about considering we're all in the middle of the woods, but brownies were known for cleaning, outside or not.

"Yeah, I need to burn off some steam." I spoke while I bounced from one foot to the other, readying myself for what was to come.

"Everyone, get into position," Baron's voice called out to us all, and we all moved to get into position with the warm-ups. Luana rose her hand as if she was lifting nothing and multiple thin pillars of the earth jutted out of the ground in uneven rows around us. It reminded me of the same type of training my father used to have me do when I was younger. The only thing they were missing was the brown sacks for heads filled with straw.

Sometimes, my pada would draw faces on them with me before we would train. It was one memory I always held close to me. I tucked it away and stretched while watching all the others do the course before me. First went the handful of Earth Dryads that were here, and I admired how, although being on the more dainty side, they all moved with such a force, a purpose, as if they were as hard as the stone they wielded. Another thing I tucked in my mind because it was something I'd have to learn soon.

As of now, the only thing I could wield was water, and I could move some wind after what Ace taught me and the little bit of practicing I had done.

Oof. I still had so much to learn. The thought alone riddled me with anxiety and dread. Which was exactly what I came here to get rid of. I needed to work out all the frustration thrumming through my bones, down to my damn soul.

When Baron finally called my name, Luana raised the pillars of rock again as if they weren't all shattered to pieces only moments ago from the others before me. Baron looked me over and gave me a nod to begin and I rolled back on my heels, moving the blood coursing through my veins faster, before I called out to the water under the forest floor. It snaked up around my legs and arms and then I lunged forward into the rocks, slicing and jabbing at the pillars. And then they shifted. They moved around the surrounding space before one by one; they barreled in my direction and they forced me to blast them apart with my water before they took me out.

I centered myself. My water circled me like a savaged kraken with tendrils of blue swaying and bobbing around me in one tight circle, ready for whichever direction the next attack would come from.

"I think we should give her a little more fellas. What do you think?" Baron spoke up and when I glanced around, everyone was looking at me.

It was me against everyone here. They raised their arms with the gifts the gods had blessed them with, circling their fingers, water, fire, stones, or their weapons before they all got into a fighting formation.

I glanced over at Baron, but he only gave me a smug smile. "Let's see what you got, Peacebringer." He said, before he nodded at everyone to begin and they all came at me in small groups of three.

The pillars began rotating wildly. The heat of the flames licked the surrounding grounds, but I kept my circle taut. My waterlike tentacles whipping and slicing at anyone who got too close. The Fire Fae launched fire balls, while the Earth Dryads suddenly made the earth fall under my feet. I pushed my water under my heels so I could stand on it to remain steady as I skated across my water to avoid the giant balls of fire. An Orc barrelled at me at full speed with a machete type blade the size of my body as he swung it in my direction and I fell backwards to dodge it. The breeze of death whispered past my face.

Once I made it back to my feet and I looked over at him, his jutted teeth were longer than Hinkys, wearing some type of large animal pelt on his back that had sharp claws and teeth. He was shirtless, and nothing but ripped muscle. He wore large brown trousers that seemed to be held up with multiple straps of leather. And one large strap connected his large spiked shoulder plate onto his right shoulder. I sensed it was iron even from the distance and my mind wandered to all the fae he had probably tackled and killed with it.

"That's not for you, Peacebringer. We're only having some fun." He sneered as he ran for me again, his heavy booted steps echoing off the trees. The only thing that was running through my head was how fucked I was as the rest of the group followed behind him.

CHAPTER FORTY-FIVE
EMELYN

I hadn't planned on being pummeled to a pulp by some of the best fighters in the resistance, but it was technically what I wanted, to get some of the weight of my emotions off my chest.

My lungs burned, my head pounded, and I was crusted in blood and sweat by the time Baron called a quits. We all crowded around the campfire drinking water from our skins. The exhaustion settled over all of us. Our shoulders sagged as we all sat perched on some logs the Orc had dragged over from the woods.

"What's your name?" I asked the Orc as Ace came up from beside me to sit next to me and Luana.

"Ugan," he said as he held out his huge hand to shake mine. "Nice to finally be introduced to you, Emelyn. Sorry if I was too rough on you. I figured the Peacebringer could handle it." He said it with a wink.

I wagged my head, "just because that is my title doesn't mean I know how it works yet." I huffed a breath.

He chuckled, "I'm sure we'll get you there in no time, plenty of people here who would be honored to teach you how to wield your abilities." He said, grabbing a long branch and poking at the fire. Shay sauntered out of the shadows and greeted Baron with a kiss before joining us around the fire.

"Have you seen Crow?" I blurted it out, not caring who was around.

Shay gave me a sympathetic look, "he's gone, Atreya sent him off to Ember to figure out what's happening after the Fire Fae camp incident, and Westwell." She said, and Baron gripped his arms around her waist.

"Where is Atreya now?" I asked.

"She's in her quarters going over some evacuation plans, we're not moving now but we will soon, she fears Valla is coming for you."

"I should go, you guys have built a safe place here, I'm only endangering you by staying."

"No, this place may seem safe, but as long as Embers emperor is in power, no where is safe, not even here." She paused a moment glancing around, "can we talk in private?" She asked and I looked to Ace and he nodded his head for me to go with her. Baron released Shay from his hold and we started walking through the woods. The bright fire light grew dim the further we got away.

Shay glanced back, making sure we were alone before continuing. "I talked to Atreya and Emeris about how we could learn more about your abilities."

"The dragon?" My brow pinched with confusion but Shay kept speaking.

"Ris suggested taking you to Draken and asking for his permission to get into the library of knowledge. you're the Peacebringer, he would open it for you."

"What are you talking about, how did you talk to Emeris? She's a dragon."

Shay grinned, "I know," she huffed and paused her steps to look at me."There is a place called Magni Island, it is protected by an acient type of magic, like a glammour but for an entire piece of land. Nobody knows of it, the only reason Atreya, Baron, and myself know it exsists is because I became friends with the dragons a long time ago. The island has been home to the dragons since before the war, they can talk to you on it, I flew to Magni today because Emeris wanted to talk to me. Apparently, the library houses all the knowledge about our world, including the Peacebringer. Draken guards the library, and may hold the key to what we need to do next." She said and my mouth parted, could this place hold all the answers I needed? I didn't want to waist anymore time.

"How do we get there?" I asked, my heartbeat began pounding in my chest. My body was exhausted but now with all this information my mind was awake and spiraling.

"We fly, but not today, we will be moving most of base camp soon to ensure Valla stays off our heels." She said and my shoulders sagged a little from relief and from disappointment. I wanted to get there now, but I also knew I was exhausted and needed rest if I was going to embark on a whole new journey. I nodded and glanced back over my shoulder to where the campfire was a speck in the distance.

"Come on, it's been a long day, let's get back to everyone." She said as she placed a gentle hand on my shoulder, "you can't save the world in one night Emelyn, don't be to hard on yourself." Shay said it with a small smile.

"Thank you," I said and followed her back to the campfire.

I walked to the hot spring with Ace to clean up after the long day I had, I caught him up on what was happening and all the things Shay had told me. Afterwards he walked me to my room, I was defeated and tired.

The tug in my chest had eased a bit, but I was sure it would be back full force by morning.

I was wrong.

By the time I lay in bed staring up at the blank, wood grain ceiling, the raw tug of emotions began clawing at my chest again. Making it feel as though a bear was sitting on me but trying to tear out of me at the same time.

I tossed and turned most of the night, unsure if it had only been minutes or hours. Trying to push down the misery and then something cold and familiar coated my skin.

The fear sent a chill down my spine and gooseflesh across my neck. I lurched to my feet, hastily throwing back on my fighting leathers and boots, grabbing my weapons, before rushing out the door. I rushed to the ropes, throwing myself off the wooden planked ledge from the trees. My knees bent from the harsh impact on the soil. I ran in the direction of Atreyas quarters, but a darkness distracted me.

A bird was flying through the trees, not just any bird, a bird made of shadows. A shadow crow. I followed it, never taking my eyes off of it until suddenly it was swooping down and I halted my steps. My breathing was rapid, my chest was heaving. I couldn't hear anything over my own heartbeat in my ears. It landed on Atreyas arm, she glanced at me with worried eyes as she tugged the note free from the shadows and the bird dissipated to nothing.

"What does it say?" I asked, barley able to hear myself speak. She unwrapped the small discolored piece of parchment, and her fear was palatable.

"Run." She said it, and then said it again, "run." she rushed into her quarters before coming back out with a large horn of some kind and blowing it for all to hear. "Run!" She screamed at me, "It's a warning, Ember is here! We have to go now!"

The screams and cries started as Atreya began shouting commands in every direction as she rushed through the base camp. Crow had sent her a warning. Something was happening. And the fear spreading across my skin, coating me like a silky sheet, let me know exactly what it was. Who it was.

The Prince of Ember.

Atreya recognized the knowing look in my eyes before she spoke again.

"We have to clear out the camp. You need to go with Shay," she calmed her voice, and regained her barrings like a true leader in the midst of chaos.

"No, I'm not leaving with all these people still here."

"Emelyn–"

"I'll gather Ace, and a few others to hold them off as long as we can to give you all the chance to escape." She glanced around at the chaos unfolding and didn't have time to argue before she nodded her head.

"Fine. But meet us at the forest's edge. You'll be with shay when all this is over. We have to get you to Magni."

I agreed before taking off in the direction she had just come from. I blew out my call to Ace, sending my whistle through the trees hoping it would only take him a moment to get to me.

I waited a beat, then two, before he swooped down and landed in front of me, his wings outstretched and ready for whatever was to come.

"He's here." was all I said, and he understood who I was referring too. Luana rushed up to our side, along with Maeve and Sedrin, all in fighting leathers draped in blades of all different sizes and ready to attack.

"Let's move." I said as I turned in the direction that everyone was running from and seen smoke barrel between the trees and an orange glow took over the night.

We moved together as one, killing any fire Fae soldiers that would burst through the treeline as smoke and flames began spreading across the ground. Sweat beaded my brow as I wielded my water and battle axe, sinking both into as many soldiers as possible until a roar echoed across the sky.

Emeris flew down, Shay riding confidently on her back as she blasted waves of fire down on the first wave of soldiers before circling around to do it again.

"Go! Now!" She shouted once she was close enough to us, Shay was giving us a moment to run, to meet back up with Atreya.

I signed to everyone "time to go" as we all turned on our heels and headed straight for the treeline. Ace glanced at me and I gave him a nod in understanding. "Go, I'll be fine." I shouted as he grabbed Luana and wrapped her into his arms and took off, and Sedrin did the same with Maeve.

Blood flooded into my legs to make them move faster against the roaring flames behind me. And then I felt the icy mask of fear coat my skin again. When I turned to glance over my shoulder, Kade was walking through the flames, fully dressed in Embers armor, looking like Iros, the god of suns and fire.

I paused for only a moment and his honeycomb eyes met mine, before they darkened, giving him a more deadly look as he continued to move toward me, slowly, as if he had all the time in the world to catch me. A sly grin tugged on the corners of his lips. The flames didn't touch him, as if they feared him.

I lurched into a sprint, nearly at the forest's edge and when I saw the opening between the trees in front of me, nothing but the bright stars and moon in the sky compared to the bright orange of flames and the wrath of the sun behind me. A shadow swooped down from the sky. And then another and another. One very much larger than the other two and once I finally broke through the tree line, Emeris was there with Shay on her back. Along with Ace and Sedrin.

"Come on, we have to go!" Shay shouted and Ace sat Luana down to let her join the rest of the scrambling rebellion and when I glanced back at Luana, I made a choice.

"No," I turned and signed to Ace as he walked toward me and he looked at me, confused. "They are after me, if I leave the Rebellion, they'll follow me. You're staying with them Ace."

"No, I'm not leaving you alone." Ace argued.

"Yes, you are. You must." Ace's eyes bounced between me and Luana as I continued, "I will be back, I promise, but please, stay." I grabbed his forearms and brought his forehead to mine. He took a moment to look at me, my eyes desperately pleading before he looked away. He kept shaking his head.

No no no...

"Ace, we don't have time, you're staying with them, keep them safe. Promise me." I pleaded.

he growled under his breath. "Fine. I promise." He signed, "but come back in one piece."

"I will." I swore it. "Mai lao kahi," I murmured under my breath and he pulled me into a rib crushing hug before Shay interrupted.

"Time to go!" shay shouted again as flames burst to life behind us. Ace released me before grabbing Luana and cradling her in his arms again, launching back into the skies, giving me one last glance as he flew in the direction the Rebellion was running to. I climbed up Emeris quickly with Shay before she sent her off into the skies, when I turned to glance at the carnage below, I was left with taunting words echoing in my mind from before.

He was the predator, and I was the prey.

THANK YOU

Thank you for reading! If you enjoyed Fate Of Water And Wind please consider leaving a review on: Goodreads, Amazon, Storygraph, or your personal social media.

Follow along with Lashell's author journey for future stories.

<u>The Osparia Series Reading Order:</u>

Prequel: Ashes In The Wind & Islands Of Ash

Book One: Fate Of Water & Wind

Book Two: Wrath Of Suns & Shadows

Book Three: War Of Fire & Fortune

ACKNOWLEDGMENTS

First and foremost I want to thank my amazing readers! Thank you for all the love and support and for loving these characters as much as I do.

Thank you to my beautiful children for being patient with me (or at least trying to be) as I wrote this story and continue to write new adventures.

To my mom: thank you for teaching and instilling in me that if you want something in life, you can't just wish it to be, you have to work hard to get it. I wouldn't be where I am today without that advice growing up.

To my brother: if you ever read this (that's doubtful) but if you do... no you didn't...

To the amazing community of friends I've made on TikTok: Thank you, from the bottom of my heart, for your support and for welcoming me into the bookish community. Without you, I wouldn't have ever published. You all inspired me to reach for the stars and write the dang thing!

To Norma Gambini from Normas Nook Proofreading: Thank you for all of your support and amazing eagle eyes!

To Lylah Taylor: Thank you for being my alpha reader.

To Miblart; Thank you for the beautiful cover.

ABOUT THE AUTHOR

Lashell Rain is a foodie fueled by a shameless amount of caffeine and a passion for storytelling. The Texas native lives at home with her two beautiful kids. Between being a mom by day, and a writer by night, she brought her dreams of becoming an author into a reality—by flying by the seat of her pants.

www.ingramcontent.com/pod-product-compliance
Lightning Source LLC
Chambersburg PA
CBHW050853210726
48290CB00004B/1204